"Talented Colby Hodge delivers space adventure at a breathtaking clip! Fans of *Star Wars* and Riddick will love *Stargazer*."
—*New York Times* Bestselling Author Susan Grant

"A pulse-pounding futuristic thriller. Hodge has created a genuinely engaging new world. Her characters are absorbing and the story is intriguing."
—*RT BOOKreviews*

"*Stargazer* is a rousing space adventure set in a fascinating universe brought vividly to life. Exciting and action-packed, it's one of the most purely fun books I've read this year...a real thrill ride and an easy book to recommend."
—All About Romance

"Colby Hodge gives us a romping good time across the stars with this futuristic tale of romance, revenge and renewal. ...*Stargazer* is a delightful tale that will carry the reader along for an enjoyable jaunt away from the everyday world."
—Fresh Fiction

"A page-turner with all the magic, mayhem, and romance one could wish for."
—*Romance Reviews Today*

"Colby Hodge has done a fantastic job in creating a story that will capture and hold readers until the last page. I look forward to reading more of her work."
—A Romance Review

ON THE BRINK

"What's wrong with him?" Joah asked.

"He appears to be wounded," Tess volunteered.

Joah bent over her shoulder to take a closer look and nudged the stranger's side with the toe of his boot. "Looks like he must have wrapped himself up and then come looking for help." Joah glanced over his shoulder toward the mountains. "He might have friends out there or he might have enemies. Maybe we should just throw him back in and let him be someone else's problem."

A cold shiver ran down Tess's back. "You can't do that."

Why did she care about what happened to this strange man? Hadn't she wished for him to just disappear?

Tess felt as if she were standing on the edge of a precipice. She knew, without thinking about it, that what she was about to do would change her life forever. For better or worse, she could not say.

Other *Love Spell* books by Colby Hodge:

STARGAZER

Colby Hodge

Shooting Star

LOVE SPELL NEW YORK CITY

LOVE SPELL®

December 2006

Published by

Dorchester Publishing Co., Inc.
200 Madison Avenue
New York, NY 10016

ISBN 0-505-52628-X

The name "Love Spell" and its logo are trademarks of Dorchester Publishing Co., Inc.

Printed in the United States of America.

Visit us on the web at www.dorchesterpub.com.

Shooting Star

Prologue

It was parade day. It was also his birthday. The boy, impatient with the maid who dressed him, broke away from her constant fussing and ran through the luxuriously appointed apartment to his mother's room.

His little brother was there, clinging to her skirts with his thumb stuck deep into his mouth as always. The child's face brightened at the sight of his older brother.

"Ben!" he said in his baby voice as he popped his thumb out and then back in.

Their mother gently touched the golden-brown hair of the child at her side and then removed his hand from her skirt so she could kneel to welcome the older son.

"Happy birthday, Ben," Rowena said and swept her son into a warm hug.

"Is the parade really for me, Mother?" Ben asked.

1

"Yes. Your father and the people want to honor the day of your birth," she said.

No need to tell the boy that it was just an excuse for his father to demonstrate his wealth and power to the people. With twenty-one sons, all of whom were to be held in high esteem by the population, there were almost constant celebrations and parades through the streets of the capital.

"Your father will come for you and honor you on this day," Rowena continued as she checked to make sure that the innocent face before her was clean and his clothing was appropriate. His eyes, so blue, looked up at her with childish excitement. She straightened a wayward curl over his forehead.

Not that it really mattered what the boy looked like. His father, the esteemed leader of their world, would stop at the appropriate place and display Ben before the people. He would be announced as the twelfth heir to the throne. This day only his mother would recognize the insignificant ranking of her son's birth. She was nothing but a lesser wife who had been gifted to the emperor by her father as part of a peace treaty. Her youthful beauty and grace had been prominently displayed at the time. She'd been welcomed into the emperor's bed, obediently done her duty, and then presented him with another son.

Perhaps if she had given him a daughter, it would have been a novelty and she would have earned a higher place in the order of wives.

Instead she'd borne another son in a long succession of sons. Her child was just one more proof of the never-ending greatness and sexual prowess of the emperor. And when the emperor had noticed her son do something exceptional one day during his warrior training, he was pleased enough to grace to the almost forgotten wife with a visit. The result was another son, Stefan Andreas, declared the twentieth heir to the throne. Another wife had given him number twenty-one. There would probably be more. Why even bother to count them after the heir and the spare? Both had been born to the same wife. The first wife. The honored wife.

"Did you have your breakfast?" Rowena asked. It would be a long day for the boy. An exciting day.

"Yes, Mother.

"Good." She smiled at him. His face held the promise of masculine good looks. The softness of childhood was giving way to the angles and planes of manhood. He had the same look as her brother, dead these many years, with his hair of golden brown and his bright blue eyes. And young Stefan looked just like him also.

How dear Stefanas's memory was to her after his death so many years ago in the planetary wars. His loss had devastated her father. The result was a treaty and her life as a gift to the conqueror of their planet.

"It's time to go," she said. She took Ben's hand into hers and with the other took the hand of his brother. Then she led them to the balcony that overlooked the main thoroughfare of the capital city.

In the distance the shield wall that protected the capital could be seen. It shimmered beneath the assault of the two suns at their zenith in the bright yellow sky. The people were grateful for the shield wall; it protected them from their enemies. They were also grateful for the strength of their emperor and his armies. After all, without him they would be at the mercy of the universe.

Or so the emperor told them.

All the wives were gathered on the common balcony that faced the street. Their apartments were linked together by the balcony on one side and a private courtyard on the other. They all were dressed in their best, with their children at their sides. All had come forth to celebrate the birthday of son number twelve, Rubikhan Benjamin, born to the mighty emperor and his fourth wife, the Princess Rowena of the planet Kalember.

The banners proclaimed it. The heralds proclaimed it. The broadcasters proclaimed it, placing the proper spin on all of it for those unfortunate enough to have to watch from their homes. The emperor is great. The emperor is strong. Long live the emperor.

"Doesn't the emperor look magnificent?"

"Isn't the Princess Rowena beautiful, even if she is getting on in years?"

"How handsome the young prince is growing."
"The very image of his father." Or so they were told to report. All of the young princes were the image of their father. *Thus his difficulty in telling them apart*, one broadcaster thought to herself. No room for such spoken witticism. Not if she wanted to succeed. She read the script as it ran across the screen before her.

"The young prince is now twelve years old. It is reported by his tutors that Prince Rubikhan Benjamin is exceptional in all of his classes, especially his weapons training. He has a natural ability that astounds those who watch him." The broadcaster checked her screen to verify the last sentence, which seemed different from the usual rote message that she was required to repeat at each birthday. Yes, she had read correctly. A sentence had been added. The young prince must be exceptional to have something different added to his publicity release.

"We look forward to seeing him lead our warriors someday," she added with a genuine smile.

The cameras focused on the balcony and the women and children gathered there. Seven wives and twenty sons were lined up along it. They were all there but the eldest. He had moved into the palace with his father a long time ago.

As it happened, Rowena and her sons occupied the apartment next to that of the first wife. The first wife had given the emperor his heir and three other sons. Her fourth son was only a few weeks younger than Ben. The boy glared at Ben, his face pale and sour. Could he be jealous? He had his own honors coming in just a few weeks, after all. Rowena took a half step forward to shelter her son from the vicious looks coming his way.

The other boy's name was Dyson. He had chubby cheeks, weak blue eyes and white blond hair. Why did she dislike his looks? Was it because he resembled his mother so closely?

"Look, Mother," Ben said.

The heralds were passing, carrying banners with his name. Next there was a hover pod with a soldier on board who was being honored for some great accomplishment. A huge monitor hanging on the side of one of the buildings showed a close-up of the soldier, with subtitles extolling his feats. The soldier seemed bored as he slowly drove the small hover craft down the street lined with wildly cheering people. But he did wave to them, which drove the mob to frenzied screams of celebration.

Next there were various officers and the current

top celebrities. It was getting close to the arts awards day. The top runners were all on open hover pods, wearing their best smiles as they blew kisses to the crowd. One especially handsome actor flashed his famous smile, and the women gathered along the street below screamed in appreciation at the treat.

"Where's my father?" Ben asked. Impatient as always, he stepped closer to the balcony's edge and looked toward his father's residence, ignoring the honorees that were lined up right below his nose. Dyson stepped forward also, blocking Ben's view.

Rowena's face remained composed. She would not show her annoyance. Since they were close in age, Dyson shared a tutor with Ben and the sessions had become a competition instead of a class.

Rowena had advised Ben to ignore Dyson's behavior. The boy's true nature would show itself, just as his mother's had, at least to the other wives. She had given birth to the heir. Why did she always feel the need to remind them of it?

"He'll be here," Rowena assured him.

How many times had Ben actually seen his father? Twenty, maybe, that she could remember. But the boy had never been with him one on one for any length of time. Their contacts had always been in passing. There would be a comment on his growth, a question about his studies, and the typical urging to keep the boy's focus where it should be.

Today would be different, however. Today Ben was twelve and he would go with his father to the governmental palace and eat dinner with him while his father told him his plans for the future. He would be introduced to those in power. He would be honored by all who came into his presence.

Today would be different. Her son was special. Rowena knew it. She had watched him, taught him, he would excel. He would be noticed. He would earn his place by his father's side. He would accomplish great things. He would see what needed to be changed and he would make changes.

After today, things would be different.

Rowena bent over Ben's shoulder and inconspicuously pointed toward the east.

"There he is," she said into his ear. Ben's hands tightened on the balcony rail, his knuckles white with the strength of his grip.

How could the emperor be missed? His hover pod was, of course, riding higher than the rest. It was bigger, as expected; it needed to be because of the bodyguards, the pair of huge black Newfs that never left the emperor's side, and the personal driver. The sides of the hover pod were covered with clear plexi to protect the esteemed leader of the people, and the top was covered with an ornate crownlike molding, indicative of the high position of its passenger.

The heralds stopped below the balcony. Soldiers and security officers lined up. The stairs were cleared. The hover pod stopped and the emperor stepped out onto the platform that had been placed there for that purpose.

He waved to the cheering crowd and proceeded up the steps with the two huge Newfs following. An assistant brought up the rear; under his arm he carried a large clear celpad and stylus, which was no doubt the only way he could keep track of all the details of the day.

The emperor looked dashing yet elegant in his

uniform. A man for the people. The protector of the planet. A loving father intent on visiting his son.

Rowena placed her hands on Ben's shoulders and without a word he stepped back, holding himself at attention as he'd been taught. They waited for his father.

The emperor waved to the crowd once more as he reached the summit of the stairs. He took a few steps and then stopped. The Newfs quickly sat down behind their master, patiently waiting for the next subtle command.

Ben's father stopped in front of Dyson.

"So you are turning twelve?" he said.

"Yes, sir," Dyson responded with a bright smile. It wasn't a lie. He was turning twelve. In just a few days.

Ben's shoulders tensed under Rowena's hands. She squeezed her fingers over the tense muscles. *Patience, my son.* Rowena's eyes darted toward the assistant, who stood at attention behind the emperor, and implored him with her lovely blue eyes.

The man shrugged his shoulders after checking his celpad.

Dyson's mother's face held a self-satisfied smile. *He has the wrong child.*

Who would dare to point that out? Who among them was brave enough to risk embarrassing the emperor? Surely he would realize his mistake? If Dyson had any honor he would admit that he was not today's honoree. If Dyson's mother was the woman she pretended to be, she could smooth the error over and turn the situation into a victory for the emperor. Why didn't she do something?

Because it was her son being noticed. Not Rowena's. Why was she so vindictive? It wasn't as if

Rowena got any of the emperor's attention. She was long forgotten, as she had hoped to be. She couldn't stand the man. The thought of him sickened her. Yes, he was handsome; yes, he was strong; and yes, he was seductive. But he was also a shallow pool, without even so much as a ripple of feeling for those who should be dear to him.

Rowena didn't dare make a sound lest she seem jealous or weak. She had to remain strong and without emotion. It was the only way they would survive the day. It was the only way they could survive the rest of their lives. They could not show emotion. Doing so would only weaken their position, and their position was tenuous at best. Did the man not even know which woman was the mother of which child? Could he not recognize the mother, at least, and then determine the correct son?

Politics ran deep in the colony of wives, just as it did everywhere else in the universe.

"Let us go, then, and celebrate," the emperor said. He took Dyson's hand and led him to the rail. He lifted their joint hands together in a signal of victory. The crowd seemed confused, but cheered as always.

The people had no choice in that.

Hand in hand, the two went down the steps to the hover pod with the canines and the assistant following, as they always did.

Rowena felt the trembling of Ben's muscles beneath her hands.

It didn't show. His posture remained erect, his gaze focused on the crowd below.

Be strong, my son.

They remained still, all of them on the balcony, until the hover pod disappeared from sight.

There were looks of sympathy from the lesser wives. There was a smile of victory on the first wife's face. They all moved inside until the only ones remaining on the balcony were Rowena, Ben, and Stefan.

A servant, quietly sympathetic, took Stefan inside. "I don't understand," Ben said finally as the first sun dipped behind their building, creating long shadows that contrasted with the orange hue of the sky. "It's *my* birthday," he continued with a sigh.

"He made a mistake," Rowena said. The all-powerful, all-knowing had made a mistake.

"Doesn't he know me? Doesn't he know who I am?"

How could she explain it? How do you tell a boy that his father doesn't really care? That his birthday celebration was all for show, just an excuse for pageantry and pomp? There was only one son who concerned the emperor. The heir, who even now had his own room close to his father, so that he could learn how best to rule.

"You and Dyson are close in age. Perhaps he got the dates confused."

"But my name is everywhere," Ben pointed out. "He must have known it is my birthday, not Dyson's."

Not if he didn't know the difference between the two boys. And not only did the emperor not know which was which, but his assistant didn't know, either. After all, he had been the one whispering in the emperor's ear.

There was no excuse for the error. A father should know his sons. He should know all of them.

Rowena didn't know what to say.

"Why didn't you tell him it was me?" Ben asked.

He took a step forward, removing himself from contact with his mother. Her hands reached for him, then dropped as Ben stepped to the balcony rail and gripped it once more.

A gentle breeze, herald of the coming sunset, ruffled the banners that proclaimed his name. Even now they were being removed from the parade route, the workers busily efficient so that nothing of this day would remain. After all, they had to prepare for the next celebration.

"You didn't tell him," Ben said. His voice cracked on the words. Whether from emotion or just the fact that he had begun the change into manhood, Rowena couldn't tell. His shoulders remained straight and his spine rigid as he looked out over the street.

I didn't tell him.

Chapter One

Ruben didn't like the way things were going. Not at all. The well-endowed woman who just a few microns earlier was rubbing the inside of his thigh as a prelude to warming his sheets had suddenly disappeared from his side as a blaster was pressed against his ear.

Not exactly what he was hoping to find by his ear. As a matter of fact, his ear was still moist from the woman's tongue and the promises of rapture she'd made as she guided him to her room above the tavern.

He had come to the dreary outpost with his ship's hold full of mining supplies, food stores, and a goodly supply of Oasian Ale. He'd also brought with him a burning need for some companionship. The long trips spent in cryo sleep were wearing on him.

Ruben was lonely. He hated to admit it, but it was

the truth. At least he knew a quick cure for the emptiness he felt inside.

Ruben had quickly identified the woman who'd sauntered up to his table as a professional, a rapture slave, a woman trained and then sold by dealers to service the lonely men who traveled to the ends of the known universe to seek their fortunes. That didn't matter to him. What did matter was that she was available and seemed almost eager to please him. In no time at all she was guiding him to her room over the bar with a promise of pleasures to come in her eyes. If only he'd realized that she was just figuring out what she was going to spend her credits on.

The old adage "You get what you pay for" entered his mind as his eyes adjusted to the darkness that surrounded him. Obviously, someone had offered her more credits to lead him into a trap than she thought she would have earned for her companionship.

If only she knew how generous he was with his credits and his other . . . assets.

"Keep your hands where I can see them," a voice growled beside him.

"If I can't see them, how do I know you can?" Ruben asked casually. The voice came from the other side of the blaster. He thought he'd recognized it but couldn't put a face to it, at least not yet.

"Always a smart-ass," the voice said. "It won't help you now."

"So I guess you know me," Ruben said, grinning into the darkness. Or else his reputation had preceded him.

He was able to make out shadows now. Too bad Shaun wasn't here. With his friend and former partner's ability to see in the dark, Ruben would have made short work of this opponent and they'd be back down in the tavern enjoying a drink. Was there anyone else lurking in the shadows that he should know about? He casually flexed his wrist to make sure that his weapon was ready as he slowly raised his hands.

"We've met," the voice said. "Of course, at the time I didn't know there was a price on your head. Or maybe that's something new you've added to your résumé."

What?

This was news to Ruben. Big news.

"There's a price on my head?" Ruben asked, hoping he didn't sound as shocked as he felt.

"Just came over the SNN last night," the voice informed him. "750,000 credits for your capture. Imagine how happy I was when I heard that the *Shooting Star* had arrived this afternoon with her hold full of supplies."

"Glad I made your day," Ruben said. "Did the Senate News Network happen to mention what I'm wanted for?"

"As a matter of fact, it did," the voice continued. "Murder and conspiracy to commit murder. Also smuggling and dealing in deadly substances."

"And whom did I supposedly kill?"

"The Emperor Rashad DeMarco Monaco of the planet Amanor."

Ruben was glad for the darkness. The two men hoping to capture him couldn't see the look on his face. He knew there were two now. A shadow by the bed had moved.

Time to go.

"You'd think I'd be worth more than that," Ruben said. "After all, that is quite an impressive list of crimes I've been accused of."

In the next micron he threw a shoulder into the body holding the blaster, and with a quick flick of his wrist hurled a blade across the room. He was rewarded with the sound of a body hitting the floor at the same instant that the blaster bombarded the ceiling with a quick burst.

Ruben dashed toward the bed, yanked his blade from its target, and dove through the window.

He fell on the metal overhang that sheltered the tavern from the heavy rain that constantly pelted the mining post. He rolled across the roof and landed on his feet in the mud that had accumulated upon the oily pavement. It sucked at the soles of his boots as he took off at a run toward the primitive spaceport, pulses from the blaster chasing at his heels.

Ruben heard shouts behind him and kept running until he reached the hangar. He pressed the button on the remote he kept with him at all times, and the hatch at the side of the *Shooting Star* opened just as he hit the ramp.

"Welcome back, sir," the Encrypted Language Intelligence said in its silky feminine voice. He'd installed it sometime after Shaun had retired and he'd realized that he didn't want another partner.

"Fire the engines," Ruben yelled. "We're leaving now!" Luckily, he'd already refueled. That was always the first thing he did when he landed.

"Engines started," Eli replied. "Anything else I can do for you?"

Ruben slammed into his seat and checked the com. "Yeah, get us out of here." He recognized the face of the man who stared at the plexi shield of his ship in frustration. Knowing that it was impenetrable did not stop his pursuer from shooting at him anyway.

"Beat you again, Forrest!" Ruben yelped in glee as he grabbed the control. "Unlucky at cards, unlucky at life," he added as the *Shooting Star* rose gracefully from her dock and hovered for a moment, tauntingly hanging over his enemy. In the next micron she was gone, shooting through the bank of clouds overhead and into the stratosphere.

"Check security," Ruben said, "and set coordinates for the closest hyperport."

There was no pursuit from below. He had not expected any. He had seen the other ships in the hangar when he'd landed. None of them could touch the *Shooting Star*, especially when she was traveling light, as she was now.

He had hoped to make a deal for some of the natural resources that the mines had to offer. The hard charcoal they mined had been around since before recorded time and was still valuable as a fuel source in the smaller settlements that were constantly cropping up on outlying planets.

Settlers were venturing further, trying to get out from beneath the Senate's thumb. They sought the peace and solitude of distance from the center of the universe. But distance also meant giving up modern sources of energy and having to rely on ancient forms.

Most of the settlers didn't seem to mind. And they were always ready to trade when he landed with his hold full of supplies.

It helped that what he brought to the outlying

planets was quality stuff, courtesy of his friend and former partner Shaun Phoenix.

Several factions in the universe would pay anything to know the hiding place of Shaun Phoenix and his consort, the Royal Princess Lilly of Oasis. Foremost among them were the Circe. The race of mostly physic women had long protected their power by destroying any male child who showed signs of being born with the psychic talent they used to control others. Those who held the power of their race were on a quest to gain unlimited dominion over the universe. Ruben made it a top priority to avoid the Circe and their cursed collars in his travels. That was one experience he did not want to repeat.

He knew they would put a collar on him again if he crossed their path. They would do anything in their power to find Shaun, the lost son of a Circe witch.

"What is our destination?" Eli asked.

"Oasis."

"Entering hyperport in ten," Eli informed him as it began the countdown to the jump.

Oasis, the garden planet of the universe, was the last place the Circe would think to look for Shaun and Lilly. In their logical minds, the couple would hide as far away from their home planet as they could get. The newlyweds were counting on that assumption to keep them safe, deep within the wild regions of the planet.

But then again those few did not know the real story.

I'll be damned before I lead anyone to my friends.

Ruben flexed the wrist where he wore the blade.

The blade was a special and private gift from his father when he realized he had slighted Ruben on his twelfth birthday. Older than history, it came from mystical origins. The weapon consisted of ten razor-sharp blades that could be individually thrown then retrieved into a solid mass with only a slight flick of his wrist. It took a special talent to throw the blade and wear it. It was almost as if the weapon sensed the will of its bearer.

His father had given it to him when he realized that Rubikhan Benjamin was the only son who had the talent to use it. It also was a part of his mother's dowry, something that young Ben did not find out until she died a few years later and her credentials were circulated during the time of mourning.

The blade had served him well—better than anything else he'd received from his parents. Sure, he had gotten an education to be envied and more training in the art of war than the highest-ranking Legion officers, but the only thing that Ruben took with him when he left his home planet was the blade. And the skills to use it.

His father had told him at one time that he was meant to be a warrior. But he had left that life behind a long time ago. Being a warrior for his father meant being a pawn. He'd rather be dead.

But instead, it was his father who was dead.

And Ruben was wanted for his murder.

Chapter Two

"Ten," Tess said. Her eyes darted to Boone and back to the trader. Eye contact was an important part of the game. But not as important as keeping her son safe.

"Fifteen," the vendor replied. He looked bored.

Tess ran her hands over the smooth leather of the boots. Her own were ruined after years of hard work in the vineyards and in the house of Joah, the man who'd bought her as a slave when she was nothing more than a girl of seventeen.

Her boots had been relatively new when her previous owner suddenly dropped ship on this solitary planet and sold her to the first man he found. Joah had told her she was to be a housekeeper, but as soon as she saw his son, she knew his words for a lie. And even though she'd tried to protect herself, the son had had his way with her. Then the son had died in an accident and Joah had, indeed, put her to work as his housekeeper. Unfortunately for her, Joah cared little for the condition of anything he owned, and so she was still wearing the boots she'd had on when he'd purchased her from the slave traders seven years earlier.

Her feet had grown a size after the birth of her son Boone, and the heels were worn, the leather scuffed beyond repair. She really needed the boots.

"Mema, let's go." Boone tugged on her arm. The crowd bumped and jostled against them in the marketplace.

"Shhh, Boone," she said as she pretended to examine the quality of the leather, frowning as if it wasn't even worth the ten credits she had offered. Ky, the huge black Newf that was Boone's protector and constant companion, watched her with tongue lolling from his dark head.

Tess mentally calculated the credits in her pocket. Her weavings fetched a decent price, but it still frustrated her to know that the vendor who purchased them would more than quadruple his investment when he resold them. Unfortunately, she possessed neither the rank nor the resources to sell them directly to persons who searched for quality fabrics such as those she made on Joah's long-dead wife's loom.

At six years of age, Boone was quickly outgrowing his clothes. A stop at an earlier stall had produced boots for him, but they both desperately needed new coats. She would have to choose.

"Twelve." Tess tried to keep the desperation out of her voice.

The vendor looked at her in disgust, but then his eyes did a slow perusal of her tall, slim body before finally flicking down to her worn boots.

Tess placed a hand protectively on Boone's shoulder. She heard the heavy panting of Ky behind her as the huge animal rose to his feet.

What did it matter what this man thought of her? Yes, she was nothing more than a slave, but at least she was spared the humility of being a rapture whore. She was clean, and so was her son. Her dark, wavy hair was captured in a neat twist at the nape of her neck, and her gray-green eyes could look into the man's with honesty and some degree of pride.

"Twelve," the vendor agreed.

Tess's face did not betray her joy and relief.

"Do you want to wear them?" the man asked.

"No," she said. If Joah saw her with new boots, he might try to sell them and then she would be barefoot. She'd scuff them up a bit and bring them out when he was dull-witted with wine.

She placed her purchase in the bottom of her bag and took Boone's hand as she slung it over her shoulder.

They wandered among the booths with the crowd, Tess keeping a sharp eye out for Qazar addicts and for a heavy coat that would get Boone through the winter months. She had already made up her mind to fashion herself a coat by weaving together strips of fabric from the clothing that Boone had outgrown. And depending on the price of a coat, she might have a few credits left over to purchase some sort of toy for him.

You would think that his grandfather would provide for him, since Boone was his only heir. But ever since the death of his son four years past, Joah did nothing but worry over his vineyards and drink the fine wines that he produced each year. Even now he was off selling the latest vintage to one of the vendors that supplied the better taverns on the planet.

Tess had long thought he'd be better off selling his wares to someone who ran off-planet, but Joah was set in his ways. As far as she knew, his acquisition of her was the only time he'd ever made a purchase that came from off-planet. The women who were native to the place were wise enough to say away from Joah and his son.

Joah thought the old ways were best. Tess considered herself lucky that the old man thought her taboo since her son had bedded her. Having his son crawl on her had been bad enough.

Tess often shuddered at the prospect of Joah using her body. Despite his beliefs, he still watched her as if he was considering it. Tess always made sure she was safe in her pallet beside Boone's bed when Joah started his drinking at night. Many a time the old man walked into the room and stood over her, just watching as she pretended to sleep. Tess was certain he would never try anything in front of Boone.

Or maybe he was just afraid of Ky.

Tess was grateful for the presence of the Newf. Ever since he had crawled out of the deep woods two years ago, he had attached himself to Boone. It might be out of gratitude for her care when he was so close to death, or it might be because he felt a kinship with the boy. Tess didn't care what the reasons were. Nor did she wonder anymore where the animal had come from or why he had been beaten so badly. She just knew that with Ky around, they were safe. No one would dare approach them when they saw the size of the animal. His broad black back nearly reached Tess's waist, and his head was on the same level as Boone's.

But not for long. Not the way her son was growing.

"We need to find you a coat," she said, guiding Boone away from a vendor selling sweets and toward a display of children's clothes. She would see how many credits she had left after she purchased the necessities. Then they could think about a treat.

Maybe she could find one for Ky also.

Boone protested, of course. It wasn't often that they got to come to the capital city, and it was an exciting place for a boy whose only companion was Ky. Joah didn't understand or care that Boone should be exposed to children his own age. His own son never had been and he had turned out fine. Fine as far as Joah was concerned.

Tess was glad Joah's son was dead. She was also glad that Boone had her looks, instead of the looks of his father. As much as she loved her son, her greatest fear was that he would turn out to be just like his father. Deliberately cruel. Her body still bore the scars of his perversions.

Yet she considered herself lucky. She was raised to be a rapture whore after being sold from the orphan's home on a planet whose name she could not remember. Strange that she could not remember her home planet. She could not remember anything about her life except that she could read and write.

She did not even know exactly how old she'd been when she came to the slave trader, except that she was old enough to be blossoming into youthful womanhood. Unfortunately, her temperament did not match the purpose her owner had for her. After a few years of training, he grew tired of her tirades and stubbornness, and since he couldn't beat her, fearing that it would mar her looks, he stopped off at the first planet they passed and sold her off. He needed to be rid of her before she became a bad influence on the rest of his investments. No need to waste more time training her. She was worthless to him. He thought it a great revenge that she would be nothing more than a housekeeper for the rest of her life.

Tess knew she was better off here than in the bowels of a mining planet, or worse yet, a prison planet. She heard the stories whispered by the ones who were lucky enough to escape those horrors. She had suffered a cruel husband for a few years, but she had Boone to show for it. She considered herself lucky that her owner had sold her off before he'd had her fixed and left her unable to bear children.

Tess was fortunate. If she could just hang on until Joah died and Boone inherited the vineyard . . . He was the son of a free man. He could inherit.

As long as Joah didn't do anything foolish, they would be fine.

The coat she chose for Boone was big, but that was her intent. It would last longer, as long as he didn't lose it, or shred it while playing in the woods on the edge of the property. It would do. She stuffed the purchase into her pack and slung it over her shoulder.

"Spare credits?"

The beggar surprised her even though she had been watching out for them. The hand he held out trembled, and his eyes were bloodshot. His lips held the deep blue tint of a Qazar addict. Even in this peaceful world ignored by the universe, there was despair. And the despair seemed to be growing more and more each day.

Ky stepped up beside her and let out a low growl.

The beggar disappeared back into the shadows behind the vendors, and Tess let out a sigh of relief.

She had three credits left. And the smell of sweet cake drew them close.

"Mema?" Boone asked.

"Yes." She smiled, the beggar already forgotten. Tess ran her fingers through his dark hair. "And a small toy too."

With Ky at his side, Boone ran toward the toy vendor's cart while she paid for the cake. She watched as he stared wide-eyed at the display and then settled on a ship. It was sleek in design, modeled after one of the Senate fighters she had seen as a young girl.

"Can I?" Boone asked.

Tess looked at the ship. It was made of a dense metal with a flame pattern painted on the side. It would last, although the paint would most likely chip off in time.

Joah would not approve. It represented the things he abhorred. He detested technology in any form. Most of the people living in the countryside felt the same. Those who resided in the city were a bit more advanced, but not much. At least they acknowledged that technology had its purpose.

"You must keep it from Joah," Tess said.

"I will," Boone promised. His green eyes lifted with his smile. He understood the way things were. His mother walked a narrow rope. He would lose his toy if Joah found out, but Tess would receive the punishment. He would be careful. He had learned much in his short life.

Tess paid for the ship. She had enough coin left for them to share a fizzy drink.

"When I am big, I shall fly a ship like this," Boone

said as they walked on, eating sticky cake and sharing the drink. It was a fine day. The weather in the city was warmer than at the base of the mountains, where Joah's property was.

"That would be grand," Tess agreed as Boone made the engine of the spacecraft hum by using his voice as his hand guided it to imaginary star systems.

Tess stopped in her tracks.

Garvin. The sight of the neighboring farmer gave her a sudden chill on what she had thought to be a warm day. The man had long wanted her and was continually making offers for her to Joah. Joah knew that if he sold her off, he'd be responsible for raising Boone, and he didn't quite have the patience for that. Still, Tess lived in constant fear that when he was deep in his cups, he would give in to Garvin's pressure and she'd find herself separated from her son.

Garvin was always touching her, pushing up against her whenever he had the chance. There were few here who would stop him, especially since she bore the mark of slave on her shoulder. It was a constant curse to her that Garvin was in partnership with Joah and made the thick cobalt glass bottles that held the sweet wine Joah produced.

Tess pulled Boone after her as she made for the shelter of a large warehouse behind the stalls.

The building was cavernous, mostly used for storage during the winter months, almost empty now when the weather was clear and dry. Still, Tess was cautious as they crept inside and moved along a wall piled high with empty crates.

"What are we doing, Mema?" Boone asked. Ky followed along behind him, silent on his huge paws, watchful as always.

"Hiding," Tess whispered.

"From Master Joah's friend?" he whispered back.

Tess took a moment to look at her son as they crept along the shadowed wall. How could he be so wise at such a young age? How much had he seen and understood as he watched the adults in his life? If only she could take him away from Joah. Away from the vineyard. Away from this planet. If only they could find a place where they could live as free people do.

Joah would never allow it. And even if and when he died and Boone inherited, she would still have to deal with Garvin.

Boone would own me.

In all her wishful thinking, that thought had never crossed her mind until now.

"I wouldn't do that if I were you." It was a man's threatening voice, but he was not speaking to her.

Tess dropped into a crouch and pulled Boone down with her, holding his hand tightly. Ky, on the other side of Boone, perked his ears up, listening with great interest to the strange voices that echoed in the empty shell of the building.

Tess pulled Boone behind her and placed a firm hand on Ky's collar to keep him quiet. If the animal thought there was a threat to Boone, she wouldn't be able to hold him. The dog merely watched, looking with interest through an opening in the stack of crates.

Tess put her head next to Ky's and watched the argument unfold.

"You didn't tell me what you were planning, Dyson," the younger of the two men said. He was facing her, and his eyes were so blue that she could see the color from her hiding place. He was tall and lean, his young face earnestly handsome, his golden-brown hair curling around his shoulders.

"You jumped at the chance to make some credits, Stef," the larger one said. He raised a hand threateningly. A hand that was missing the smallest finger. "That was all the information you needed at the time."

A low growl rumbled in Ky's throat. Tess looked around to see if they could make an escape. Unfortunately, the way they'd come in was in clear view of the two men who were arguing. There were large wooden barrels stacked close to where they talked, and now a woman in a strangely ornate hat and a long robe made an appearance from behind them.

The larger man looked ominous even with his back turned toward Tess's hiding place. His hair was pale blond and his build was threatening, even though he appeared to have more fat than muscle. He was a sharp contrast to the smooth grace of his companion, who appeared to Tess to be younger than she.

"I don't mind making credits, but not at the expense of someone's life," the one called Stef continued. "Just count me out of this deal."

"Sorry, Brother. No backing out." The larger one looked at the woman in the hat and robes.

Tess got a look at the woman's eyes as she turned toward her companion. They were colorless, vacant. A chill went down Tess's spine as another growl rumbled deep in Ky's chest. The hackles rose on his back and Tess tightened her grip. Why did the woman's eyes seem so familiar? Surely she would recall seeing eyes like that.

"Mema?" Boone whispered. His face was ghastly pale in the dim light.

Suddenly the prospect of facing Garvin didn't seem so bad.

Two more men appeared from behind the barrels. They were both dressed in black, and one held a glowing circle in his hand.

"Half-brother," Stefan said, his bright blue eyes on the two men.

"I'm more your brother than the one who left you," the bigger man said. "I'm the one who wanted to share the wealth with you." He spread his arms expansively as if sharing a great treasure.

"Tell your witch to leave me be," Stefan warned.

"Tell her yourself," Dyson replied. He crossed his arms casually across his chest.

Tess watched in shock as the young man dropped to his knees with a scream of pain. Was he hurt? What had happened? Had a weapon been fired?

At the same instant, Ky broke away from her grip and charged through the crates, toppling them in every direction. As suddenly as he'd dropped to his knees, the young man jumped up and ran for the opposite door.

"Ky!" Boone screamed.

The woman looked their way, and Tess saw pure evil in her gaze. Ky knocked over one of the barrels, and cobalt blue glass shattered onto the floor.

Tess gathered her son in her arms and took off running toward the exit, her pack slamming against her back. If need be, she would dump it, regardless of the loss. The air in the building had grown icy with malevolence, and Tess had no doubt their very lives were at stake.

To her surprise, Ky was beside them as they ran through the door. Perhaps Boone's scream had turned him back. Tess didn't have time to think about it. She bolted through the door and disappeared into the crowded streets with her son safe in her arms.

Chapter Three

Ruben blinked awake as his cryo cycle ended and automatically reached for his water bottle. He was always so thirsty when he awakened.

Why had he dreamed about Stefan? The last time he'd seen his brother was fifteen years earlier. Stefan had been just a child, barely five solar years. Ruben had no idea what he looked like now.

"Entering Oasis Hyperport," Eli said. "I hope you had a nice rest."

Ruben rolled his eyes. Sometimes Eli sounded almost too personal. What was the point of flirting if you couldn't follow it up with a little physical contact?

A quick check on his com let him know he was right where he should be. Trusting the AI was something he had issues with, even after all these years. Maybe it was because of the feminine voice.

"Identify," came a voice over the monitor.

"A sailor lost at sea," Ruben replied.

"Welcome back, Starshooter," replied the pilot of a patrolling fighter. "Don't have any bounty hunters on your tail, do you?"

"Good news travels fast, I hear," Ruben replied. He wasn't worried about the pilot or anyone else on Oasis turning him in. He had proven his worth in the skies over Oasis during the Ravigan war five solar years ago. "So what's with the extra security?" he asked. "Or is this all for me?" He looked through the plexi as the fighter settled in next to him.

"Sorry, Starshooter," the pilot replied, "although I could use some extra credits. We're on the lookout for Qazar smugglers." Ruben could see the pilot's face grinning in the cockpit of his fighter. "Got any on you?"

"Hey, even I have my limits," Ruben said into the com. He had seen his share of addicts. He'd even been offered a chance to try Qazar. Those who endorsed it said the drug gave users unlimited power and the ability to see beyond the end of the universe. Unfortunately, it was also highly addictive. Addicts would kill for it. It was easier to kill than resist the cravings. Fortunately, its habituates were easy to spot because of their bright blue lips. "Has it gotten that bad?"

"It's an epidemic," the pilot reported. "But so far we've managed to avoid it on Oasis." The pilot saluted him. "Safe stars," he said and dropped off of Ruben's wing.

"Safe stars," Ruben replied.

So the news of the price on his head had reached Oasis. Not surprising, since it had been on the SNN network. Shaun and his father-in-law, Michael, kept a close eye on the happenings of the universe. It was their way of heading off any trouble that might come toward Oasis.

Ruben's ship gracefully sliced into the cool, clear skies of Oasis. It never ceased to amaze him to see how bright and pure the colors were here. The population of the planet had taken care of their natural resources. Everything they used was recycled, and since there was no industry of any kind, the planet remained untainted.

Perfect patchwork fields came into view, dotted with small settlements of farmers. Ruben flew over neat lines of orchards and long rows of buildings used to house animals. Random patches of flowers broke up the smooth organization of the fields, and crystal blue rivers could be seen, winding their way through the countryside.

Shaun and Lilly would be expecting him. The pilot who had greeted him would have alerted them to his coming as soon as he hit the skies above Oasis. Ruben's stomach was already growling with the thought of the good food and good companionship that he was soon to enjoy.

The terrain below became wilder as he flew closer to the equator of the planet. Soon he could see the ocean swirling turquoise, cerulean, and then emerald as he flew toward an array of islands cropping up from the water.

They had been formed long ago by volcanoes. One of the smaller ones held a lake of the purest silver. Ruben moved the control forward and the *Shooting Star* began her descent, losing herself in the bright rays of the sun.

The ship skimmed over the water, Ruben taking joy in seeing just how close he could come to the surface, which was completely still except for the ripples caused by his exhaust. Ahead of him was a cave, barely noticeable in the uneven surface of the volcano.

Ruben knew it well. He reduced the power in his thrusters and the *Shooting Star* gracefully settled into the landing bay.

Shaun was waiting for him.

"Been busy, have you?" Shaun asked as Ruben walked through the hatch.

"You know me," Ruben replied. "I'm the terror of the universe."

"No, you're the scourge. Qazar is the terror."

"Thanks for clearing that up." Ruben looked into the pale gray eyes of his friend. He could tell Shaun was worried about him. "So how's the family?" he asked, changing the subject.

They walked into the labyrinth of tunnels that led to the villa carved into the opposite side of the volcano.

"Zander and Elle have grown a bunch since your last visit, and Lilly is the same." Ruben heard the pride and love in his friend's voice.

"Has Zander—" Ruben began.

"No," Shaun said. The tunnels were dark now. Ruben didn't have to see his friend's face to know that he was concerned about his son.

The twins, named Alexander and Arielle, were now four solar years. Very few even knew of their birth. Their very existence had to remain hidden from the Circe, who would be desperate to lay their hands upon the offspring of a male and female of their race.

"Hey, not everyone can see in the dark, you

know," Ruben reminded him. The tunnels were pitch-black as they went into the depths of the mountainside.

"Sorry," Shaun said. "Lights." A series of beacons lit up and trailed away into the tunnels.

"Encrypted Language Intelligence?" Ruben asked.

"Yes."

"How did we live without it? At least my Eli keeps reminding me that I can't live without it."

"Want me back?" Shaun asked.

"Nope. Besides, the co-seat is still broken."

"You still haven't fixed that? What's wrong? Can't you find a woman who's good with her hands?"

"She was great with her hands," Ruben replied with a grin. "How do you think it got broken in the first place?"

Shaun laughed out loud as the tunnel expanded into a wide cavern. They had almost reached the villa. Soon they walked through an intricately carved archway with broad wooden doors.

Exquisitely woven tapestries covered the stone walls. Plush rugs covered the smooth, polished floors. Couches and chairs were arranged in intimate seating groups, suggesting nights of fellowship before the wide fireplace with the carved mantelpiece.

Beyond, on a balcony that seemed to be floating among the clouds, Ruben could see Lilly and the twins, Zander and Elle; the sweet sound of wind chimes joined in with their laughter. Lilly, delicate and graceful, turned toward him with a wide smile. The children, miniatures of their parents, ran to Ruben with squeals of delight and wrapped their arms around his legs in greeting.

"Do you need some help staying out of trouble?" Lilly asked as she gave him a quick hug and a kiss on the cheek. Her pale gray eyes twinkled mischievously as she smiled up at him.

"Not if it involves any of your torture," Ruben replied, referring to Lilly's ability to plant images of horrible consequences in his mind. She was training him to repel any mind probes the Circe might use against him. Since he knew about the children, he had to be wary. So far, he had managed to stay well away from any contact with the evil race of women telepaths.

"Is something wrong?" Lilly asked quickly as the thought flashed across his mind.

"You mean besides the fact that I'm wanted for several high-profile crimes?"

"We're so sorry about your father," Lilly said.

Shaun handed Ruben a glass of Oasian Ale. He remained silent. Ruben had told his friends about his estranged relationship with his father several years ago.

"His murder is not surprising considering who he was, and what he was," Ruben said carelessly as he tossed down the ale. "What happened, exactly?" He saw Lilly's eyes on him. She knew he was hiding something.

Shaun handed him a PDV and he flipped it open. The Senate logo appeared on the small screen, indicating that the digital had been downloaded from SNN. Shaun, like most rulers in the universe, kept his ear tuned to the latest news from each planet.

"News from the planet Amanor," the beautiful announcer said on the handheld screen. Funny how her beauty didn't take away any of the ugliness of the news. "High Marshall Emperor Rashad De-Marco Monaco has been assassinated, along with his heir, Prince Rashad the Second. An attempt has also been made on Prince Dyson DeMarco. Reports are that Prince Dyson, who is number thirteen in line to inherit by Amanor law, was uninjured in the attack, which occurred on the planet Lavign.

"The prime suspect in the assassination is Prince Stefan Andreas, who is number twenty in line for the throne. The prince has not been seen since the attack on his father and half-brothers. Prince Stefan has a full brother, Prince Rubikhan Benjamin, who is also wanted in the attacks. It is not clear, however, if Prince Rubikhan is alive or dead. He was outlawed by his father fifteen solar years ago."

Ruben was amazed to see an image of his face appear on the screen alongside that of Stefan. At least he thought the other picture was Stefan. The resemblance was striking.

"I guess my cover is blown," Ruben said.

"At the present time, there are thirty-eight princes, all in line to inherit their father's position," the newscaster added with a wry smile.

Yet another tribute to his father's sexual prowess.

"In other news," the woman continued, "Senate and Legion personnel are working in unison to find the source of the new cult drug Qazar . . ." Ruben snapped the PDV shut and handed it to Shaun, who was giving him the same penetrating look as Lilly. He knew his friend was tempted to probe his mind to get a sense of what he was feeling.

"He was a bastard," Ruben said simply.

"Is there a chance that your brother had anything to do with the assassination?" Shaun asked.

"I don't know," Ruben said. "He was only a boy when I left. I don't know what he's like. I can't say that I'd blame him. I know I wanted to kill our father many times."

"Perhaps there was an attempt on your brother's life also," Shaun commented. "And that's why he's missing."

"You mean he could be dead and we just don't know about it?" Ruben asked. He walked out to the balcony, his mind swirling.

So much had happened. Was Stefan involved somehow in their father's assassination? Or was he a victim also? And did this have anything to do with the dream Ruben had had while in cryo?

He grabbed the smooth rail of the balcony and looked out over the jungle that fell away to the ocean. As usual, the colors were vivid and brilliant, the vista a thing of beauty to behold. Beneath him he could hear the sound of a waterfall as it sprang forth from the mountain and tumbled down into the sea.

A ship was coming in, flying the same course that he had taken, and circling around to the lake behind. The sun caught its reflection and dazzled his eyes.

"Michael," Shaun explained as he joined him. "Come to see his grandchildren."

"I had a dream about Stefan while I was in cryo," Ruben said. "I wonder if it means anything."

"Why don't you tell us about him?" Lilly said as she stepped onto the balcony. "You've never mentioned your brother in all the years we've known you."

Talk about Stefan?

Ruben had made a career of not telling anyone about anything.

The children played quietly on a mat on the balcony.

Their excitement over seeing him again had passed, their minds easily distracted.

If only it were that easy for the rest of us.

Elle talked to her doll and Zander shot at imagined raiders with a toy spaceship that was decorated with brightly painted flames on the side.

It was a peaceful setting. A place of contentment. It was the total opposite of his life since leaving his home planet.

His hands gripped the balcony rail.

"You've never mentioned your mother either," Lilly urged gently.

Ruben turned to Lilly and gave her a dazzling smile. It was the same smile that saved him dozens of credits when he sat in a myriad of taverns dotting the underside of the galaxy. The smile that made women fall over each other in their eagerness to warm his sheets. The smile that had gotten him out of more trouble than he cared to remember.

"Ow!" he yelped as the nerve endings in his nether region sensed the assault of a set of pincers.

"Don't try to con me, Ruben." Lilly graced him with a sweet smile.

Shaun, standing next to the balcony, suddenly found something fascinating in the landscape below. Ruben could see the wide set of his friend's shoulders shaking as he fought to control his laughter.

"As if I could," Ruben said as he shook his head to dispel the pain she'd placed in his mind. "Or would."

"If you don't want to talk about it, then just say so," Lilly said.

Ruben resisted the urge to place his hand over his groin, just to make sure everything was still attached.

"It's just that I've never even thought about him in all these years," Ruben began.

"Was that a conscious decision?" Lilly asked. "Not to think about him? Or did you make yourself put him out of your mind?"

"Does it matter?" Ruben asked.

Shaun gave him a dangerous look. Ruben threw up his hands in mock surrender.

And then with perfect timing, Michael walked in.

The children ran to their grandfather, who gathered both of them up in his arms and carried them out to where Ruben, Shaun, and Lilly were standing.

Though Shaun was the official ruler of Oasis, Michael handled the day-to-day running of the government. Ruben recalled that the last time he'd visited, Shaun was excitedly talking about a thing called democracy and was hoping to implement it on the planet. It sounded like a giant popularity contest to Ruben, but it might just work in a place such as Oasis. Especially if Shaun were the one running for election.

"Just so you know," Michael said to Ruben with a big grin. "We're supposed to turn you in to the Senate."

"What's the matter?" Ruben asked. "Isn't the big guy paying you enough?"

Chapter Four

My mind is my own.

Ruben felt the soft brush of Lilly's presence as her mind entered his with the gentle grace of a butterfly. A sense of relief filled him as he realized he could sense her probes. That was a good thing. He should be prepared in case the Circe ever caught up with him.

"You can't let your fears be known, Ruben," Lilly said out loud.

She was sitting before him with her legs crossed in a position that he would never be able to achieve. Her face was calm but serious, and her light gray eyes pierced his soul.

"Try once more, and this time clear your mind of everything," Lilly said. She pushed stray locks of her ash-brown hair behind her ears and straightened her back as she settled into position.

My mind is my own. Ruben began the litany again.

It was the only weapon that could be used to fight the Circe, if one's will was strong enough.

Once more Lilly entered into contact.

No other may possess it.

Strong-willed. That was what his mother always said about him. She also said that he reminded her of her brother.

Stefan . . . his brother. Stefan was in trouble. He could feel the fear. It was overwhelming, the urge to run. The urge to hide. Stefan . . .

"Ruben?" Lilly asked. "Something is troubling you."

Ruben blinked as he realized Lilly was speaking out loud.

"I've got a price on my head, Lilly," he said dryly. "It causes me some concern."

Lilly dismissed the comment with a wave of her hand. "You're doing a good job of blocking me."

Ruben allowed himself a smile of satisfaction. Blocking was something he was great at. He'd actually suggested this practice session so he wouldn't have to talk about his family.

"Try again," Lilly instructed. The look of determination on her face was a challenge.

Ruben closed his eyes and began once more.

I see your mother . . .

Cold chills ran down his spine. With catlike grace Ruben jumped to his feet and walked to the balcony. He placed his hands, hands that would rather be on the controls of the *Shooting Star* than anywhere else in the galaxy, on the thick stone banister that overlooked the ocean. He stared at the dancing treetops against the deepening sky. The tinkling chimes above him gave evidence of the strength of the breeze.

Lilly moved gracefully, silently, beside him and placed a delicate hand next to his. His knuckles showed white as he tightened his grip on the rail. A vision of himself as a boy on his twelfth birthday flashed through his mind.

"You've told us of your father, Ruben, but never of your mother or your brother Stefan," Lilly said. "All we know is that she died and you left to seek your fortunes elsewhere." Lilly placed a hand on his arm. "What troubles you, dear friend?"

Ruben knew Lilly well enough to know that this was not the time for his tavern charm.

How should he answer her?

Inside the villa, Shaun and Michael had their heads together. It was amazing how quickly Shaun had taken to being the leader of an entire planet. But when Ruben reflected, it really wasn't amazing at all. He'd always sensed that his friend was destined for great things. And a great love.

The children were once more playing on the rug, quietly content, oblivious to the fact that people would kill just to possess them.

There was absolutely no reason for him not to tell Lilly about his past. What did he have to lose?

"Our mother died quite suddenly. One day she was perfectly fine and then she developed a fever and was dead within two days. I hated my father so I left. I hid on a freighter and got off-planet. The pilot found me and gave me a choice. Either be jettisoned into space with the garbage, or go to work for him. He soon discovered I had a knack for flying and made me his partner. I was fourteen when I left. By the time I was nineteen, I had my own ship. I met Shaun a few years later, and the rest you know."

"You still haven't mentioned your brother," Lily pointed out gently.

Ruben turned to look over the vista. "His name is Stefan Andreas. He's nine years younger than I. My father rewarded my mother with a conjugal visit because I impressed him with my weapons training," he said bitterly. Ruben had always known that his mother hated his father. He knew she was nothing more than a peace offering to the emperor. "Stef was the result of that reward."

"So he was only five when he lost his mother and his brother?"

"Too young to remember either one of us," Ruben said.

"But old enough to feel abandoned."

Ruben gave Lilly a sideways look.

"How would you feel if it had been you?"

"It was me, Lilly," Ruben said angrily. "My father did not recognize me on the most important day of my life. He chose my half-brother to honor instead of me."

"We all make mistakes, Ruben."

"Tell me that you wouldn't recognize your own children, under any circumstances. Tell me that Shaun couldn't tell his apart even if he had fifty of them."

Lilly looked toward Shaun in the other room and smiled.

"It wouldn't surprise me a bit if my father had fifty or more children, if you count the ones that aren't royal."

"Yet you have only one true brother. He's the only family you have."

"And I thought you were my family," Ruben said,

flashing his devilish grin at her. It was quickly followed by a yelp as the banister seemed to turn to molten steel before his eyes.

"You know we love you, Ruben," Lilly said with a saucy smile. "So do you want to practice some more? Maybe if you practice, it won't be so easy for me to—"

Ruben threw his hands up in mock surrender. "Anything, just quit zapping me with your brain, Princess."

Ruben lifted an eyebrow at the children, who were hiding fits of giggles behind their hands. He followed Lilly back into the villa and settled into place on the floor.

My mind is my own.

Ruben scrunched his eyes shut and held them tight, fighting against the image of a Circe before him. He didn't recognize her; though her eyes were the same color as Lilly's, they were vacant, soulless, and pale.

Stefan was in trouble.

Lilly was trying to distract him by using Stefan. He'd show her. He'd build a mental wall that was as solid as the stone of the mountain protecting this villa. She wouldn't get in this time. Lilly was not going to penetrate his defenses.

My mind is my own.

Stefan . . .

No other may possess it.

Help me, Brother . . .

I will keep my mind.

"Ruben?" Lilly said.

He blinked. "Good try, Princess."

"That wasn't me."

"What?"

"The Circe. That wasn't me."

"You didn't plant her in my mind?"

"No. I don't know her. I've never seen her before."

"So what does it mean?"

"Something you don't want to hear."

"But how is that possible?" Ruben jumped to his feet again. "How can Stefan suddenly be communicating with me telepathically? After all these years? He probably doesn't even remember me."

Lilly joined him as he made his way to the balcony. "Maybe you're more open to such communication now. Or maybe it's a link somehow between me and this other Circe."

"So perhaps she's the reason why Stefan is missing? Could she be the one who's responsible for the assassinations? Could you be seeing what she's seeing?"

"It could be. I really don't know if it's possible."

"But how can we be sure that was Stefan? I haven't seen him in fifteen years. Except for that digital image, I wouldn't even know what he looks like."

Lilly placed a gentle hand on his arm. "I saw him too, Ruben. He looks just like you."

"He does?"

"From what I could see. He's younger. He's softer around the face. His hair is the same color as yours, but long." Lilly placed a hand at her shoulder to signify the length of Stefan's hair.

"That's what I saw," Ruben said. "So what should I do?"

"What do you want to do?"

47

That was a loaded question if ever he'd heard one.

What should he do? Better yet, what could he do? He didn't even know where Stefan was. Was he at home? On Amanor?

Doubtful.

Ruben shook his head.

"How would I even find him? He's got to be in hiding, if he's still alive."

"Perhaps we should look deeper and see if there's something that might lead you to him," Lilly suggested.

"You mean inside my head?"

"Yes."

Ruben rubbed his forehead. A dull ache settled between his eyes.

"I guess it's worth a try," he said. He looked toward the sky. For some strange reason, the thought of looking deeper made him feel . . . trapped. "Can we do it out here?"

"Yes," Lilly said. "You don't even have to move." She placed the index and middle finger of her left hand alongside his temple. "Just think about Stefan."

How could he? It was such a long time since he'd allowed himself to think about Stef.

Ruben let his mind drift. He felt Lilly drifting with him, and the realization that she could see the things he kept locked away hit him like a blast of solar wind.

"Be at peace, Ruben," her voice whispered inside his head.

Ben . . .

His mother's voice called to him.

Ruben fought it. He didn't want to be a child

48

again. He didn't want to feel the pain of someone else controlling his life.

He didn't want to see his mother.

"Your name is Ben," Lilly said in his mind. He sensed her smile.

Too much . . . too close . . . my secrets . . . my life . . .

A scream. A boy screamed. Stefan? Did Stef ever scream like that? Ruben shook his head. Not in his memory.

Lilly was gone. Ruben blinked as awareness came to him. His mind searched for a memory, but the scream had been in the present. It was here. It was now.

"What happened?" Michael asked as he rushed onto the balcony.

Ruben's mind settled on the chaos around him. Lilly held Zander in her arms. The boy was pale as death. Shaun was beside her, his hand on Zander's face, searching for whatever had injured his son.

"He saw the mother die," Elle said. She didn't seem to be concerned about her brother although she stood by her father's knee. Shaun knelt by her side as she spoke.

"What?" Lilly gasped, her face full of shock.

"The baby's mother died," Elle explained. "Zander saw it and showed me in my mind."

"Zander saw it?" Shaun asked. "Who died? Where?"

"It was the mother. The bad woman said, 'Let her die,' and then she took the little girl away. The little girl saw it and cried, and Zander heard her." Elle's voice was perfectly serious. Perfectly calm.

"Wake up, Zander," Elle said. "Mother is frightened now."

The boy's pale gray eyes fluttered.

"The little girl is sad," Zander said as he regained consciousness. But the voice was not his own. The sound of it sent a chill up Ruben's spine.

"Can you see anything?" Shaun asked Lilly.

Lilly placed her hand on her son's temple just as she'd done earlier with Ruben.

"No," she said. "I see nothing."

Shaun placed his hand on the opposite side of Zander's face.

Ruben watched beside Michael as the parents linked their minds and delved into the unknown region of their son's mind.

"She's gone now," Elle said. "They took her away."

"Can I play?" Zander asked, his voice once again his own.

Ruben realized that the boy still held his toy tightly clutched in his hand.

Lilly ran a quick hand over her son's forehead.

"Yes," she said. She looked at Shaun, confusion plainly written on her face as Zander went back to his imagined flights.

"What happened?" Michael asked, his concern evident.

"I don't know," Lilly said. "He saw something. Somewhere." She stepped to the banister.

"Maybe you should look inside Elle?" Shaun suggested as he moved to her side.

Lilly clutched her arms at her elbows. She seemed chilled, and Ruben felt the wind rising up from the falls below. Shaun wrapped his arms around Lilly as she looked back toward the children.

"Maybe some memories are better left inside,"

Ruben said. "What he saw, or Elle saw . . . it sounds bad."

"I don't know," Lilly said. She worried her lip with her teeth. "I've never experienced anything like this." She looked at Ruben. "Maybe it's connected somehow to you and your brother."

Chapter Five

"Do you think what happened with Zander has anything to do with what I experienced?" Ruben asked Shaun. The two men stood on the balcony and looked out over the night-shrouded vista. Dinner was long over and Lilly was putting the children to bed.

"I don't know," Shaun admitted. "Zander has been an enigma to both of us since the day he was born. Maybe we were just expecting too much out of him." Shaun went back to pondering the view. Ruben did not have to be a telepath to know that his friend was worried about his son.

They stood in companionable silence, watching the night sky. A meteor streaked by, falling across the heavens.

"Make a wish," Shaun said quietly as they watched the meteor burn out.

Michael joined the two men on the balcony as

they sampled brandy from fine crystal, all made on Oasis.

"What exactly did you see?" Michael asked.

Ruben gently held the delicate snifter between his long, lean fingers.

What did I see?

"I saw Stef. But it was more as if I were looking through his eyes at what was happening. He was arguing with someone." Images started to settle into place as he thought about the vision. "It was Dyson," he said angrily. "And there was a witch there too."

The glass stem snapped in his hand and the bowl of the snifter shattered on the stone floor.

"Dyson. Isn't he your brother too?" Michael asked.

"Half-brother," Ruben corrected.

"I thought there was an attempt on his life also," Shaun said. "On another planet?"

"Is there any chance that your brother was perhaps in league with Dyson and they had a falling-out?" Michael asked.

"I don't know," Ruben said. "Stefan was only a boy when I left. I don't know what he's like. But in my dream, I definitely sensed danger to him."

"Danger from whom?" Michael asked.

"I think it was from a Circe. I know I saw a witch, and she seemed evil, threatening."

"Could the Circe be behind your father's assassination?" Shaun asked.

"What does Amanor have that the Circe would want?"

"Power," Ruben replied. "The armies are enormous. My father believed his strength lay in training and in numbers. He defeated all the planets in the system and they all came under his rule. The Senate negotiated a treaty with him to keep him from extending his rule into the other systems."

"So what did your father get out of the treaty?" Shaun asked. "If he was that powerful, they must have offered him something."

"I was too young when it happened to remember. But I do know that my father felt like he was a divine ruler. His conceit knew no boundaries."

"That kind of power would have tremendous appeal to the Circe," Shaun said. "Will your father's armies follow them?"

"I guess it depends on who winds up taking the throne," Ruben said. "There are, or were, thirty-eight of us in line. Thirty-seven without me. I guess the chances are pretty good that one of us didn't feel like taking the lesser role."

"No doubt one of them aspired to something better than being a prince in waiting," Shaun said.

"I can think of one right off the top of my head," Ruben said. "But since there was an attempt on his life also, I guess I'm wrong."

The two men looked at him in confusion.

"Dyson," Ruben explained. "He's a few weeks younger than I, so we were always placed together with the tutors. I hated him nearly as much as I hated my father. But that doesn't make him a murderer."

"So what are you going to do?" Shaun asked.

Ruben looked out over the darkness that covered the valley below. He heard the clink of ice and felt a moment of regret at breaking his glass until he realized that Michael had poured him another drink.

Ruben swirled the amber liquid in his glass before he brought it to his lips and downed it with one swallow. It was meant to be sipped, not inhaled, and his throat burned as the brandy poured into his gullet.

"I'm going to find my brother," he said finally.

"Want some company?" Shaun asked with a wry grin on his face.

Ruben shook his head. His friend was needed here with his family. "I doubt Eli would let you back on board the ship."

Where should he start his search?

That was the question on his mind as he guided the *Shooting Star* toward the hyperport above Oasis the following day.

Should he go back to Amanor?

His stomach turned at the thought. And he sensed that Stefan wasn't there.

You're letting this psychic stuff get to you.

Ruben had always been practical. He knew his world, and he knew his limits. His main means of protection was his casual approach to life. He was a smuggler when and where needed, and a trader when the Legion or Senate Protectorate came calling. He didn't appear dangerous. That was Shaun's specialty. Yet he could take care of himself, and his ability with his blade was enough to keep most adversaries at a distance.

Usually, he'd talked his way out of trouble, and paid a few fines and gone on his way when his words and charm had not worked. He made a good living and enjoyed himself whenever he had a chance.

But now he sensed that his intuition was correct. Stefan wasn't on Amanor.

"Bring up planet Lavign," he instructed Eli. A

three-dimensional display hovered over his com with his present location on one side and the planet Lavign on the other.

"Should I plot the course?" Eli asked with its silky voice.

Stefan had been missing since before the assassinations. Dyson was reported to have survived an attack on the planet Lavign.

It was as good a place to start as any.

"Plot course."

"Yes, dear," Eli replied.

Ruben's face twisted into a scowl. When had Eli gotten to be so . . . fresh? He really needed to do something about it, and soon. And he should probably fix the co-seat too, he reminded himself as he caught the crazy angle of the seat out of the corner of his eye.

"Course laid in," Eli said. "Estimated time of arrival, five solar days. Will you sleep now?"

"Yes," Ruben said and prepared himself for cryo.

I wonder if I'll dream about Stefan.

Ky was acting strange. Tess watched from the window as the Newf stood at the edge of the woods, sniffing the air. The stream that formed the border between Joah's land and the forest tumbled furiously past the huge animal, drowning out any noise that might have come from the woods. Ky ignored the water as usual. He never drank from the stream, and would only occasionally immerse himself in the icy cold water on exceptionally hot days.

Joah's heifer, on the other hand, was wild for the water. She'd take up permanent residence in the stream if Tess let her. And every time she escaped her pen and got into the water, she would become crazier than usual. She'd stagger about with glassy eyes, and her milk would be useless for days. Another thing that Joah would usually blame on Tess. Was it her fault that the heifer was crazy?

Tess wiped the last pot dry and put it in the cupboard. She hung the towel on the rack and wiped an imaginary crumb from the table.

Joah was in the winery. No doubt he'd be drunk soon. Tess shuddered at the prospect of Joah coming into Boone's room and standing over her pallet as he usually did. At least she didn't have to worry about Garvin tonight. There had been no sign of him in the time since she'd escaped his notice in the marketplace.

A shiver went down her spine, but Tess ignored it. The evil she'd seen in the strange woman's eyes haunted her dreams, confusing her with disturbing visions of a childhood she couldn't remember.

Who was the young man?

What trouble had befallen him?

Was he still alive?

Why should it concern me?

The scene they had stumbled across in the warehouse troubled her. She couldn't help worrying that something terrible had happened to the young man.

Stefan. His name was Stefan.

And she knew there wasn't a thing she could do about it.

Joah had not mentioned anything about a body being discovered or a crime committed. Even without the convenience of modern media, news traveled fast in the outlying settlements via the gossip they all engaged in while trading their wares. And something such as this, if it had happened, would warrant special visits just to keep each other informed.

The strangers were most likely offworlders. They had to be. Their manner of dress was strange, and their appearance was rich compared to that of the locals. But what were they doing here? Were they traders? Had they taken the young man with them and left, or were they still around?

The sudden memory of the Qazar addict gave Tess pause. Could the strangers have something to do with Qazar? The drug had to come from somewhere. Were the men and the strange woman she had seen responsible for its presence on the planet?

Tess dared not mention the incident to Joah. That would just bring undue attention to herself, something she tried hard to avoid. It was best just to go on and pretend as if nothing had happened.

His name was Stefan . . . I'll never forget his eyes . . . or hers . . .

Dusk was falling. Ky still sat by the stream, watching, listening, and waiting.

What was he waiting for?

"Boone?" Tess called out.

"I'm here."

Tess walked into the other room where Boone sat at the table looking at a book of pictures with simple words beneath them. The book was so old that the pictures were faded and the corners of the binding were well worn. But it was a good way to begin teaching him to recognize letters and form words. He was better with numbers.

How long would it be before he outgrew her fundamental teaching? Her own education, which she did not remember receiving, had been sorely lacking. There was a school in the community, but Joah wouldn't hear of Boone attending. He didn't want the boy learning anything new. The reality was that he didn't want Boone to know more than he did.

"Time for bed," Tess said. "Go tell Ky to come in," she added as Boone reluctantly closed the book.

Tess always slept easier with Ky close by. Ky tolerated Joah but had no allegiance to him. His heart belonged to Boone and by default Tess.

Tess put the book away and picked up a few scraps of paper and a small piece of lead that Boone had practiced his letters with. If only she had thought to buy him some things to help with his lessons on their last trip to the market instead of wasting her last few credits on fizzies and sweet cake.

And a toy. Tess picked up the metal starship as Boone ran to the heavy wooden door and pulled it open with two hands.

"Ky!" he called out. "Come."

Tess placed the toy in her pocket and picked up a basket from the floor. She continued to clean off the table, placing her shears in the basket, along with the strips of fabric she was cutting from the clothing Boone had outgrown. The next step would be to weave the strips together on the loom. Her plans were to use her old coat as a lining and piece the weaving on top of it. The extra layer would give her coat the bulk to keep her warm through the winter.

The wind that came down from the mountains in winter was icy cold on a good day. Most of the time, it cut clear through her and took her breath away.

Winter was still a long way off. But her free time was so short . . .

"He won't come, Mema," Boone said. "He keeps looking at the mountain."

Tess stored the basket under the loom and made sure Boone's things were safely tucked away on a shelf.

"We'll go get him," she said and took Boone's hand.

The night air was warm, and the insects that inhabited the woods gave a rousing chorus that could barely be heard over the rushing of the stream. The sky was cloudless, and countless stars pricked the night with their brilliance. Light poured from the window of the winery. Tess hoped to herself that Joah would stay inside.

"Look," Boone said. "The heifer is out."

Tess looked toward the small pen adjacent to the shed, and sure enough, the gate was wide open. How had the animal managed to do it?

Maybe that was why Ky refused to come in. Forever vigilant, he knew the heifer needed to be captured and returned to her pen.

"Let's see if we can find her," Tess said.

Ky turned his head as they approached the stream.

"Where is she?" Tess asked the huge animal.

"Show us," Boone added.

Ky turned his head toward the woods and gathered his powerful body for a leap. He cleared the stream and waited with his head turned back for Tess and Boone to join him.

Tess held on to Boone's hand as she hopped onto a stone in the middle of the stream. She hoped that neither one of them would fall in. Even in the middle of summer, the water was frigid, and she hated the sweet, metallic smell of it. She couldn't blame Ky for not drinking it. She had tasted it once, and that was all it took to convince her the water from the well was best for drinking.

So why did the heifer like it so?

There was a narrow trail that led to a clearing on a knoll above Joah's land. That was where they usually found the heifer when she was having one of her adventures.

Ky led the way but he stopped frequently, testing the air with his nose, his huge ear flaps perked, listening. The sound of the stream was lower here, the sounds of the insects louder as they sang their chorus, confident the birds that hunted them were asleep in their nests.

Except for the worrats. One swooped dangerously close to Tess's head and flew off, screaming its shrill cry.

The disgusting creatures usually hunted close to the mountains. The flying reptiles hated light of any kind and stayed away from the small outposts of civilization gathered in the valley below.

Boone covered his ears with his hands, and Tess felt like doing the same.

She hated worrats with a passion.

They moved on. The insects became louder, the trail darker.

I should have brought a beacon.

Ky crashed on ahead, his tail wagging, swooping against the underbrush. The clearing should be close.

The stars shone with brilliance overhead as the trees parted and Tess and Boone walked into the clearing. Ky barked once and the heifer bawled in return and took off down the other side of the knoll.

"Ftttt." Tess swallowed the curse. She did not want to spend the night chasing the recalcitrant beast.

Chapter Six

"Talk to me, sweetheart."

Ruben knew he was in trouble. The hair on the back of his neck had stood straight up since the moment he'd woken on cue from his cryo.

"Check coordinates," he barked.

"Checking," Eli sighed. "Again."

"Well?"

"Coming into planet Lavign," Eli said. "Star system—"

"I've got all that," Ruben said as he looked at the com. Something was definitely amiss. "What's wrong?" he wondered out loud.

"All systems fine," Eli said.

"I wasn't talking to you," Ruben snapped. He was tempted to shut off the voice mode. "See if we've got a tracer," he added. "And now I *am* talking to you."

"Searching," Eli said in what sounded like a huffy tone.

"There's nothing there," she said after a moment. "A thorough sweep shows no tracers. Ship is perfectly balanced," it added.

"Women," Ruben muttered, referring to Eli. "They never tell you how they really feel."

He'd never even heard of the planet Lavign until he'd seen the SNN broadcast. A quick review from the files on Oasis showed that Lavign was a recent addition to the Senate charts, settled less than a hundred solar years under the inhabitant code number 127, which meant religious restrictions.

Most likely a planet full of crazies with strange ideas of what society should be like.

But even crazies needed things. Things that he could provide. Traders were always welcome on these out-of-the-way settlements. Traders meant news and fresh supplies, and both were always in demand.

So what was Dyson doing on the planet Lavign? Had his half-brother suddenly become religious?

Dyson has probably announced himself as their lord and master.

That was one quick way to become a target for assassination. Not that Dyson needed any help in that department.

He was always such a—

Ruben decided to quit thinking about his half-brother as he did a manual check. The *Shooting Star* passed the check with her usual flying colors.

Eli remained silent. She was probably pouting because he'd done the manual check.

Ruben set the angle of entry into the atmosphere and searched for his water bottle. It wasn't in its usual place, and he realized that he had forgotten to fill it before leaving Oasis. He'd had other things on his mind. He'd have to go aft to find some water, but the prickling on the back of his neck kept him in place. With control in hand, he wondered why he had not been hailed from below.

"Anything on the com?" he asked.

"I'd be sure to let you know," Eli replied.

She was definitely pouting.

Surely they had some sort of security set up on the planet. Ruben opened his hailing frequencies.

"See if you can raise someone," he instructed.

"I have," Eli replied.

"Do it again."

Next thing you know, she . . . it . . . was going to expect presents.

"Standard hailing frequencies," Ruben added. At least he was doing his part. He had no intention of coming in unannounced.

"Warning," Eli said. "Unknown craft approaching from below." A shrill jangle from the com let him know that she . . . it . . . wasn't making up the danger.

"This is *Shooting Star* calling the planet Lavign," Ruben yelled into the com as he punched off a warning beacon. "Repeat, *Shooting Star* calling Lavign. Request landing coordinates."

Nothing. Ruben did a quick visual of the deepening sky. He was coming in during a glorious sunset. He could just see the curve of the sun dipping over the edge of the planet and the orange-pink brilliance of the sky above it.

It reminded him of Oasis. Clean and pure.

"Are you sure there's something out there?" he asked.

"Yes. But if you don't believe me, you can check for yourself."

His com showed a blip. There was another craft out there somewhere. It should be close enough for a visual, but a crafty pilot could hide in the glare from the sun and use its reflection as a cloak.

He'd done it himself, many a time.

"Repeat, *Shooting Star* calling planet Lavign. I am unarmed and seeking coordinates for landing."

No response. The sun, now gone, gave way to a clear black sky.

"Show me the geopoll," Ruben barked out.

It was a handy tool to have when smuggling, especially when he was trying to avoid interaction with Senate outposts. Infrared under the three-dimensional image showed sparse population by humans and animals. The terrain was rolling, with mountains showing in the distance. No industry visible of any kind. There were no lights sparkling from below to show the location of a city, and no power blip to indicate an energy source.

The night skies, brightly lit with millions of stars, looked as if he could reach through the plexi and gather a handful. The absence of light below gave the illusion that the stars were close and tempting, a treasure to be collected.

Maybe he should have done some more research before taking off on his quest to find his brother. It would have made more sense than just going by his gut.

Another alarm went off with a whoop. "We've been locked," Eli said calmly. Someone was targeting him. Where was the other ship? What was after him?

Ruben didn't have time to think about it as the single blip on his screen suddenly split in two. He'd been fired upon. He pulled the *Shooting Star* into a quick roll to the port side, and the ship responded gracefully.

From the corner of his eye Ruben caught a quick flash as the missile passed on by and exploded in the atmosphere. The light from the blast bounced off something solid.

There was another ship out there. His screen showed the blip was somewhere above him.

"My sensors indicate that the other ship is now above us," Eli said.

"Yeah, I already figured that out, sweetheart."

What he wouldn't give to have Shaun sitting up in the gun turret right now. The empty co-pilot seat beside him reminded him more of his solitude than he cared to admit. Maybe he should fix it, once this ride was over.

He flipped on the screen that gave him a visual link with the turret and pushed the control forward so the screen was aimed toward the atmosphere above.

He saw it on the screen. The absence of light. The craft that was after him was as black as the night sky. Deliberately. Whoever was flying it did not want to be seen. It was a clever idea and would be handy on a cloudy night, but tonight, when the stars were dazzling in their brilliance, the craft blocked them from view.

If this ship was part of the planetary defense system, then why the need for camouflage? The settlers were within their rights to protect their skies from invaders.

The back of his neck told him his attacker was not planetary defense. Just maybe, this camouflaged ship had something to do with his brother's disappearance. He'd come here looking for answers, and obviously, someone did not want the questions asked.

"Look for a place to land," Ruben commanded.

He needed to get away from his attackers. And he'd better do it quick, before whoever it was figured out that he was about to fly up—

Too late. Ruben caught the impression of a dive, but it was hard to track the ship visually once it started its countermeasures.

"Warning. Warning. Attack imminent," Eli said.

"You've got to be kidding."

He should have taken out his opponent when he'd had the chance. But it wasn't as if the *Shooting Star* was a Falcon and fully loaded with armament.

The blip on his screen told him his pursuer was still there, and he'd better do something quick.

Ruben didn't bother with a visual check as he armed his missiles. All these years operating as a smuggler and he'd never used them. He'd never had a reason. Shaun and the turret gun had gotten the *Shooting Star* out of more scrapes than he could count. He couldn't even say for sure the last time he'd bothered to check the proton chambers.

It was time to make his move. The blip was behind him now and coming fast.

Too fast . . . Ruben's curse exploded from his lips at the exact same time that he took the control and kicked in a quick burst of hyperion. Another second's delay and he'd have been a meteor shower, falling to the planet below.

* * *

"Look," Boone said, pointing skyward.

A flash showed in the sky, extremely close to the mountain.

"Was that a shooting star?" he asked. "Should I make a wish?"

"Always," Tess said. Boone closed his eyes tight and held on to his mother's hand. "Done?" she asked when he looked up at her, his green eyes looking black in the darkness.

"Yes," he said. "I can't tell you what it is or it won't come true."

"Just let me know when it does," Tess said, and they moved on.

Another flash burst above them, lighting the entire sky.

"There's another one," Boone said.

"Maybe that was lightning," Tess observed. "It sure was big."

"It's different," Boone said simply as the sky once again lit up.

It was. Not jagged as usual and the sky was cloudless.

It seemed to be a night of strange occurrences. Tess felt an uncontrollable urge to grab Boone up and run from the strange light, back to the relative safety of the farm. She looked for Ky, who had taken off after the heifer.

Before she had a chance to call out, Ky growled and turned from chasing the heifer. He ran toward them at full speed.

Why did the ground feel as if it were moving?

The roar from above was so sudden that it threw them to the ground. Boone cried out as Tess fell on him. Her breath left her body in a whoosh as Ky landed on top of her. She gasped for air but could not draw a breath with her diaphragm flattened as it was between Boone and Ky. A mighty wind poured over them with a noise so loud that she would have screamed if she'd had any air to do it. She had to move, but found herself paralyzed.

What is happening? . . . Boone . . .

The *Shooting Star* had taken a hit.

He was losing pressure in the cargo bay.

"Pressure leak. Cargo bay."

Ruben slapped a button on the com. That would shut her up. He didn't need any help communicating with the *Shooting Star.* He knew exactly what she was capable of.

"Come on, baby," he urged the ship as he fought for control. He knew that if he'd been in the stratosphere, he would be nothing more than an imploded mass of metal right now.

He was going to have to ditch.

But not without a fight.

The hyperion burst had taken him out of range, but not for long. He knew the mysterious dark ship would be closing in on him for the kill.

"I hope you've got something left, sweetheart."

Ruben punched the dials on his com. He blew his spare tank, knowing that the gases would form a harmless cerulean cloud in the pristine oxygen of the planet. It would also make his attacker think he was on his last legs.

He couldn't have more than a few seconds left. Ruben jerked back on the control and the *Shooting Star* pushed her curved nose into the air.

Ruben watched the blip on his screen as he silently

urged his craft upward. He knew he only had one chance before she gave out on him.

NOW!

Ruben threw the lever above his head as his pursuer flew into the cloud, right beneath and behind his position. He felt the shudder as the cargo hold separated from the module that held the cockpit, his personal quarters, and the mechanical operations of the *Shooting Star*.

Like a bomb, the hold fell, straight out of the sky, its trajectory right on target.

"Yes!" Ruben whooped as he felt the explosion beneath him. It was more than he'd hoped for.

The answering shudder from the *Shooting Star* was not part of the celebration. Alarms sounded, more noise to distract him.

"Shut up!" Ruben barked.

It had to be shrapnel. The noise was enough to kill him. If he survived this, he was going to do some serious work on his systems.

He didn't have time to admire the ball of flame that shot up from the ground below as his enemy exploded upon contact.

"Sorry," Ruben muttered as an apology to the inhabitants below. It was all he could offer at the moment. He had his own crash to avoid.

If he could. He summoned the geopoll again with the flip of a switch. There was a clearing ahead. Unfortunately, it was in the same vicinity as the crash.

"I hope there's no one out for an evening stroll," he said.

If there was, they were in for a show. Ruben said a silent prayer as he lowered his emergency landing gear. What was left of the *Shooting Star* was designed for a quick getaway and a bay landing. Ruben was certain of his skills and knew his craft like he knew his own body, but a drop-like-a-stone landing was something he'd never tried before.

He only had one chance to get it right.

"Come on, baby," he urged as he saw the treetops getting closer. If only he could make it to the clearing, he had a chance of not ripping her belly out.

He felt the popping of the treetops as he skirted along and then dropped lower, willing the craft on by sheer willpower.

And then suddenly he realized he'd run out of room. He was headed straight for the ball of fire that was all that was left of his enemy.

He jerked her nose up and the engines stalled. The *Shooting Star* fell to the earth, landing on her tail with a thud before she toppled over.

Ruben was catapulted from his chair and slammed against the co-pilot's seat before being thrown on the com. Pain exploded in his side and in his ankle as he felt himself falling toward the earth with his ship. The entire clearing was aglow with the light from the fire, but for him, the light was fading fast. The impact of the ship hitting the earth threw him to the deck, and the world went dark.

Chapter Seven

She couldn't breathe. She couldn't scream. The world was ending and she couldn't draw her last breath.

Tess squirmed beneath Ky. She knew Boone was alive by the sound of his panicked cries. Ky moved, finally. She felt him rise to his feet as oxygen flooded her lungs.

Gratefully she sucked it in as she flopped over on her back and looked up at the night sky.

Except she couldn't see it.

The world was on fire, or at least part of it.

"What happened?" Boone asked as he climbed to his feet.

"I don't know," she answered. She grabbed Boone and felt him. His arms. His legs. She frantically placed her hands on his face. "Are you hurt?"

"No," he said. He looked toward the fire. "The trees are burning."

"I know." The flames reflected red in the center of his bright green eyes.

"Did something crash from the sky?"

Tess shook her head. "I don't know. Probably." She was still trying to figure it out.

Tess pulled Boone toward her as they watched the flames, wide-eyed in apprehension. Ky stood beside them, his ears perked and tongue lolling as the heifer charged into the clearing and ran past them, bawling as if she herself were on fire.

Tess and Boone watched as she ran by and turned to follow her wild escape.

They were stopped in their tracks by the sight of a spacecraft half buried in the earth in what used to be the clearing. Used to be, because the size of the craft filled the area on top of the knoll.

Tess blinked her eyes.

The ship was still there.

What is happening?

Ky was already sniffing around the thing, curiously investigating in his own way to see if it was a hazard to Boone.

His tail was wagging. He stopped at the cockpit and barked at the clear plexi that covered it.

"Stay here," Tess instructed her son as she unsteadily rose to her feet and dusted her hands on the back of her pants.

Ky scratched at the dirt beneath the plexi and looked hopefully toward Tess as she tentatively approached the craft.

Ky whined.

At first, Tess saw nothing in the plexi but the reflection of the flames behind her. She placed her hands on either side of her face and leaned her forehead against the cool plexi to peer inside.

"Is it a starship?" Boone asked. He had ignored her command, of course. He ran his hand over the curve of the ship. "Do you think someone's inside?"

"I can't tell," she said. She moved over the wide expanse of window. She caught sight of a flashing red light, possibly an alarm, and blinking lights in the ship's command center. There were two chairs, both turned askew, one seriously damaged; what looked like a panel of some sort was hanging precariously by some wires.

There had to be someone inside, didn't there? She had traveled on a much larger ship than this before coming to Lavign and she remembered it being equipped with escape pods. But this craft didn't seem large enough. It didn't even seem large enough to travel in deep space. Was it in itself an escape pod from something much larger?

Tess looked back at the fire behind them.

A million thoughts flooded her mind as Boone plastered his face to the plexi below her.

What had happened? Was there another ship? Was that the reason for the fire? Had a battle taken place? They'd seen the bursts in the night sky; obviously, something catastrophic had happened. Were there other craft even now flying above, marking this place with their sensors?

What should she do?

"Mema!"

Grab Boone and run.

"I see something," he said.

75

Ky barked. Boone went to where Ky was scratching at the side of the craft.

No, no, no!

"Don't touch anything," Tess said, too late. She heard a whoosh of pressurized air.

"Boone, don't go in there," she warned in vain. To Boone, who dreamed of travel in the stars, this was a dream come true.

"But Ky went in," he protested. She heard the hollow echo of his voice. He was already inside.

Tess ran around the front of the ship and found a hatch, halfway open on the side.

She did not hesitate. Her son was inside. She could hear the sound of footsteps and the clanking of metal as whatever was inside shifted.

"Boone!" she yelled. "Don't move!"

The light from the emergency beacons was dim, but she could see some detail. She was in a small corridor opposite what appeared to be sleeping quarters. A narrow bunk was bolted to the wall on the opposite side. A door hung open to her right, and there was a sealed bulkhead to her left. The half-open door revealed a lavatory, complete with shower. She stepped on something as she moved toward the front of the ship. She lifted her foot in apprehension and saw that it was nothing more than some personal items that had spilled out from the bathroom. She kicked a hairbrush and razor back into the lavatory with the toe of her boot.

How in the world had Ky fit through here?

"Mema?"

"Don't touch anything," she instructed once again.

"There's someone here," he said. Boone's voice sounded hollow in the dark recess of the craft.

The fire beyond had burned itself down to nothing more than embers. Tess's eyes strained to see in the darkness. The flashing red light did nothing to help her night vision, but she could make out the shadows of Boone and Ky in the cockpit. There was no room for her inside, so she grabbed the Newf's collar and pushed him out as she wedged herself past him.

There. Below the console. Boone pointed.

A long leg extended out on the floor. The flashing of the light caught the reflection of liquid on the floor.

Blood.

"Is he dead?" Boone asked.

Tess hoped for a moment that he was.

Cautiously she looked beneath the console.

It was a man. Dressed simply in dark pants with several pockets down the side and a plain white shirt. No insignia of any kind that she could see.

She placed her hand against the part of his neck that was exposed above his shirt collar. The skin was surprisingly warm, and she could feel the steady thump of his blood-flow, even if it was pooling on the floor beneath him.

"He's alive," she said, almost regretfully.

Trouble is coming . . .

Her mind screamed in unison with all the alarms and flashing lights operating in the small area.

At that moment they all shut down. Tess looked around to see Boone smiling at her.

"Don't touch anything else," she cautioned as she saw his hand poised over the console. How had he known which button to push? Or had he just been extremely lucky? The next one would most likely detonate the ship.

"See if you can find a light," she said. Giving him something to do would keep him from blowing them into oblivion, she hoped.

The man was tall. Much taller than she was. How could she even move him? Should she move him?

Maybe she should get Joah.

Where was Joah? Surely he had noticed the crash. And the fire . . . unless he was drunk.

The man was bleeding. It was hard to see beneath the console, but the puddle at her feet was growing.

A bright light hit her face. Boone returned with a beacon in hand.

"Shine it under there," Tess instructed.

Her heart froze in her throat when she saw the pale face in the bright light. It was the man from the warehouse. Or was it? Tess took the light from Boone so she could give the stranger a closer look.

Are you Stefan?

There were the same high cheekbones, the same long, straight nose. Straight brows over eyes closed from an obvious blow to the head. There was a narrow cut at his temple.

Are the eyes the same piercing blue?

The hair was short, cut to the nape in back and around the ears on the side, but it was the same warm brown she remembered. Tess pushed back the spiky locks that were matted to his forehead by blood.

He seemed older, somehow. Leaner. More chiseled. Mature. His jaw was covered with a slight growth of beard, most likely the result of an induced sleep that a lot of the deep-space travelers used. Who was he? Where had he come from? And most important, was his being here a danger to her son?

"Mema?" Boone barely whispered, as if afraid the man on the floor might wake up. "Is he the man we saw before?"

"I don't think so," Tess answered. She was not sure if her answer was more to assure herself or to comfort her son.

Where was the blood coming from?

Tess moved the light slowly down the long length of the man's lean torso. A reflection caught her eye and she looked closer.

A piece of metal protruded through his shirt. This part of his body was pressed to the front of the ship, so Tess had to move around to get a closer look.

The wound was in the side of his abdomen. The blood on the front was slight, so there must be more damage in the back.

Tess placed her hand on the man's side and pulled his torso toward her. She was rewarded with a groan of pain and the sight of more metal protruding from his back. Somehow, in the crash, he had impaled himself on a piece of the co-pilot's seat.

Which meant she would have to pull it out.

Should I?

The implications of what had just happened in the clearing suddenly flooded her, and the desire to grab Boone and run caused her to tremble.

Who and why was someone fighting in the skies above Lavign? Did it have anything to do with the scene in the warehouse she had stumbled upon? It had to. The man lying before her, possibly dying, looked just like the young man called Stefan.

What should she do?

As if in answer, the man groaned once more and moved his head. Tess moved the light to shine on his face and saw the full lower lip move.

"He's talking," Boone whispered.

Tess leaned in close to hear.

"Stef . . . Stefan." The words were slurred, but there was no doubt in her mind what he'd said.

Run!

Her mind screamed, but she knew she would never be able to look into Boone's eyes again if she left this man to die.

Joah would most likely beat her.

What should she do?

"Let's see if we can move him to the bunk," Tess said finally, her decision made. Carefully she pulled the man out by his arm. But despite her care, his head hit the metal floor with a klunk as he came out from beneath the console.

"Sorry," Tess said as she positioned herself behind his shoulders. "Boone, grab his feet."

Another groan sounded when Boone grabbed his ankles. Tess made a face. She hoped they weren't doing more harm than good.

They managed to squeeze past the seats with only one or two bumps and one groan. Ky got in the way, of course, and Tess had to push the animal away with her hip. She could see from the dim emergency lighting that a trail of blood dripped beneath the man. Suddenly Boone slipped in it, dropping both of the man's legs with a thud as he recovered his balance.

"Sorry," he said with a grin, mimicking Tess.

She resisted the urge to laugh. He reminded her so much of herself sometimes that it scared her.

And besides, this was a serious situation they were in. Yet hysterical laughter threatened to pour forth.

"Pick him up," she instructed as she bit the inside of her cheek to keep her emotions at bay. "Gently."

"Why don't you just kill me?" a voice slurred beneath her.

Tess yelped and threw up her hands, then immediately grabbed for him as he once again hit the metal floor with a thud.

She bent over to catch a glimpse of bright blue eyes trying to focus on her face.

"I . . . was . . . just . . . kid . . ."

They fluttered shut as he slid back into unconsciousness.

"Did we kill him?" Boone asked.

"Not yet," Tess said as she felt for his pulse. "Run and get the light."

Boone did as he was told and quickly returned. He shone the light over the man's torso, and Tess's stomach heaved when she saw that the piece of metal had gone deeper through his abdomen. It was now clearly protruding through his shirt.

"What are you going to do?" Boone asked.

"Pull it out," Tess replied. "Let's see if we can get him on the bed."

Once again they picked him up. Ky watched and then padded after them into the small cabin as they slowly lowered the patient on the bunk.

"Ky—move," Tess commanded in frustration.

Ky whined and kept his eyes on the bunk.

"Boone, look around for some bandages. And please don't touch anything that blinks."

"There," he said, pointing the light behind her.

A cabinet was built into the wall and covered with a plexi door. Inside was a box marked with wings, the universal sign for medicine. Tess opened the cabinet and was amazed to find that everything inside was intact, though jumbled. She bumped her hand on a silver flask while reaching for the medical kit and immediately recognized its purpose.

"Brandy," she informed Boone as she opened the vial and sniffed its contents.

He nodded in complete agreement.

No more excuses . . .

Tess took a deep breath to gather her senses as she looked at the man lying on the bunk. She opened the kit and found the tube of adhesive used for pulling wounds together and sealing them shut. It might work on a cut finger, but there was definitely not enough to treat this wound.

She was certain that he needed more medical technology than what she could offer. He probably needed more than what the entire planet had to offer. The one surgeon she knew on Lavign used a needle and thread such as she used to mend clothing. Wounds such as this required more advanced care.

She found scissors in the kit. Boone held the light, and she used the scissors to rip the shirt open, exposing a wide breadth of smoothly chiseled chest.

Tess swallowed hard.

"Shine the light there," she instructed Boone, and the light danced over the sheen of sweat gathering on the man's skin.

She could actually count the ridges in his abdomen, Tess realized as she looked closely at the piece of metal that jutted through from back to front.

The spike seemed smooth and as thick as her middle finger. She didn't think it would make much difference if it came out the front or the back. She just needed to get it done so they could leave before someone showed up. A vision of the woman with the evil eyes filled her mind, causing a shiver to go down her spine.

Tess placed one hand firmly on the muscles of his abdomen and with the other firmly gripped the spike and pulled it through. She followed up by pouring brandy on the wound.

The man never moved.

"We must stop the bleeding," Tess explained to Boone.

She made two pads from the roll in the medical box, coated them with brandy, and placed them over the wounds.

"I hope he doesn't have any injuries . . . inside," she said, more to herself than Boone, who was doing a great job of holding the light steady.

With the aid of her teeth she ripped the shirt and tied it tightly around the wound. She found a blanket on the floor and covered him up, pausing a moment to look once more at the strange yet familiar face of the man.

Is he looking for Stefan?

"Let's go," she said.

I don't really know anything.

Boone looked at her in confusion.

"Before Joah comes," she added.

Boone turned off the beacon and set it on the bunk close to the man's hand. Tess had to smile at his consideration and then added the flask. He'd probably be in pain when he woke up . . . if he woke up.

She couldn't worry about that. She had to protect Boone.

"Come on, Ky."

The Newf seemed hesitant.

"Ky," Boone called out.

He came, but almost grudgingly. Once she knew Ky was following, Tess hurried down the trail. They must get back before Joah discovered they were gone.

They found the heifer standing in the stream. Ky went after her with teeth bared and chased her back to her pen. Tess knew her milk would be spoiled for days.

"Go to bed," she told Boone as she closed up the pen.

The light was still shining from the window of the winery. She didn't bother peeking inside. She knew Joah would be passed out, drunk, and likely to stay that way the rest of the night. He'd most likely die some night after one of his drunks. At least she hoped so.

Tonight was as good a night as any, in Tess's mind.

Ky stopped at the door, his eyes and ears turned toward the clearing on the ridge across the stream.

"Come on," Tess said and pulled him in by his collar.

She quickly sought her pallet on the floor next to Boone's bed.

But sleep was a long time coming.

Chapter Eight

Images came and then danced away as if he were gazing at them through water. His mother's face shimmered and faded into that of his brother, which turned into Lilly's face and then, most puzzling of all, into that of a woman with clear gray-green eyes. He did not recognize her, but knew her to be significant.

Through it all he heard a childish voice calling out and thought it must be Stefan.

But his brother was nowhere to be found.

He could hear the water. It was far off in the distance, calling to him like the images beneath the surface of his dreams. He was so thirsty.

It was the pain that finally woke him. The dim light that greeted him seemed to be natural. Morning or night, he could not tell, nor did he care as he lay in his bunk and tried to focus his eyes on the ceiling panels overhead.

So which felt worse, his side or his ankle? Ruben

COLBY HODGE

tried to decide as his mind filtered the pieces of information that swam to the surface.

He had crashed. He was in whatever was left of the *Shooting Star.*

So what was he doing in his bunk with a flask in one hand and a beacon in the other?

And who had wrapped his stomach up so tight that he could scarcely breathe?

Ruben slowly and carefully rolled to a sitting position, his side screaming in agony the entire time.

His ankle joined in the chorus as soon as he placed his feet on the floor.

But that was nothing compared to the explosion that went off in his head.

When the capacity for conscious thought returned, he opened the flask and took a long draw of its contents.

Shaun's brandy. And the flask a gift from his friends as he'd started his quest. How long had he been gone? How long since the crash?

The brandy didn't help his thirst at all. He needed water. He could hear it running, there, somewhere. Just the sound of it made his craving worse.

There was water in his ship, close at hand.

Ruben looked down the length of his torso. He was soaking wet with sweat. He had been wearing a shirt when he crashed.

Technically, he still wore it. It was damp, no doubt from the moisture that covered his bare chest and back. Should he look at the damage beneath it?

The pain he felt was enough to dissuade him.

Someone was here.

Someone had cared for him. Was the Good Samaritan still around?

He stood, and his head exploded again. Ruben braced his long arms against the ceiling as he waited for the solar burst before his eyes to stop.

At least his ankle was supporting him, in spite of the pain. He took a hesitant step and grabbed on to the door frame.

"Hello?" he called out.

Nothing.

The ship still had power. The flash of light from the cockpit was reassuring. How much damage was there? He'd have to run a check.

But first he needed water.

He hobbled a few steps to the lavatory and turned the tap over the small sink attached to the wall.

Nothing. No pressure at all. Of course the main tank had gone with the cargo hold, but there still should be something in the reserve housed beneath the deck. The problem was either structural or engineering. He hoped for the latter. As long as the *Shooting Star* was in one piece, he'd have a chance of getting out of here.

Wherever here was.

So thirsty.

Ruben looked in the mirror on the wall above the sink. A deep, narrow cut at his temple explained the headache. He probably had something for that in his kit, which was back in his cabin. He probably should seal the cut. He wiped the moisture off his forehead. He felt warm. Very warm.

Why hadn't the person who'd doctored his other wound not done it for him? Ruben tentatively pulled his shirt away to look at his side. All he saw was a pad tied over the skin. He felt rather than saw the wound in his back.

He pulled the shirt firmly back into place. He could tell without seeing it that the wound was bad.

He looked back in the mirror, trying to summon his memory of the crash. He could see it. The tree-tops rushing beneath him, the ground coming up to meet him, the sudden impact and the falling.

Ruben's hand went to his side. He'd impaled himself on something. A woman's face flashed before him, vague and misty, her eyes bright and clear in the darkness of his mind. He did not recognize her. Had she been the one who'd helped him? Had she carried him to his bunk? Was there someone else?

If only Lilly were here . . . and Shaun.

Now was not the time to succumb to loneliness.

Best shut down the power so he'd be able to charge back up when the time came. If the time came.

His ankle protested as he made his way forward. Ruben had the feeling that the only things keeping him upright were the sturdy boots he wore. His ankle didn't feel broken, but he had done something to it.

He blinked hard when he reached the cockpit and looked through the shield. At first, as he looked at the earth rising up around the plexi he thought perhaps he'd crashed at a crazy angle. But his ability to stand up fairly straight in the ship told him that the *Shooting Star* was pretty much buried in the earth.

He was going to have to dig her out . . . but not right now. Now he needed water.

Even with his great thirst and the sudden awareness that he was more than likely running a fever, his mind was on his ship. Ruben fell into his seat and checked the com. There was no way he could run a thorough check. Not the way he was feeling at the moment. He noticed that the side hatch alarm was on as he powered down. The hatch was open, which meant someone had been here. That answered the question of whether or not someone had helped him.

But it also led to several others.

He noticed that the co-pilot seat was broken partly away.

Guess I'll really have to fix it now.

He reached under the com for his water bottle, but it was missing, more than likely shaken loose in the crash. He looked around the floor, but if it was there, he couldn't see it. He had to have water.

Ruben made his way back to the hatch. He found it halfway open, as he expected. It had lost pressure in its controls. Something else he'd have to attend to, once he found the water he could still hear.

It was definitely morning. The planet's sun cut through the peaks of the mountains that rose up beyond the treetops. A deep gulp of air reminded him of Oasis. But the vista gave proof that this planet was much wilder, more untamed.

His quick study when setting his course for Lavign had indicated that the settlements had only been here around a hundred solar years.

How long did it take for a planet to be tamed?

He stepped out of the ship and found that the sound of rushing water was much louder. He had landed in a clearing of some sort, on a rise, as far as he could tell. The treetops fell away from it, and in the distance he could see a flash of sunlight bouncing off something shiny. Ruben wondered if it was a settlement of some sort.

He had to find the water.

Ruben took a stumbling step and then righted himself. He took a moment to test his ankle and decided his thirst was much greater than the pain he felt.

He found a trail, falling away out of the clearing and leading into a deep wood. It made sense to follow it down, so he proceeded.

His hand went without thought to his wrist as he realized that this was most likely a game trail he was following and he might run into some kind of animal.

His blade was gone. Missing.

He never wore it in cryo. It was probably still in its place in the cockpit.

His thirst and the pain he felt all over now kept him going downhill. He knew he didn't have the strength to fight, even if it meant his life.

He was so thirsty.

The sound of rushing water seemed louder.

The treetops melded together overhead, blocking out the sunlight. This land was wild and primitive, and the trail he was following was so narrow that branches brushed his arms and ferns touched his ankles.

He could barely hear the call of the birds flitting around in the dense wood. The rushing of the stream overpowered any noise they made.

He was getting closer. The nose was so loud it filled his head.

His ankle pained him, his side pained him, and he wasn't sure if it was the blow to the head or his fever that made the things around him seem distorted.

All Ruben knew was that he had to find the water.

He stumbled forward along the path. A branch whipped against him and tore at the bare skin of his chest. Ruben ignored it. All he wanted was something to drink.

The light filtered in, brighter. The trail widened a bit and the brush didn't seem as dense.

He could see the sunlight reflecting off the water, teasing his eyes as it played hide and seek with him through the underbrush and the thick trunks of the trees.

And then suddenly he was there.

Ruben dropped to his knees at the bank, ignoring the pain that shot up from his ankle.

He scooped up the liquid and brought it to his parched mouth.

It tasted strange: metallic, sickeningly sweet, yet cool.

It was like swallowing shards of ice as he gulped it down.

He felt a tingling inside. It started in his stomach and then spread as if small bursts of tazers were going off through his nervous system.

Ruben took another gulp.

And another.

He splashed it on his face and over his chest, rinsing off his sweat.

The wound on his temple screamed as the water hit it. The wound in his side doubled him over as the water trickled past his shirt and the padding.

What is wrong with me?

Ruben grimaced in pain as he rocked on his knees. His vision blurred and he blinked. Something was coming toward him. Something big and dark.

When the water seeped into the wound in his side, the breath left his body in shock. The pain radiated out, and he groaned as he pitched forward into the water.

His last conscious thought was that the stream would carry him away. There was no way he could fight the strength of the current.

As the water poured into his wounds, he decided he didn't want to fight. It was easier just to close his eyes and let the stream take him.

Chapter Nine

The day was sure to be hot. Rain would be welcome. Tess looked up toward the vineyards and the neat rows of grapevines growing upon their trellises. Joah must have opened the drip irrigation system that was fed by the stream. The water filled the channels and trickled down into the root systems of the vines.

Off to the side she saw the giant draft horses standing beneath a low, wide tree, sheltered from the heat of the day in their pasture. Occasionally they would swish their long, thick tails to chase off the insects that hovered over their wide backs.

Tess wiped the sweat from her forehead and wearily picked up a basket and small spade as she went through the back door to the kitchen garden. She was already exhausted, and her day had barely started. What little sleep she had gotten the night before had been filled with visions of the injured pilot, the young man Stefan, the woman with the strange, evil eyes, and most bizarre of all, the Qazar addict she had seen in town.

She wondered briefly what Ky was stirred up about. She could hear his deep-throated calls from the front of the house. He was probably chasing off some varmint that had come searching for an easy bite in the trash pile that was slowly decomposing in the heat of summer.

It wasn't until she heard Boone frantically calling for her that she put the basket of vegetables down on a work table and ran between the shed and house toward the sound.

Boone was downstream, right at the edge of the property. He knew not to go past the tree that marked the boundary. Ky was farther down, the front half of his large body in the water. He appeared to be pulling something with his huge jaws as he backed out of the stream.

Tess's heart sank as she saw the limp form of the man appear on the bank. But what had she expected? That he'd just go away? Disappear? Die?

He must have come down the trail and fallen into the stream.

Maybe he'd drowned.

A quick look toward the vineyards revealed Joah heading their way.

There was nothing she could do to turn him back. Tess ran to Boone and Ky.

"It's the man," Boone said as Tess fell to her knees beside the bedraggled form.

His arm was bleeding where Ky had held it to

drag him out of the stream. The cut on his forehead was tinged with bright blue and red crystals.

Tess tentatively touched a finger to the crystals and immediately pulled it away. The tip of her finger felt scalded.

"Is he alive?" Boone asked.

Tess bent her head to the stranger's pale lips. She felt a frigid kiss of air hit her cheek.

"Yes, but barely," she replied. She touched her hand to the neck where his pulse should be. His skin felt like ice, and the blood was barely moving.

"What is it?" Joah asked as he ran up.

"A man," Boone said.

"Well, where did he come from?"

Tess bit her lip as she waited for the blows that were sure to come as soon as Joah found out that she had known about the man since last night.

"Ky found him in the stream," Boone said.

Joah looked down at the man and then upstream. "He must have come down the trail from the mountains," he observed. "Just like your beast."

Tess didn't know if she should be grateful that Boone had lied. Or maybe he had just omitted part of the truth. Ky *had* found the man in the stream. It was a technicality that she did not have time to deal with at present. She was more concerned about what Joah's plans were.

"What's wrong with him?" he asked.

"He appears to be wounded," Tess volunteered.

Joah bent over her shoulder to take a closer look and nudged the man's side with the toe of his boot. "Looks like he must have wrapped himself up and then come looking for help." Joah glanced over his shoulder toward the mountains. "He might have friends out there or he might have enemies. Maybe we should just throw him back in and let him be someone else's problem."

A cold shiver ran down Tess's back.

"You mean let him die?" Boone asked. He looked up at Joah with trembling lips, his green eyes wide with shock.

"Better him than us," Joah said. "He's an off-worlder. Not from around here."

"But you said we should help our neighbors," Boone said, quoting from Joah's weekly lesson at the meetinghouse.

"He's not our neighbor," Joah replied.

"But—" Boone protested.

"Enough!" Joah cried. "Go to the house."

Tess recognized the stubborn tilt of Boone's chin as she turned to face Joah. "You can't do this," she said firmly.

"Get to the house, Boone," Joah commanded.

Ky growled low in his throat as Joah raised his arm and pointed to the house.

"Go, Boone," Tess said quietly, her eyes steady as she looked at Joah.

"Take the beast with you," Joah added, his eyes unwavering also.

"Come on, Ky," Boone said.

Ky did not move.

"Ky!" Boone called out. "Come!"

Ky moved next to Tess.

"Come get him, Boone," Tess said. She took hold of Ky's collar. She knew well the look in Joah's eyes. It usually came after a night of heavy drinking. He was in no mood to be challenged.

Yet she was about to do that very thing.

Boone took hold of Ky's collar. Tess knew there was no way her son could move the Newf if he didn't want to go. She just hoped that his devotion to Boone would be enough to keep him out of harm's way.

"Go with Boone," she urged the Newf as Boone tugged on his collar.

Ky obeyed, reluctantly.

"You can't do this," she repeated as Boone and Ky walked away.

Why did she care what happened to this strange man? Hadn't she wished for him to just disappear?

Tess felt as if she were standing on the edge of a precipice. She knew, without thinking about it, that what she was about to do would change her life forever. Whether for better or worse, she could not say.

"I'll do what's best for me and mine," Joah replied. "Now help me throw him back in."

She had to do what she could to save the man. She had to do it for Boone. He had to grow up knowing what was right and what was wrong.

All she would get was a beating. Wasn't a beating worth a man's life? Tess looked down at the pale, handsome face. Was it her imagination or were his lips moving?

"Do you want your grandson to think of you as a murderer?" She raised her chin as Boone had done moments before.

Tess knew the blow was coming, but that knowledge did not prepare her for the violence of it. It spun her around and she fell, landing on top of the man who lay at her feet.

Far off in the distance, she could hear Boone's

cries and howls from Ky. At least Boone had known enough to lock him inside.

Joah grabbed her hair and pulled. Tess placed her hands over his to keep him from yanking her hair out as he hauled her to her feet.

She was amazed to see the stranger's piercing blue eyes looking up at her as she settled unsteadily on her feet. Joah spun her around to face him.

"You watch your mouth," Joah ground out from between gritted teeth. "Now grab his feet so we can throw him back in."

"I can't let you do this, Joah," Tess said.

She felt her lip split as he hit her again. This time she managed to stay on her feet. The next blow knocked her flat.

Tess looked up at the clear blue sky as she attempted to gather her scattered thoughts.

He'll just beat me senseless and then throw the man in the stream himself.

Then so be it. She had to do what she could to stop a murder.

For Boone.

"I've heard all the sass I'm going to hear from you, girl," Joah threatened. He stood over her with his chest heaving from exertion. His white hair, sparse as it was on top, stood up at the ends, and his nose, usually red from drinking, had turned purple with rage.

Tess didn't move a muscle as she watched the strange man stagger to his feet behind Joah. He grimaced in pain as he placed his hand against the wound in his side. His blue eyes seemed to widen in recognition as he looked at Tess.

I'm in for it now.

Joah clenched his fists. Was it possible that he did not know the man was standing behind him?

"Am I interrupting something?" the man said. Was he grinning? It sure seemed as if he was.

Tess quickly placed the knuckles of her left hand to her mouth to keep from laughing out loud.

Joah looked as if he'd seen a ghost. He spun around and backed away as the man towered over him with his hand still pressed to his side.

How could he be standing there so tall when just a few moments earlier she had thought him close to death? He still looked ill. His skin, stretched tight over the muscles of his face, was a pale, pasty color with a lavender tinge beneath the surface. Tess imagined that the wound in his side looked a lot like the one on his forehead.

The man took a hesitant step toward Tess and held out his hand to her. He cocked an eyebrow expectantly.

Tess placed her hand in his. He was deathly cold. He must be using every ounce of his strength to stand. She got up and was even more surprised when he lifted his hand toward her face.

Her first instinct was to move back, but a gentle smile reassured her as his long finger wiped away the blood that trickled from her lip.

Joah sputtered as Boone and Ky ran down from the house.

"Are you the one?" the man asked Tess. His piercing blue eyes seemed to look straight through her.

She looked warily at Joah.

"Who are you?" she asked as she looked back at the man.

"Do . . . you . . . know . . . my . . . brother?" he asked weakly.

"He's awake," Boone called out gleefully as he joined the strange trio by the stream.

"Stefan," the man added. His face was deathly pale, but his eyes remained fixed upon her, piercing her with their intense blue color.

"What's he talking about?" Joah asked. "Who are you?" he demanded. "Where do you come from?"

"Er . . . Ben . . ." The man's words were slurred now. Tess saw the truth in his eyes. What little bit of strength he had used to save her was quickly fading. He would pass out again, and then Joah would have his way.

"Help me get him to the house," she said to Boone and placed her arm around the stranger's waist just as his blue eyes closed beneath dark lashes.

Boone ran to the man's side and held on.

"You've got to walk to the house or you're a dead man," she whispered in the man's ear.

His head lolled forward, but he took a step.

"He said his name is Ben," Boone informed her as if she had not heard.

Ky fell in behind them.

"Ben," Tess said. "Walk." She took as much of his weight as she could. She knew Joah was watching them. She also knew that once she got the man to the house, he would be safe. Joah would never harm a guest under his own roof. He was mean, but he did have a set of principles that he lived by.

"Sl . . . slave . . . drive . . . er."

Tess tried not to laugh at the absurdity of it all. She, a slave, was saving a stranger's life. And yet the stranger was calling her a slave driver.

Maybe she was dreaming the entire episode. Maybe she'd roll over and wake up and find herself on the pallet in Boone's room.

Better yet, maybe she'd wake up and find herself a child once more, only this time she'd have a mother and a father who loved and adored her and she would not end up sold as a slave to an evil man on a backward planet.

But then she wouldn't have Boone either.

"Keep on walking," she urged.

"Ben," Boone added.

"Ben," she repeated. They were literally dragging him as they reached the step up to the wooden porch.

"Where should we put him?" Boone asked as they stumbled through the door with their burden.

"In there," Tess said, using her chin to point to the room that she never entered. It was Boone's father's room, although she never would refer to him that way. She never referred to him at all unless she could help it. Joah never talked about his son either, not since he had been crushed by several large wine kegs.

If not for Boone, it would be as if he'd never existed. They stumbled through the door and dropped their burden onto the bed.

"Whether he lives or dies, it's all on your head now," Joah said from the doorway.

"At least with me he has a chance, Joah," Tess said. "That's more than you were going to give him."

When had she gotten so bold?

Joah took a step into the room and was greeted by a throaty growl from Ky.

"You'd best hope that whoever done this doesn't come looking for him," Joah threatened.

Tess looked down at he man on the bed.

Her life had already changed.

Chapter Ten

Tess took a moment from her chores to peek in on the man, who still thrashed weakly, fighting the sheets. For three days he'd fought a battle with his dreams. For three nights she had wiped his brow, trickled well water into his mouth, and looked in bewilderment at the blue-tinged wounds on his head, back, and abdomen. How could they be healing so quickly?

"He's still sleeping," Boone informed her from his place on the woven rug next to the bed. Ky lay beside him. They both stayed there during the days. Boone did his lessons and played with his spaceship, crashing it over and over again onto the faded rug, his imagination reenacting the scene in the clearing on top of the hill.

Tess allowed their presence; it freed her up to do her work. She knew that Boone would alert her to any change in the man's . . . Ben's . . . condition.

There had been _____ _____
carried him into t_____

The first night th_____ _____
lized blood had come_____ _____
protruding from his ski____ _____
was amazed to hear the__ _____
as she dropped them one_____ ____
The last had issued forth fro__ _____
the second night. It made sen__ _____ ___ ___
about it. That wound was the de_____ __ __ the
way through to his back. Still, she _____red what
had caused the strange crystals. No__ the wounds
were healing, or appeared to be. And quickly. They
resembled injuries a few weeks old instead of a few
days. If not for the dark bluish color of the raw,
puckered skin, she would have been pleased with
his progress.

At least there was no danger of the man . . .
Ben . . . bleeding to death.

His name is Ben.

Tess walked to the side of the bed and touched her
hand to his forehead. It was cool to the touch.

"Wake up, Ben," she said. If he were feverish, his
restless state would make sense. It seemed as if he
were trapped inside himself, fighting demons whose
names only he knew. He murmured them occasionally as he tossed his handsome, beard-stubbled face
over the pillow. He spoke strange words and the
names of people she assumed he knew. Shaun, Lilly,
and the one she recognized . . . Stefan.

Stefan is his brother.

Tess was exhausted. After three nights of sitting
by the stranger's bedside, the lack of sleep was
catching up with her. Joah had made it clear that the

ponsibility. And she would be
ever repercussions resulted from
recovery.

gest of all was that she could not keep Ky
ay from the man. The Newf waited until Boone
was settled for the night and then joined her in her
night watch, closely watching the struggles of the
man . . . Ben . . . as he mumbled strange names and
fought his nightmares.

Tess was grateful for the Newf's solid presence at
night, especially when Joah stood drunkenly in the
doorway and harangued her with vague threats.

She heard the slamming of the door as Joah came
into the house. No doubt he was looking for his
dinner. It was ready. All she had to do was put it before him.

"The heifer is out," Joah said angrily as he walked
toward her.

Tess bit her tongue. The last thing she'd done before coming in to fix dinner was check the heifer's
pen. It had been secure. Joah had probably let the
animal out just so he'd have an excuse to beat Tess.
He was angry about the stranger. He was angry that
the man was in his son's room. But most of all, he
was angry that Tess had defied him.

"I'll find her as soon as I fix your plate," she said,
keeping her eyes down. She wouldn't look up. Every
time she did, Joah hit her, even when Boone was
watching, as he was now.

"Hurry up about it," Joah snapped. He tossed a
look toward the bed and then stomped off to the
table.

"I'll find her," Boone volunteered. "Ky and I can
do it."

Tess's heart swelled as she looked into the boy's earnest face. He never said anything when Joah hit her, but she knew it bothered him. Tess was glad he never asked her about the beatings. She wouldn't know how to begin to explain them to him.

Perhaps tonight she could snatch some sleep. Or maybe work on her coat while she watched over the man . . . Ben. He'd said his name was Ben . . . not that it mattered to her.

"No, I'll do it," she said, placing a hand on her son's dark hair. "I could use some fresh air."

She looked once more at Ben.

Stefan is his brother.

Somehow that knowledge didn't make her feel any better.

"Get in here!" Joah yelled.

Tess jumped, and Boone with her. She should have gone immediately to fix Joah's plate and she knew it.

"Stay here," she said to Boone as he raced toward the table.

He's trying to protect me.

"Boone," she cried. "No!"

"I'll fix your plate," he called out as he ran ahead.

Tess's boots felt heavy as she walked the ten steps to reach the stove. She saw the years stretching ahead of her. She saw herself older and weaker, unable to recover from Joah's heavy hand. She saw Boone growing up an angry young man. She saw him furious in his passionate youth as his hands closed around Joah's neck and he choked the life out of him for daring to strike his mother. She saw it all as she walked to the stove and took the plate from her son's hands. He stood on tiptoe to scoop stew from the pot.

She was powerless to change their fate.

Boone held his hands out, waiting to take the plate to Joah.

Tess hesitated. She shouldn't let him do it. But the thought of another beating was enough to bring tears, unbidden, to her eyes.

"I got it," Boone said, calling over his shoulder to Joah, who was watching them both carefully.

Tess gave him the plate and placed a piece of bread with the stew. She turned her back on Joah to fix Boone's plate. She felt her skin crawl, knowing Joah's eyes were still upon her . . . waiting . . . watching for anything he could use as provocation.

"Hmmm, it looks really good tonight, doesn't it?" Boone said.

He was trying to distract Joah.

Boone shouldn't have to live this way.

"I'd best go fetch the heifer," Tess said. She wanted neither of them to see her tears. She placed Boone's full plate on the counter and took off through the door with Ky on her heels.

If only they could run away. If only she could take Boone and leave this planet. But it wouldn't happen. It couldn't happen.

Tess stood in the settling darkness, listening to the sounds of the stream rushing by. Clouds gathered over the mountaintops in the distance, blocking out the setting of the sun. She swiped at the tears on her cheek as Ky leaned heavily against her hip, almost knocking her off balance with his compassion.

Her mind chased after endless and fruitless scenarios. The only ships that ever landed on Lavign were traders, and she had no credits to bribe them with, or to pay for passage. There was no place she could run. There was no one to help her.

She was no different from the heifer, always yearning for something she could not have.

"Ftttt," she hissed when she saw the heifer in the stream, her face buried in the water as she drank, her sides heaving with the effort. What was wrong with her?

Tess went to fetch her. She saw a flash of light over the mountains. Was it lightning? Or more star fighting?

What exactly had happened the night that Ben had crashed? There must have been a battle of some sort in the skies above Lavign. What did it all mean? She had been so busy and so worried about the happenings of the present that she hadn't had time to think about that night. Boone had questioned her a few times with curiosity, but she'd quickly shushed him. It wouldn't do either of them any good if Joah found out that she had helped the man after his crash, bandaged his wound, then said nothing.

Come to think of it, she was surprised that Joah had not found the ship on the knoll. Of course, he never ventured over the stream. His joints were too stiff to make the jump easily. But still, she thought he might have gone looking, just to see if there really was some threat to his family.

Perhaps she should go and look around the clearing herself.

And what would you do if you found someone?

Tess stopped in her tracks. What would she do? What should she do? Her biggest problem was time. She didn't have any. Unless she wanted to sneak out in the middle of the night to go exploring. She was much too weary even to consider that.

Light flashed once more in the clouds over the mountains.

What if the heifer took off toward the knoll again? Then she wouldn't have any choice but to go after her.

A bang from the house startled her out of her reverie. She'd better get back before Joah caught her just standing around.

"Come on, Ky," Tess said and moved toward the stream. The heifer stayed where she was and continued to drink as if she would never get another drop. Tess managed to grab the strap of leather around her neck without having to step in the water. The heifer protested, of course, and jerked away, but Ky jumped in and nipped at her flank. The heifer bawled and jumped up beside Tess.

Ky shook himself off as he joined the pair on solid ground. Droplets of water hit Tess on the cheek. She touched her hand to the skin and wondered why it felt as if she'd just been pelted with hail. Ky let out a huff of disgust and fell in behind the heifer, who was not happy about being forced back to her pen.

What is wrong with her?

Once more her milk would be worthless, bitter and blue for several days until she got the water from the stream out of her system.

Blue . . . Like Ben's wounds.

Something was wrong with the water. Tess had always thought it tasted strange and kept Boone away from it. Ky hated it, but the heifer loved it.

Tess shoved the heifer through the gate of her pen and latched it securely behind her. She took a moment to look toward the vineyards.

Joah used the stream to irrigate the vines. There was nothing wrong with the wine, however. He never had any trouble selling it. Dealers were always ready to pay his price.

And yet Ben, who had fallen into the stream, had exhibited strange symptoms. Was the water the reason why he was still unconscious?

Or was it just because he had suffered a blow to his head?

"Get ahold of yourself," Tess said. Ky looked at her as if she were speaking to him.

"I'm just tired," she explained to the Newf. Ky's dark eyes gave her sympathy.

So tired.

Wearily she turned back to the house and the pile of work that awaited her. She paused when she saw Joah stomping his way toward the winery. She hoped he'd drink himself into a stupor again tonight.

If only he'd drink himself to death.

If only.

"Boone?" Tess called out as she came into the house. "Time to do your lessons."

"I'm doing them, Mema," he called back. Tess knew without looking that he was on the rug next to Ben's bed with his books spread out before him. She stood in the doorway to the room as Ky moved past her and took up his new station beside Ben's bed.

"I thought he might be lonely," Boone explained. His toy spacecraft sat on the rug beside him.

Without thinking about it, Tess crossed over and placed her hand on Ben's forehead.

"Wake up, Ben," she said.

Chapter Eleven

Ruben blinked against the bright sunlight that burned his eyelids. What a night! If he felt this bad, there had better be someone handy to make him feel better. Whoever she was, he hoped she had gotten the number of the shuttle . . . ouch . . . that had run over him . . . multiple times.

He felt horrible. The slightest movement was painful. Had he been in a fight?

His eyes finally opened and blearily focused on a whitewashed ceiling while he tried to get his mind to identify the strange humming noise in his ear. And what was that huffing that accompanied the humming? Why was the side of his face hot and slick? Was he bleeding?

Ruben was amazed to find that his arm worked as he raised his hand up to his face. His side, however, was another story. Pain shot through him as he wiped his cheek and spread his fingers before his eyes. No blood, but the fingers were moist.

"Errrrrrr." The rumbling came from something close by, and Ruben turned his head and came face to face with a large square head and lolling tongue.

Well, that explained the huffing. It was a Newf, and it was panting.

Ruben's eyes swam for a moment before they focused on the room.

There was a Newf next to him. He had not seen a Newf since he'd left Amanor.

Where was he?

Ruben took the time to examine the rest of his surroundings as his eyes darted from corner to corner. The room was simple and plain. Nothing more than a bed and a few pegs on the wall holding some random pieces of clothing.

His clothes?

Ruben suddenly realized that he was naked, covered with nothing more than a sheet. A cold sheet at that. He skin felt icy.

The humming still sounded. Ruben cautiously twisted his head and saw a small boy with dark hair.

The boy sat on the floor and swooped his hand through the air, flying what looked like a toy spaceship. An achingly familiar toy starship.

"Zander?" His voice cracked hoarsely. How long had it been since he'd used it?

The boy jumped to his feet and stared at him with vivid green eyes.

"Mema!" he yelled. His eyes never left Ruben's face.

The Newf scrambled to its feet, and Ruben was amazed to see that the animal's back stood higher than the bed he was lying on. The breed was bigger than he remembered. Or maybe it just seemed smaller in his memories because the animals had always flanked his father, who was bigger than life.

Was he on Amanor?

His mind circled, trying to recall exactly what had happened to him. He had crashed. Had he crashed? His memory was fogged by a swirling blue haze.

Ruben tuned his ears to exterior noises. There was no familiar hum of machinery. No sounds of flight in the sky. No chatter of people.

Nothing but the song of a bird and the rising of a breeze. In the distance he could hear a faint slap-slap sound and beyond a distant roar that for some strange reason made him lick in lips in thirst.

And footsteps.

"Boone?"

A woman slipped into the room. Ruben saw dark hair twisted up neatly, bright hazel eyes beneath dark lashes, and a hint of freckles splattered across her nose. She was tall and almost painfully thin. Her face was bruised, and her lip had been split recently. A work-hardened hand touched the hair on the boy's head.

She was his mother. It was obvious by the looks of both of them.

"He's awake," the boy said and pointed to Ruben.

The woman moved toward the bed, and Ruben suddenly became very conscious of his lack of attire. Who had undressed him? Why?

"Greetings," she said. There was no smile of reassurance added as she bent to straighten the sheet.

Ruben wished he were at least wearing his pants.

Her hands were efficient as they smoothed the sheet around his legs to her satisfaction.

"Er, greetings." Ruben slowly pushed himself up to his elbows and wondered if he would be able to move quickly if needed. "Where am I?"

"Lavign," she said stiffly as she checked the clothing hanging on the pegs. Ruben recognized one of the items as his pants. He wondered what had happened to his shirt.

He also wondered what he had done to offend her.

"How did I get here?" he asked.

"You crashed," the boy said. His toy quickly went into what Ruben supposed was a reenactment, complete with an explosion of noise from the boy's pursed lips.

"We found you in the stream," she said. Panic chased across her face, which was still pretty despite the marks on it.

Ruben's head swam as he tried to remember what had happened.

He was Ruben. He was a smuggler. His craft was the *Shooting Star*. He had been attacked as soon as he hit the atmosphere of this planet. He was looking for his brother.

And this woman knew where Stefan was. He was sure of it. He recognized her from . . . someplace. And quite obviously, she didn't want to talk to him.

Ruben loved a challenge. Especially one as pretty as this. But if there was a son, then there had to be a father . . . someplace.

"Thank you," he said. "I guess you saved my life."

She didn't seem too thrilled about it.

"You have a wound in your side. It goes all the

way through," she said, pointing to his side. "You also took a blow to the head. Your ankle is swollen, but I don't think it's broken."

Ruben's hand followed her extremely impersonal inventory. His side felt raw, his forehead tender, and his ankle, when he flexed it, painful. She could have been reading a bill of lading by her tone.

He also understood what she had left unsaid. *You're not welcome here. Hurry up and leave. You are an inconvenience to me.*

"What did I do, crash into your flower garden or something?" he asked with what he hoped was his charming grin. "I can pay for my care."

At least, he had possessed credits when he'd crashed.

"You'll have to take that up with Joah. It's his roof you're sheltered under." She had managed to talk to him without once looking at him.

"Is Joah your husband?" Ruben asked.

"No," she said. "He's . . . he's . . . he owns the place." She finally looked at him with eyes full of panic.

She was terrified of something. Ruben wondered what it could be. Surely it wasn't the fact that he was here.

Or maybe it was. She knew about Stefan. She had to. Why else had he seen her in his dream?

Or was everything just conspiring to confuse him?

One thing, he knew for sure. He couldn't just ask her. Not right now.

"Do you need anything?" she asked as she gripped her upper arms with her hands.

There were a lot of things he needed. He needed to know what had happened. He needed to know why he'd been attacked as soon as he entered the planet's air space. He needed to know where his brother was. He needed to know who was responsible for pinning his father's assassination on him. He needed to know if his ship was all right. He needed his pants. And he was thirsty.

"Water?" he asked, adding a smile.

She nodded, turned, and then stopped. She looked at the boy and then at him, as if wondering if it was safe to leave the child there.

"What's your name?" Ruben asked the boy.

"Boone," he said and stepped close to the bed. The Newf stood next to him, watching with great intelligence showing in his dark eyes.

The creature was as big as a space pod. Apparently, the woman realized that the Newf would protect her son, so she left.

"And him?" Ruben asked.

"Ky."

Ruben held out his hand, palm down and the animal gave it an obligatory sniff.

Might as well get down to the important stuff while the woman was gone.

"Where's your father?"

"I don't have one," Boone said.

Ruben considered the possibilities brought up by that answer while Boone posed a question of his own.

"Where do you come from?"

"Out there," Ruben replied, pointing up. "Where's my ship?"

"On the knoll. Mema doesn't want Master Joah to know that we found you in your ship."

Jackpot!

"When did you find me?"

"We were there when you crashed. We were chasing the heifer."

"You saw me crash?" *And what does a heifer have to do with anything?*

"Yes." Boone went through the reenactment once more.

"How's my ship?"

"It's in the ground."

Ruben scratched the growth on his chin and tried to figure that one out.

"Is it fast?" Boone asked.

"When I need it to be," Ruben answered. "Your mom said you found me in a stream."

"Ky did. The next day. Master Joah wanted to throw you back in so you'd die, but Mema wouldn't let him."

Ruben decided that he really liked this kid. And his mother. This Master Joah, on the other hand . . .

"Your Mema works for Master Joah?" he asked.

"Yes. She cooks and cleans and keeps the garden and washes our clothes and teaches me my lessons and takes care of the heifer and the chickens and—"

Ruben held his hand up to stop the recitation. "She sounds like a busy lady."

"And she took care of you," Boone added and let out his breath. "She pulled a rod out of your side," he said almost reverently.

So that's what had happened to him. He really should have fixed that seat.

"What happened to her face?" Ruben asked. The kid was a font of information.

Boone looked down at the once-bright rug. "Master Joah hit her," he said quietly. "A lot."

Ruben felt the boy's frustration, and his own

started to roil inside. What kind of man was this Joah? A vision flashed across his mind, one of a woman falling on him by the bank of a roaring stream and a stooped old man looking at her in rage.

"What's your mema's name?"

"Tess."

"Tess." He tried it out. "I like it. It's a pretty name for a pretty lady."

She walked in then, carrying a tray with a pitcher of water and a glass. She placed it on a small table next to the bed and looked down at him with her arms folded.

"Thanks," he said. "Tess."

"Ftttt," she hissed and looked down at Boone.

Boone was oblivious. He picked up the pitcher, poured the glass full, and handed it to Ruben.

"Thanks, little guy," Ruben said with a smile as he took the glass. He drained it in one long gulp and held it out for more.

"I really don't think you should be drinking like that," Tess said. "After all, you've hardly swallowed anything in the past few days."

"And here I didn't think you cared."

She looked as if she wanted to strangle him. Boone refilled the glass, and Ruben tilted it up and drained it as he had the first.

"Just how long has it been?" Ruben asked. He suddenly realized he was starving. He hadn't eaten since leaving Oasis.

"Four days," Boone said when Tess seemed disinclined to answer.

"Since you seem to be feeling so much better, I'll fix you some soup," she said finally. "I'm sure that you are now capable of taking care of the rest of your . . . needs." She shot a pointed look right below his waist.

Ruben had the decency to look away in embarrassment as the realization came over him that she *had* seen to his . . . needs while he was unconscious. She had seen all there was to see and apparently found him lacking in some way. He also realized his behavior was no way to thank her for saving his life.

And one need that she referred to was suddenly pressing. He probably shouldn't have drunk so much water, so fast.

"Er, where's the lav?" he asked.

Tess pointed toward the wall behind him. "Out there," she said and left.

He shifted uncomfortably under the sheet.

"What's a lav?" Boone asked.

"The place where you go," Ruben replied, still trying to figure out why he should go "out there."

"Oh," Boone said. "We call it the necessary house. It's outside."

"Hand me my pants," Ruben said. "Doesn't it get cold in the wintertime? Why don't you have it in the house?"

Boone handed him his pants. "I don't know, that's just where it is," he said.

Ruben managed to sit up and swing his legs over the side of the bed. He wondered how he'd be able to stand with his swollen ankle. He looked at his side and let out a low whistle.

"I guess I'm lucky to be alive," he said. "But why is the scar blue?" He touched a finger to the puckered skin at his side, then touched the wound on his forehead, wondering if it looked the same.

Boone shrugged at the question, his green eyes wide with wonder. "Do that again," he asked.

"What?"

"That noise," Boone said, looking in fascination at Ruben's mouth.

Ruben whistled, and the boy immediately pursed his lips to give it a try while Ruben pulled his pants on beneath the sheet.

"We'll practice later," Ruben said. "Help me up."

He used Boone's shoulder as a crutch and pulled himself up. To his surprise, the Newf came to his side, also helping to support the bad ankle. Ruben grinned down at the pair who were both looking up at him expectantly.

"Show me the way," he said, and they haltingly made their way to the door.

They went out through a bigger room that held a table and a few worn overstuffed chairs. A huge wooden contraption took up one entire wall. It had a series of pedals beneath it, and thick cords were strung between the slats. There was a bench before it, and Ruben wondered what purpose the contraption could possibly serve. The basket of colorful fabric strips beside it and a bright rug on the floor brought it all together in his mind.

Tess made rugs.

Why?

His door was one of three that led off the big room. There was also a door in the middle of one wall that led outside. All he saw beyond it was green.

"This way," Boone said and turned Ruben toward the back of the house. They made their way into another room, where Tess was standing over a stove that had to be older than time. He saw flames shimmering beneath a pot that she stirred.

"Where am I?" he said again as he hobbled through toward another door. "What is this place?"

They walked out onto a covered porch, and he saw a garden, a large tower with metal blades turning in the breeze, and some other buildings that he did not have the time or inclination to figure out at the moment.

Boone pointed to a narrow shack at the end of a trail of smooth stones.

"The necessary," he announced.

Ruben lifted an eyebrow as they hobbled down the path. As he opened the door, his nostrils were assaulted with a horrible smell and he realized that inside there was just a hole in the ground and a wooden seat. The bright sunlight that streamed though two small openings in the exterior wall did nothing to cheer up the interior.

"When you've got to go, you've got to go," he told himself as he stood before the hole.

It wasn't until he saw that the fluid coming out of him was bright blue that he realized he was in trouble.

Chapter Twelve

Tess listened to the sounds of Ben making his way across the porch with the help of Boone and Ky.

She really shouldn't allow Boone to spend so much time with Ben. Having a pilot practically crash-land in his lap was a dream come true for a young boy who was always dreaming of the stars. But it would be a mistake to let him get attached to Ben. It would only lead to disappointment.

The best thing that could happen for all of them would be Ben's swift departure. If only he would get in his ship and fly away before Joah found it, or before whomever he was battling with came looking for him.

But he was hurt and his ship was buried in the dirt on top of the ridge. And it might be damaged beyond repair. How could he fix it if it was? Lavign had no technology at all beyond the small spaceport where traders occasionally came in.

What would she do if he asked her about Stefan again? How did he know that she had seen his brother?

Tess stirred the soup and checked the loaf of bread that was browning on a stone in the oven. She would have to fetch more wood.

How much will he eat? Joah would surely be angry if he thought the man would cost him credits.

How long will he be here?

How attached will Boone get to this stranger from the stars?

She heard the slam of the door to the necessary. A smile curved her lips when she thought of how Ben must have reacted to such primitive accommodations. She could easily recall the convenience of modern lavatories with their hot running water and sanitized conditions. It was a luxury that she would never again know.

She heard the awkward sounds of Ben limping across the porch and deliberately kept her back turned to the door as she heard the screech of its hinges.

The back of her neck prickled as she stirred the pot. She knew he was looking at her.

"I'll bring your soup to your room," she said to the wall over the stove. Maybe she could keep Joah away from him.

She heard hesitant footsteps creaking across the worn wood floor. From the corner of her eye she saw Boone pull out a chair and sit down at the table.

"I can eat in here," Ben said. "I wouldn't want you to go to any trouble."

So Ben was walking, or limping, on his own.

She felt, rather than heard, him getting closer.

So why did she jump with a start and drop the ladle into the pot when suddenly he appeared at her side?

There was too much of him. Too much skin showing across his wide, bare chest. Too much body as he towered over her. He seemed to fill up the area around the stove and sink. It had always been an area that was all hers as no one else ever cooked or washed up afterwards. She had never been around so much . . . maleness, even after living all these years with nothing but men. Or an old man and a boy child. Ben's masculinity was very different.

He dipped a rakish eyebrow at the pot as he seemed to size her up, along with her soup.

"What did you do to me?" he asked, his blue eyes piercing through her defenses.

"What do you mean?" she asked. "I cared for you." Tess took a step back and crossed her arms defensively across her chest.

"You gave me something." He took a step closer.

"I did not." Tess took another step back and regretted it as he took another step toward her. Her face did a slow burn as she looked at all the bare flesh presented to her. She tried to step away but realized that she was trapped between him, the sink, and the stove. All three were unyielding.

He stuck his arms out on either side of her, placed them on the counter that held the sink, and slowly, carefully, leaned in so that his mouth brushed alongside her ear.

"If you didn't give me anything," he whispered, "then why is my piss blue?"

Tess felt her eyes widen in shock as he pushed himself back away from her. Tess turned and looked out the window toward the stream before looking back to find him lifting the ladle out of the pot and examining the soup.

"Nothing blue in here," he said and limped to the table. He pulled out a chair and sat down across from Boone, who was grinning as if he'd just received a great present. "I apologize for my lack of attire, but I seem to have lost my shirt," he said as he settled himself into the chair.

"That's because Mema—"

"Boone!" Tess commanded sharply, then instantly regretted it. "Go get Ben a shirt off the peg." She arched an eyebrow at him. "Please."

Boone rushed off to do her bidding, although he wasn't happy about it. Tess could tell by the set of his chin. Her heart sank as she realized it was already too late to keep her son from becoming infatuated with the stranger.

"Ben?" Ruben asked skeptically as Boone hustled away.

"That's what you told us," she said, plainly confused.

"I did?"

"Yes, when we carried you into the house." Tess's mind went back to that moment. Had she misunderstood? "You said your name was Ben."

He looked at her with a bemused expression on his face. Why did he make her feel so strange? She wondered. Looking at him was difficult. It was as if there were too much of him.

She bent to pull the bread from the stove and hastily dropped it when she burned her knuckles on the inside top of the oven. She stuck them in her mouth as tears stung her eyes.

She heard the scrape of a chair, and once more Ben limped toward her. "Let me see," he said. The thought of his coming near was more painful than her burns.

"I'm fine," Tess replied and quickly checked her hand. Blisters were already rising on her skin, so she quickly stuck her knuckles back in her mouth.

He was not to be deterred. He pulled her hand away from her mouth with a gentle tug and examined the white welts that ran across the top.

"I have something in my kit that should take the pain away," he said. His voice was husky and deep. It curled around her ears like a song. "It would be in my ship," he continued as he raised her hand close to his mouth and blew gently across the top of her knuckles, turning her knees to quivering stalks. "It would help with this, too." His finger gently brushed her split lip, leaving fire in its wake. "Do you know where my ship is?"

Tess jerked her hand away as if she had burned it again and looked up into his piercing blue eyes. Was he teasing her? Did he know that she had helped him the night of the crash and then left him alone with his injuries? What must he think?

"Here's one!" Boone announced happily as he ran into the room brandishing a worn blue shirt that had belonged to Joah's son.

Ben hooked the shirt on his finger and raised an eyebrow at it, considering its size, which was obviously too wide and too short for his frame.

Boone smiled proudly, as if he had made the shirt himself.

And the realization hit Tess that of course Ben

knew about her finding him in the ship. Boone would have told him. Boone would tell him everything without thinking twice about it.

Did Ben know she was a slave? Tess felt her face go hot and pink at the realization that this strange man might know she was nothing more than chattel.

Ben slid his long arms into the shirt, whose cuffs landed a few inches above his wrists. He held his arms out in bemusement as the tail of it dragged at the waist of his pants.

Boone laughed.

"Please tell me you didn't lose my boots," Ben said as he wiggled his long toes above the worn wooden floor.

"They're in there," Tess said, nodding toward a storage room off the kitchen. "I'm sure they've dried out by now."

He limped to the table and sat down again. "That's right," he said, his eyes once again steady on her face. ".You found me in a stream."

Why did the shirt have to make his eyes seem bluer?

"Ky found you," Boone said. "He pulled you out."

Ben held out his hand to the Newf, and Tess was amazed to see the beast move willingly to his side.

"Thanks, big guy," Ben said as he rubbed the huge head, all the while keeping his eyes on Tess. "Guess you saved my life."

Why did he have to keep looking at her like that?

With her knuckles still screaming, Tess found the knife and sliced the crusty bread. She ladled soup into a thick bowl.

"Boone," she said. "Come help." No need to get close to Ben. He could take care of himself now.

"So what is this place?" he asked as Boone carefully placed the bowl in front of him and ran back for the bread. "What's with the"—he waved his hand toward the rear—"lack of proper facilities?"

"This is how we live," Tess said. She had her back to him as she busied herself at the sink. Her hand was throbbing now, shooting pain into her upper arm.

"Why?"

"The original settlers of this planet came here to escape technology. They believed that it was a curse and that man could live better if he lived simply." She quoted Joah's rhetoric.

"I'm all for simplicity," Ruben said. "But I'm also for sanitation."

"The ways of this planet were determined long before I came here," Tess said.

"What's sanitrasion?" Boone asked.

"It's keeping things clean," Ben said. "So you're not *from* here?"

"Ftttt!" Tess whispered to herself. Had she lost all sense since this man came into their lives?

"Mema cleans everything," Boone said proudly.

"Maybe if you had better sanitation, she wouldn't have to work so hard," Ben replied. "And she could concentrate on her cooking," he added as he sipped the soup.

"Is there something wrong with my cooking?" Tess asked indignantly as she turned from the sink.

"It tastes fine," he said. "I'm just wondering if anything else on me is going to turn blue."

"That's not my fault," Tess said. "I had nothing to do with that."

Ben made a doubtful face, and Boone giggled.

Now he's got my own son doubting me.

"Boone," she said. "Go do your lessons."

"Mema," he whined.

"Now."

Tess watched in shock as Ben looked at Boone, then tilted his head toward the other room. The chair screeched across the floor as her son scooted away from the table and, with his chin jutting out stubbornly, left the room. They heard the sounds of books slamming and another chair being dragged as he sat down to do his work.

"I don't need your help with *my* son," Tess snapped, hands on her hips.

Ben casually sipped his soup. "I'm a novelty to him. I just thought he might be more cooperative if he knew I was supporting you."

Tess's jaw dropped open and then shut abruptly.

"Are you an authority on raising children? Do you perhaps have some of your own?"

"Not that I know of," he said with a sheepish grin. "But I've been around a few."

Tess suddenly realized that she was relieved to hear his answer. But that didn't take away her anger at the sheer gall of the man.

"I can take care of my son," she said. "And I have no problem with Boone's minding me. At least not so far."

"I'll try to stay out of your way," he said.

"And don't tempt him with things he can never have," she added, her anger evident. "He's stuck here and he doesn't need to be dreaming about far-away places or luxuries that he'll never know."

"He's stuck here?" Ben asked. "Are you prisoners?"

Tess felt her face go pink once more and wondered briefly if it was too late to toss him back into the stream. It seemed as if he knew exactly what questions to ask. The ones she didn't want to, or couldn't, answer.

"More soup?" she asked.

"You didn't answer my question," he said with a grin. "And I have a lot more to ask you."

Tess suddenly sensed that he used that grin like a weapon, casually disarming his victims as he moved in for the kill.

She almost laughed at the thought, but then panicked inside as she realized that he could, indeed, be a killer, for all she knew.

Joah was right. They should have let him drift on downstream to become someone else's problem.

"Who are you?" she asked. "What brought you here?"

"As I told you, my name is . . . Ben," he said, his lips twisting strangely over his name. "I'm a trader."

"What brought you here?"

Ben took a piece of his bread and dipped it in the bowl, soaking up what was left of the soup. He placed it in his mouth and carefully chewed as he haltingly rose from the table with the bowl in his hand.

He limped toward her, and Tess scooted out of his way as his progress brought him to the sink.

He made a great show of swallowing the remains of the bread and then looked in puzzlement at the pump that sat on the side of the sink. He even waved his hands below it, as if his motion would start the flow.

"Curious," he said, leaning over and peering up into the pipe.

Tess couldn't resist. She grabbed the handle, knowing that the pump was primed, and lifted it.

129

A flow of water hit him in the face and he sputtered and spewed as he came up, his cheek barely missing the pump.

He stood dripping before her and slowly lifted the tail of the shirt to wipe his face, revealing the chiseled muscles of his abdomen and the bright blue puckered skin on his side.

"Like I said." He continued mopping. "I'm a trader." Satisfied that his head was dry, although his shirt was now damp, he let it fall back into place and limped toward the other room, stopping in the door to look at her. "I answered your questions, sweet cheeks. And I expect you will answer mine." His blue eyes traveled the length of her. "Eventually," he added as he left the room.

Chapter Thirteen

Ruben allowed himself a smile as he hobbled from the room toward Boone, who was chewing on some sort of writing instrument.

Let her stew on that for a while.

She had to know something about Stefan. There was no other way to explain the fact that he had seen her in his dreams.

Or maybe his memories of that strange dream had just gotten jumbled up in the crash. He was still having a hard time distinguishing between what had really happened and what he'd dreamed. The haze that had filled his head for the past few days had left him a bit confused. He had vague recollections of a large warehouse, a rushing stream, and . . . a boy?

"What are you working on?" he asked Boone as he limped toward the table where some worn books and several sheets of old paper were scattered about.

This place really was simple. A good celpad could replace of most of the stuff lying on the table.

"Numbers," Boone said. He lifted the paper to show a series of problems.

Ky's thick tail beat on the floor as Ruben approached the table and pulled out a chair. The ankle was hurting him, and he did not want to overtax it. He needed to heal as quickly as possible.

"Where'd you get these?" he asked, pointing at the problems.

"Mema writes them for me in the mornings so I can learn things. After I do them, we look at the answers." Boone went back to his work as Ruben once more perused the room.

Everything was so primitive. There wasn't a piece of plexi or tunstun in sight. Everything was wood and pegs. There were a few metal piecings. Only a few. And what there was looked positively ancient.

"Isn't there a school you can go to?"

"Master Joah won't let me."

"I can't wait to meet this guy," Ruben commented, more to himself than Boone.

"He's in the winery," Boone said.

"Winery?" Ruben's ears perked up at the word.

"Yes, he makes wines and sells them. Master Garvin makes the bottles that we put the wine in."

"Who's Master Garvin?"

"He lives downstream."

"Is there any wine here in the house?"

"No. He keeps it in the winery."

"Oh." Ruben looked at the contraption that filled one long wall. "What's that?"

"It's a loom. Mema makes rugs and things on it."

"Does your mema ever sleep?" Ruben asked. Considering all the things that she did, it would be miraculous if she had time.

"Yes. She sleeps on the floor in my room."

"She what?"

"She sleeps on the floor next to my bed."

"Why? Doesn't she have her own bed? Or am I sleeping in it?"

"No, she won't sleep in there. It belonged to Master Joah's son. He's dead now."

Ruben chewed on that comment for a moment, trying to put all the odd facts together.

Tess worked day and night for a man who beat her. Boone didn't have a father. According to Tess, they would never leave this place. Boone wasn't allowed to go to school. And Tess slept on the floor because she refused to sleep in a dead man's bed?

His head hurt. Ruben rubbed his hand over the wound on his forehead.

Boone grinned up at him.

"What?"

"It looks like a star," he said. He put his lead to paper and dashed out the five lines that made up a lopsided star.

"It does?" Ruben touched it again. "Is there a mirror around here?"

Boone rushed off, and Ruben shook his head as he heard a door bouncing off a wall. In an instant the boy was back with a small frame in his hand. "Here," he said. "Mema keeps it next to the tub."

"Tub?"

"Yes. We wash in it. We wash us."

"Bathe?" Ruben asked. "Your body?" He recalled

133

his glimpse of the room that sheltered his boots. It didn't seem big enough for a bathing chamber and he hadn't seen a thing to bathe in, either vertical or horizontal. In fact, it looked like nothing more than a storage closet.

"Yes. Bathe," Boone said, trying the word.

Ruben held the mirror up to examine his forehead. Sure enough, right over his left eyebrow and close to his hairline was a blue starburst-shaped scar. "I must have whacked it pretty hard," he said as he looked carefully at his reflection. "I wonder if it will stay blue."

Boone shrugged his shoulders once more.

"How about you?" he asked Boone. "You got any blue on you?"

Boone laughed. "No."

"So why do I?" Ruben felt Tess's eyes on him from the doorway. She was probably furious at him for distracting Boone from his lessons.

"I don't know."

"So how about these numbers?" Ruben said, tapping a finger on the paper. "Do you know these?" If he was helping the kid with his lessons, Tess couldn't be mad at him could she? Besides, Boone was an untapped resource, ready to give up everything he knew. Maybe he knew something about Stefan. And it would be a lot easier to find out something from Boone than Tess. She would probably keep silent just to spite him. Strange that she had taken an instant dislike to him for some reason.

He could never recall its happening before. At least not with a woman.

"Yes. These are easy."

Ruben turned his head to the problems, ignoring Tess, who he knew was still watching. They were simple addition and subtraction problems with three columns of numbers.

Ruben looked at Boone. "How old are you?" he asked. Three columns was kind of advanced, he thought, for a kid Boone's size. Maybe he was older than he looked.

"Six," Boone said. He held up both hands to show the proper number on his fingers.

"You must be pretty smart. Why don't you show me what you can do?"

Boone bent his head to the problems as soft foot-steps passed by. Ruben stole a look at Tess and found her in the room he had used, stripping the sheets off the bed. She quickly replaced them with another set and carried the used ones out.

"For a moment there I thought you were kicking me out," he said with a grin as she walked by with her load.

"That's up to Joah," she tossed back at him as she passed by. Ruben watched her go, admiring the gentle swing of her backside as she walked away. Her clothes were so baggy that it was hard to determine her curves, if she had any at all.

"Does she ever smile?"

Boone looked up from his work. "Sometimes."

"I'd like to see that."

Boone grinned widely, and Ruben wondered if Tess's grin would look the same. He definitely had her chin. He looked exactly like her, except for his bright green eyes.

"How long have you been here?" Ruben asked.

"Always."

"How about your mema? Has she always been here?"

"No. She comes from the stars. Like you."

Another interesting fact to add to the Tess question.

"Did she come here with your father?"

"I don't have one," Boone said with a most serious air.

Ruben nodded his head as if this were possible while wondering why Boone didn't know anything about his father.

Or had the kid been a plant? There were places that grew embryos in tubes. They were products of genetic engineering. But that wasn't likely on this planet. How could it be? They had primitive outdoor lavs. The thought that there was a shiny, clean facility growing babies in tubes somewhere was inconceivable.

But it would explain the kid's skills with numbers. Engineered children were exceptionally smart. But why would Tess go for a plant and then come to this out-of-the-way place? What exactly was she hiding?

The situation was getting complicated. Ruben looked at the boy's profile as he went back to his work.

He couldn't be a plant. He looked just like his mother.

"How much more work do you have to do?"

"Just this page," Boone said with a hopeful look. "I can do my reading after dinner."

"Hurry up. I want to look around." And if Boone was with him, the boy could answer more questions. Maybe Ruben could even work the conversation around to Stefan.

"Do you want to go to your ship?" Boone asked excitedly. "I know where it is."

"That might be a good idea." Ruben tapped his finger on the table repeatedly. "Lessons," he said. "While you finish, I'll go get my boots."

Ruben stood up and tested the ankle. Ky rose to his feet also and followed along as he made his way to the other room to get his boots.

Ky pushed the door to the back open with his nose and padded away. Ruben found his boots, thankfully dry, and also his socks, which he determined had been washed.

Maybe he should leave Tess a few credits when he left. She had taken good care of him.

Except for the spots where he was turning blue.

And first he'd have to find his credits. They weren't in any of his pockets. Why wasn't he surprised?

A man who wanted to throw him back in a stream wouldn't think twice about going through his pockets while he was unconscious. This Master Joah sounded like a real character.

But there was always the possibility that Tess had taken them.

Ruben dismissed the idea as quickly as it came into his mind. He'd only known the woman half a day, but he was pretty certain she wasn't a thief.

As he slid on his boots he wobbled and crashed alongside a huge, dented copper tub hanging on the wall. Surely that could not be where the family bathed?

The first thing he was going to fix on the *Shooting Star* was the lav. No way was he going to fold his body into that thing.

Ruben had to laugh at himself. As if he were planning on staying around long enough to consider such things. He needed to find out all he could about Stefan and be off, hopefully with his brother.

He hobbled to the door. Tess was outside hanging the wet sheets on some sort of rope strung between two posts.

What was wrong with the people in this place? Were they just gluttons for punishment? Why work so hard if you didn't have to? Wasn't that the entire point of progress, to make things better for the human race?

"I'm done," Boone announced as he raced into the room.

"Did you do a good job?"

"Always," Boone replied. He burst through the door and Ky came bounding up to meet him. "What do you want to see first?"

"How about you show me where my ship is," Ruben said.

"It's this way," Boone said. "Mema! I'm showing Ben around," he yelled as he took off at a full run with Ky at his side.

Tess looked over her shoulder and did a slow perusal of Ruben as he haltingly stepped off the porch.

"Don't go too far," she cautioned. "I don't think you're up to it."

"It's nice to know that you care," he said, grinning at her.

He chuckled to himself over the face she made at him.

She was right. He hoped his ship was close, because what little strength he'd had upon wakening was gone.

Boone was jumping and waving to him from the

edge of a stream that was a good distance from the house.

Ruben presumed that the large, long building nearby was the winery. Beyond it he could see rows and rows of grapevines stair-stepping their way up the gentle slope that eventually dissolved into the deep woods clothing the mountains. An intricate series of wooden chutes stood along the row, and Ruben, from his visit to Oasis, realized that it was a form of irrigation, fed by the stream.

"Impressive," he admitted, knowing that without technology someone had gone to quite a bit of trouble to build it.

An animal bawled at him as he limped toward Boone. That had to be the heifer. Ruben thought. She belonged to the same breed of cattle that grazed on Oasis.

It was amazing how much Lavign reminded him of Oasis. This world had the same potential if its inhabitants were as careful as the Oasians were. And why shouldn't they succeed? They didn't have to fight the pollutants that were a result of an overworked atmosphere.

"This way!" Boone yelled.

The distance to the stream looked impossible to Ruben as his ankle screamed in protest. His side was hurting, and his head had started to throb. On top of that, an incredible thirst had made itself known deep inside his throat. The water of the stream looked so cool, so inviting. Maybe he should just immerse himself in it. Surely it would make his ankle feel better.

The *Shooting Star* could wait. He wasn't strong

enough yet. Boone had said the ship was on top of a knoll. There was no way his ankle could handle a climb right now.

He'd just soak his ankle in the stream and take a good long drink of the cool, fresh water.

Ruben waved at Boone. He'd understand.

The *Shooting Star* could wait.

He wanted to run, but his ankle wouldn't let him. Suddenly the thirst was unbearable. He licked his lips in anticipation of filling his mouth with the cool, clear water.

"Oy!"

Ruben saw Boone's face crumple in disappointment as he turned toward the winery. An old man was coming his way. Weathered and crusty, he carried an ancient piece of wood in his hand. It looked like a club.

"What's your business!" the man yelled, shaking the club in a menacing way.

Ruben realized his drink from the stream would have to wait. He had some public relations work to do. "You must be Joah," he said, grinning as he stuck out his hand. "Tell me about your winery."

Chapter Fourteen

They reeked of it. The sweet, sticky smell of the wine sickened Tess as she served up the meat and vegetables to Joah and Ben, who were laughing uproariously at the table.

And to think just a few short days ago Joah had wanted to toss their "guest" back into the stream.

Now they were carrying on like old friends. Tess could never recall hearing such laugher in the house, and certainly not at the table. Not even when Garvin showed up with his sneaky looks and whispered conferences had there been such hilarity.

Boone sat and watched with a wide smile on his face, looking back and forth between the two men as Ben regaled them with stories of space pirates and fights in taverns that had the boy literally on the edge of his seat.

Tess fought the urge to knock both of them out of their chairs with the flat edge of the old iron skillet she'd just finished scrubbing. Ben had succumbed to Joah's ways in one day.

Her ears caught snatches of the stories as she worked at the sink. When the words "women," "large breasts," and "warming my sheets" caught her ears, she resisted the urge to cut out Ben's tongue with the knife she had just placed in a crock. Slowly she turned toward the table.

"Boone," she said, grinding the words out between clenched teeth. "Time for bed."

"But, Mema," Boone protested.

"Now." The quiet resolve in her voice carried more weight than any amount of yelling would.

Joah looked at her with narrowed eyes. Tess knew he was debating whether he should strike her for interrupting the hilarity.

And then Ben gave that slight nod of his head toward Boone, just as he had earlier in the day, and her son jumped to do his bidding.

"I'm sorry," Ben said as Boone went out the back door with Ky on his heels. "Things got a bit out of control," he admitted.

Joah grunted his disdain as he poured more wine into their glasses.

"Why don't you sit down and join us?" Ben added as he pulled out a chair for her without rising. "No wonder you're so thin. You don't eat enough."

"It's not her place to sit at this table," Joah protested. "And she gets plenty to eat."

Ben seemed confused as he looked between Joah and Tess. "There's always a place for a beautiful woman."

Tess felt the heat rise up her throat and onto her face. She had eaten, taking bites as she worked at cleaning the kitchen. She would never dare to sit at the table with Joah. She was just grateful that Boone was allowed there.

"Don't be making trouble over things that are none of your concern," Joah warned Ben.

Tess stared down at the floor, dreading the look in Ben's eyes that was sure to come when he realized her status.

She heard the clink of a glass and stole a look toward the table.

"Have I told you what a genius you are?" Ben said as he held his glass of wine up to the lamp that hung over the table. "This is by far the best wine I've ever tasted."

"Ye've told me," Joah said. "Ye've also told me you are going to make me rich, but I've yet to hear how ye're going ter do it."

The clatter of Boone's feet on the back step was a welcome relief for Tess. She followed him out as he bade good night to the men.

Ben answered, but Joah ignored the boy, as usual.

"Are Ben and Master Joah going to be partners?" Boone's voice was muffled as he pulled off his shirt.

"What do you mean, partners?" Tess asked.

"Like Master Joah and Master Garvin," he explained. "With the wine."

"What makes you think that?"

"When they were in the winery, Ben said he wanted to export the wine. That means take it to another planet and sell," he said with pride. "Ben explained it to me."

"Maybe you shouldn't ask Ben so many questions," Tess suggested as she held out the baggy old shirt that Boone slept in. "And I don't want you in the winery."

"But Master Joah said I need to learn the business. And Ben said I could ask him whatever I wanted and he'd answer and then he could ask me things, too. We even shook hands on it." There was a sense of awe in Boone's voice.

Tess wasn't sure that she liked this idea. "What kind of questions does he ask you?'

"All different stuff. Where's his ship, when did you come here, where's my father—"

"What did you say?"

"I told him I didn't have one." Boone climbed into his bed while Ky made his customary three circles beside it before settling down on the floor.

"What did Master Joah say when you asked?"

"Ben doesn't ask me things in front of Master Joah," Boone said as if he and Ben had a long history between them. "He asked me if you ever smiled, too."

"He did?" Tess pulled the blanket over Boone and tucked the sides under the mattress. "And what did you say to that?"

"I said sometimes." Tess sat down on the edge of the bed. "Mema? Why don't you smile much?"

Tess felt an odd ache in her heart. "Aren't I smiling right now?" she asked. She kissed him on the forehead.

"Yes," Boone said. His hand touched the side of her face. "I like it when you smile."

"I like it when you smile, too," Tess said. She blew out the lamp.

"Mema?" Boone called to her as she reached the door. "Can you smile for Ben? He said he wanted to see it."

"I'll try," Tess said. "Now go to sleep."

She heard the men's voices raised in laughter once more as she closed the door to Boone's room. She went immediately to the front door and stepped out into the night air.

It was another warm cloudless night. Rain would be welcome, if it ever came. Tess looked off toward the mountains as she walked toward the pen to check on the heifer.

There was light flashing in the sky as there had been for several nights past. Strange how lightning would flicker around the mountains, but the storms never moved down into the valley to give them rain. But as long as the stream ran by the place, the grapes would survive, and the well seemed to be in no danger of going dry.

But it would be nice not to have to fill buckets to water the garden, nor pump the trough full for the draft horses that grazed in the field beside the house.

The heifer was secure. Tess was so grateful, she gave her an extra ration of grain. The animal buried her muzzle in the bin and took a mouthful, then raised her head and stared toward the stream as she chewed.

Tess rubbed the thick, soft neck of the animal as they both looked toward the rushing water. "I'm as bad as you are," she sighed. "Always yearning for something I can't have."

Tess leaned comfortably next to the heifer. The sound of the stream filled her senses and she let the noise wash over her, wishing that the resonance could carry her worries away as easily as the water rushed toward the unseen rivers that fed into unknown oceans far, far away.

Her son told her she didn't smile enough. Yet hadn't she always tried to take her pleasures in small things, since those were the only joys she would ever have?

She had long ago given up wanting things for herself. She knew it would never be. Not as long as Joah was alive. Not as long as she lived as a slave on Lavign.

But for Boone . . . for Boone she wanted more.

What could she give him?

If Boone were older and she knew Ben better, she would suggest that her son stow away on the pilot's ship. He seemed decent enough, even with his wild tales.

Was that the kind of life she wanted for her son? That of a drifter?

But then again, he'd have a chance to make something for himself. Of himself. Without the sour taint of Joah.

How long did she have before Joah's ways started to rub off on Boone? How long before he formed the same opinions that the old man held? How long before he turned into the same type of man as his father? . . . Tess shook her head at her ramblings. She would never consider that animal to be Boone's father.

Maybe she should convince Ben to take Boone now.

Could she face the days without her son? Would she have a reason to go on without any hope at all?

What would happen to her when Joah died? He would die eventually. If only the casks would fall and crush him as they had his son.

Tess hated thinking of Joah's son. Her skin still crawled at the thought of him, even after all these years.

At least Boone had nothing of his sire in him. Not yet.

What if Ben did take Boone? What guarantee did she have that he wouldn't just dump him off someplace to fend for himself?

Her mind chased in endless circles. Worry had been her companion so long, she didn't know what she'd do without it.

No wonder she never smiled.

The sound of voices reached her and she realized, gratefully, that Joah and Ben were on their way to the winery. Tess stole a look over the heifer's back and noticed that they both were a bit unsteady on their feet.

Ben's wobbling could be blamed on his sore ankle, she supposed. But the raucous singing that accompanied their staggering gait made her fairly certain the wine was responsible.

She hoped they would both pass out in the winery so she could enjoy some peace for the rest of the evening.

A genuine smile lit her face. She would have a bath and wash her hair. Even if it meant more work. And while her hair dried she would work on her coat. Since Ben seemed to be able to take care of himself now, she could return to her regular routine.

She might even get to sleep at a decent time tonight.

With that small bit of comfort, Tess made her way back to the house. She filled all the pots with fresh water from the pump over the sink and heated the water on the stove while she prepared the tub. She lifted it off the wall and placed it within the narrow confines of the storage room. She found a towel that was a bit frayed at the edges but in better shape than most of them and placed it on a small stool along with a hard bar of soap and an herbal mixture that she used to clean her hair.

When the water had heated to her satisfaction, she poured it into the tub and then quickly dried the pots and put them away while the water cooled a bit. Some she saved in a pitcher to rinse her hair with.

When everything was ready, Tess yanked off her boots and placed them carefully on a shelf. She dropped her clothes where she stood and kicked them aside as she tested the water with her toe.

Assured that the water would not scald her skin, she settled her body into the tub. With her knees in the air and her arms hanging on the narrow rim, she was able to lean back against the scooped-out end and let the heat of the water seep into her bones.

Don't think, don't think, don't think.

Don't think about tomorrow. Don't think about the future. Don't think about what's going to happen to Boone. For just a few moments, don't think at all.

Tess let her mind drift to a scene that came occasionally to her when she was on the edge of sleep. It would tease her mind and sometimes wake her with a start as she tried to recall whether it was real, or nothing more than the remains of yearnings from a childhood she could not remember.

She was on a beach, beside a sea of the most brilliant colors she had ever seen. How she even knew what it was, she had no clue; she had never seen so much water gathered in one place, but her mind told her it was the sea.

In her dream she was young. Not much older than Boone. She felt the sting of the wind on her cheeks as her hair whipped around her. She tasted the salt on her lips and felt the scrubbing of the sand between her toes as the water washed around her feet.

In her hand she held a shell. As far as she knew, she had never seen such a treasure, but her dream told her it was perfect. She was holding it in the palm of her hand and watching the sunlight bring the opalescent colors to life as she moved it beneath the bright sunshine. She was showing it to a boy who looked amazingly like her son.

And then she would hear someone calling her name and she'd turn and see a tall, slim woman with long, dark hair and a man with vivid green eyes coming toward her.

Then the vision would dissolve, and all she would see was a great black emptiness that stretched on forever.

The water had cooled, and Tess went about the business of bathing. She washed her face and then ran the soap down her legs, which were hairless, like the rest of her body. The hair had been permanently removed by her former owner as part of his plan to make her into a rapture slave.

She washed all she could reach before standing to work on her hair so she would not make a puddle on the floor. She lathered the mass, which reached past her shoulder blades when she let it down, then blindly reached for the pitcher to rinse.

When she turned around to grab for the towel, she saw Ben standing in the doorway with his boots in his hand, and his lower jaw somewhere around the collar of his borrowed shirt.

An eternity passed, packed into a moment.

Tess swallowed hard. The scars on her breasts were evident, the result of the twisted desires of

Joah's son. With shaking arms she tried to cover herself, and Ben's piercing blue eyes turned away in what she was sure had to be revulsion.

"I'm sorry," he mumbled as he backed away, his boots still in his hand. "I'm so sorry . . . Tess."

Tess suddenly realized that she was holding her breath; she let it out with a gasp, shaking violently with a sudden chill.

She grabbed the towel and quickly dried herself off. She wrapped it around her hair and hastily dressed in the clothes she had dropped on the floor.

On silent feet she ran to the room she shared with Boone. Ky's tail thumped a greeting as she put her pallet on the floor and hastily pulled the blanket up to her chin.

Through the wall she could hear the creak of the bed as Ben settled into it. Each sound made her breath catch in her throat.

On the other side of her she could hear Boone's steady breathing as he slumbered in innocent sleep. Tess tried to catch his rhythm, willing her own breaths to match his, but the creaks from the other side of the wall kept distracting her.

It was a long time until they stopped. And when morning finally came, Tess was not sure if they had ever stopped at all.

Chapter Fifteen

What had happened to her? The image of Tess's scars had haunted his dreams throughout the long, restless night. When he had stopped at the storage room to drop off his boots, his intent had been one of polite consideration since that was where she had seen fit to store them. He had had no idea that he would find her bathing. In his drunken state, his body had quickly reacted to the sight of a beautiful naked woman damp from her bath.

His eyes had taken in the length of her spine and the long muscles of her legs, and his body had quickened at the sight of her. Her arms were raised gracefully over her head with a pitcher poised to pour water over her long, dark hair. The sluicing motion of the water sliding through her hair had brought his attention to what appeared to be a brand on her shoulder. But before his muddled brain could identify it, he had been startled to see her turn to face him, revealing the horrible twisted scars on the sides of her breasts. Tess sucked in her breath so hard at the sight of him that he was able to count every one of her ribs. He was unable to tear his eyes away from her. It wasn't until he saw the horror in her eyes that he was able to look away . . . and apologize.

The realization of what the linked chain brand on her shoulder meant had finally driven him from the miserable prison of his bed just as the first pink of dawn touched the sky.

Tess was a slave. Which explained a lot.

But who had scarred her? What kind of pervert would do that to a woman? He must have used some kind of tool, and Ruben's mind went to the set of tools that hung on a wall in a small workshop in the winery, one of the stops on the tour that Joah had given him the previous afternoon.

Ruben's hands clenched in anger against the top rail of the fence that surrounded the pasture. He flexed them open and looked at his hands, wondering whose hands had done the damage to Tess. One of the huge beasts grazing there looked down at him with soft, dark eyes and pawed at the earth with a hoof as large as a dinner plate.

"What kind of place is this?" Ruben asked the animal, who snorted and turned toward the trough to drink.

No answer came, just the deep gulps of the animal as it drank its fill.

I came here looking for answers, and all I've found is more questions.

And getting drunk last night hadn't helped him get any answers. Ruben practically smacked his lips as he recalled the first taste of the pale blue wine

Joah had poured for him from a dusty bottle harvested in a dry year.

Joah had gone on to explain that the drier the year, the better the wine. All Ruben knew was that he had never tasted anything like it in all his travels. There was a great pile of credits to be made if he could just convince Joah that his fortune would be made in trading off-planet.

Somehow credits didn't seem so important in the light of day. But maybe another glass of that wine would make him feel better.

Ruben eyed the trough. It was deep and the water clean, except for a few stray blades of glass floating around. He swung himself over the fence and landed a bit awkwardly on his bad ankle.

He took his clothes off, sat down in the trough, and picked up the sliver of soap he'd found on the edge. His first intent this morning had been to bathe in the stream and then go up the trail to look for the *Shooting Star*. The trough seemed to be a more practical solution.

The water was warmer than the stream, but not by much. The horses looked at him with something akin to amusement as he scrubbed the soap over his face and hair and then submerged himself beneath the water to rinse. He ran his hands over his jaw. He needed a shave.

Ruben quickly finished with the soap and then took a moment to just sit in the water. He felt the cold soak into his muscles and bones and hoped that it would purge his system of the apathy that seemed to be miring him down.

He should have gone to find the *Shooting Star* as soon as he awoke. He should be working on repairs so he could get off this planet. He should have questioned Tess and Joah both about the whereabouts of Stefan.

And he should be trying to figure out who had shot him down and why.

Instead he was wasting his time chatting up a slave and her son and scheming to get more credits . . . as if he needed any. He had enough stashed away now on Oasis to live comfortably for the rest of his life.

Truth be told, he could probably support the population of a small planet with what he'd earned while tweaking the noses of every law enforcement agency in the galaxy. A planet just like this one.

Ruben splashed water on his face. What was he thinking? He must have taken a harder blow to the head than he'd originally thought. His fingers went to the wound and traced the puckered skin on his forehead.

A scar that looked like a star. A freaking blue star.

That ought to help him keep a low profile on future runs.

Ruben rose from his bath and shook the water from his body as he stepped out of the trough. The horses, startled by his bizarre behavior, tossed their heads and moved away, their huge hooves pounding the ground so hard that the earth vibrated.

Ruben used the borrowed shirt to dry off. He had no further need of it now; he had other clothes on the *Shooting Star.* His hand brushed against the wound on his side and he took a moment to examine it.

Tess had pulled a rod out of him, or so Boone had said. That took a lot of courage. It took a lot of courage to help someone in need when your own life was under the control of someone else.

Boone had said that Joah wanted to throw him, Ruben, back in the stream. Tess had stopped him. With head down in concentration, Ruben realized that he had been awake then. He remembered that Tess had fallen on him because Joah was beating her.

Beating her because she'd tried to stop Joah from murdering him. And he had somehow gotten to his feet and kept Joah from killing her. That was when Tess and Boone had practically carried him into the house.

She had asked him his name, and in his weakened state all he'd been able to get out was "Ben." That was why she called him Ben. He liked the sound of it on her lips. There was no need to correct her. It wasn't as if it would be a permanent thing.

The sound of a door banging shut brought his head up, and he watched as Tess made her way to the necessary.

Why was she a slave? He was still wondering about it when she walked back to the house, undoubtedly to start breakfast.

Ruben wadded the shirt in his hands and tossed it toward the fence. He didn't have time to get involved here. He needed to get to his ship. He needed to find his brother.

"Come on, Ky!"

Ruben looked toward the house and saw Boone and Ky coming toward him at a run.

Ruben picked up the shirt and shook it out. It was wet. It was dirty also. More work for Tess. The water in the trough was scummy, too, and he realized that Tess would probably be the one to clean it out for the horses. Luckily, it seemed to have a drain, and he pulled up the lever and watched as the water poured out onto the crusted earth.

Who needed technology? It seemed that the people of Lavign got along pretty well without it. Well, except for the lack of lavs.

Was the lack of technology the reason slavery was tolerated? How could technology, the result of man's genius, be evil and slavery acceptable?

Boone arrived just as Ruben figured out how to use the pump. He had not forgotten Tess's baptism of him the day before, so he gave the spout a wide berth as the water poured out.

"What are you doing?" Boone asked.

"Helping your mema," Ruben said. "And I want you to help her, too."

"I am," Boone said. "She said for me to find you and take you to your ship so you could leave."

Ruben's hand slid off the pump, and he grabbed a lungful of air as he reached for it once more. The pump, however, had other plans. It was primed and flowing, and the handle flew up and hit the underside of his arm.

Ruben let out a string of curses that had Boone alternating between covering his ears and laughing out loud.

"Er, don't tell your mema where you heard those words," Ruben said as he rubbed his arm. "And don't repeat them," he added firmly.

"When are you going to teach me how to whistle?" Boone asked with a wry grin on his face.

Ruben saw the mischief twinkling in the boy's bright green eyes and realized that Boone was conning him, or charming him, depending upon which way you looked at it. Boone's staying quiet about the cursing depended upon Ruben teaching him how to whistle.

The kid learned fast. It was almost scary how much he reminded him of . . .

Me.

"Go ask your mema to give me something I can eat while we're walking up to the ship," Ruben said, ruffling Boone's thick, dark hair.

"Don't you want to go inside?" the boy asked.

"No. Just grab me something. We've got work to do. As soon as I eat, I'll teach you how to whistle."

Boone took off like a shot, and Ruben pulled on the damp shirt and set off. Boone had caught up with him before he got past the winery. The boy handed him a crusty heel of bread with egg and cheese on it.

"Mema said not to drink from the stream," Boone warned as they approached the rushing water.

"Why's that?" Ruben asked as he munched on his food. It was tasty, and he understood why Joah wanted to keep her around. Everything she had prepared for him was good.

"I don't know. She just said not to."

"I guess she has her reasons," Ruben said.

Ky jumped onto a flat stone in the middle of the stream and leaped onto the opposite bank. Boone followed.

Ruben looked down at the water and wondered if his ankle would support him. Maybe he should soak it. Maybe he should just take a drink . . .

"Come on!" Boone urged. Ky was already gone, bounding up the trail.

Ruben hopped onto the stone, balanced on his good leg, and then leaped to the opposite bank.

The path soon became dark and narrow. It was nothing more than a game trail, Ruben realized, and that was probably why Joah didn't know about the *shooting star*. The old man thought he'd just wandered in from somewhere. Joah probably never came up here. The only reason Tess and Boone had come so high was because they were chasing the heifer, or so Boone had said.

But surely Joah would have noticed the crash. It must have made a horrendous noise. But Joah might not have heard it if he was drunk.

"It's not far!" Boone announced. The trail was too narrow for them to walk side by side, so Ky led the way, bounding along with endless energy.

"Teach me how to whistle," Boone reminded him.

"Just pucker up like you're going to kiss someone and blow," Ruben said.

Boone laughed at the directions and set to work getting his mouth right, turning around occasionally to show Ruben his lips. By the time the trail widened a bit, he was making some sounds.

Ruben rewarded him by whistling a tune, and Boone looked back with amazement.

Ruben whistled again when he saw the *Shooting Star*.

She was buried nose deep in the earth. It looked as if someone had scooped out a depression for her and she had burrowed in to hide. His first thought was about the landing gear. Was it still attached?

The hatch on the side was halfway open, and he hoped that none of the local wildlife had decided to move in.

"I guess we should have brought a shovel," Ruben said.

Boone answered with a wispy whistle.

"Come on," Ruben said, and they slid through the hatch. Ky moved into the interior of the ship with his nose down as Ruben stopped to check the panel beside the hatch. He found that the problem was nothing more than a loose valve, which gave him hope that everything else would be in as good shape. He'd need a tool to fix the hatch, and they were all in the cockpit.

He stopped by his cabin and found a clean shirt, then pointed out the lav to Boone.

"That's my necessary," he said with a grin.

Boone answered with a grin of his own.

"Tell your beast to stay out of the way," Ruben said as they went into the cockpit. Ky was still sniffing around and he let out a low growl as he lifted his great, shaggy head.

Ruben raised an eyebrow in question, but Ky merely sat down as if to wait for orders. Ruben tossed his head toward the back of the cockpit, and Ky obliged so Ruben could move into his seat.

He pressed a button on the com.

"Wake up, darling," he said, and Boone giggled.

"On line," Eli responded.

"Diagnostics," Ruben commanded.

"Running."

"What is that?" Boone asked.

"My ship," Ruben said. "Or maybe just the brains of it."

"Really?" Boone looked at the com in admiration.

"Yes. When it's done it will tell me if there's anything wrong with the *Shooting Star*."

"It sounds like a girl," Boone said.

"Acts like one, too," Ruben replied.

"Why do you call it *Shooting Star*?"

"That's its name."

"Why did you name it that?"

"Why do you ask so many questions?"

"You told me I could."

"I did, didn't I?" Ruben ran his hand up under the com. "I named her the *Shooting Star* because she's fast and that's what she looks like when she flies."

"We thought you were one," Boone said.

"What?"

"A shooting star. Before you crashed, we saw you in the sky. I even made a wish."

"Did it come true?"

"Not yet." Boone's eyes, already wide with excitement at being in the ship, got wider when he saw what Ruben pulled from its hiding place beneath the com. "What is that?"

Ruben held out the blade. "It's a weapon, and you have to promise me that you'll never touch it."

Boone's face fell as he carefully looked at the blade in its sheath. "Can I touch it while you're holding it?"

Ruben was tempted. But give the kid a break and he might just try something more. That's what he would have done when he was young. Younger. Not like he was old now.

"No, you can't. Your mema would skin me with it if she knew." Ruben pushed up his sleeve and strapped the blade into its usual place.

"Diagnostics complete," Eli said.

"Give me the bad news," Ruben said.

Eli began ticking off a list of systems and noted which were operating normally and which were in trouble. Ruben was relieved to hear that there was no structural damage. Also, the engine and the landing gear seemed to be fine. He'd have to make repairs to the water systems and the pressure valve and then dig the nose out to see if he could get her up high enough for launch.

"Sounds like everything is going to be all right," Ruben said.

"Can we fly her now?" Boone asked excitedly.

"No," Ruben laughed. "First we have to dig her out. And I've got to fix a few things. Starting with the hatch."

"When you get her ready, can you take me up into space?" Boone asked.

Ruben looked at the hopeful face. What could he say? He didn't want to make promises he couldn't keep.

And more than anything, he couldn't get attached to Boone.

But what harm could there be in taking the kid for a short flight?

You got shot down once . . . what if you get shot down again?

"You'll have to ask your mema about that," Ruben said, feeling smug because Boone couldn't be mad at him if Tess forbade it. He felt fairly confident that she would.

"I will!" Boone shouted in joy.

"See if you can find a tool box in there," Ruben said, pointing to a panel in the back of the cabin.

Boone quickly found it, and Ruben carried it back to the hatch, pushing Ky ahead of him since there wasn't room to pass by him.

He did a quick bypass and then repaired the broken valve. He replaced the panel and looked down at Boone who was paying rapt attention to every move he made.

"See if it works," Ruben said, pointing to the pressure pad.

Boone slapped his palm on it with gusto, and the hatch slid shut and then quickly popped open.

"There must be something in the track," Ruben said.

Boone knelt down and examined the deep groove that the door slid over. He held up a shiny object. It was as long as his finger and encrusted with tiny jet crystals.

"What is this?" Boone asked, handing it to Ruben.

Ruben looked closely at the object and rolled it in his palm, willing his mind to recall why it seemed so familiar.

And then realization struck him, leaving a hollow feeling in his gut and a twitch in the back of his neck. He recognized the item as the ornament it was, and he knew who had worn it.

A Circe had been in the *Shooting Star*.

Chapter Sixteen

What were the Circe doing on Lavign? And what were they doing in his ship? How long since they'd been here? And how long before they came looking for him?

Did they realize that the pilot of this crashed ship knew where their sworn enemy was located? Were they behind the attack on the *Shooting Star*?

Despite all his precautions, the Circe had managed to find him. He had to warn Shaun and Lilly before he was captured. But how? He was too far from Oasis to send a direct message, and if he tried to bounce a communication through the system, he might as well take out an ad on the SNN alerting the entire universe to their location.

"I've got to get out of here," Ruben said quietly.

"What is it?" Boone asked.

"Nothing," he said. Ruben slid the ornament into

163

one of his many pockets. "Let's see about fixing the water pressure."

If he had to, he'd dig all night to get the *Shooting Star* out.

"Boone, do you think you could run back down to the house and find me a shovel?"

"Sure," Boone said and took off at a full run with Ky on his heels.

How long do I have?

He should have known the Circe would show up. There had been a Circe in his dream. He'd seen Tess and Boone in his dream, and they certainly were real. And from the beginning, he'd thought the Circe were involved in his father's death.

Ruben cursed himself for being every kind of fool as he lay on his back in the lav and worked on the pressure valves behind the panel that held his water supply.

He had to make sure that everything was in good working order. There was no telling where he'd have to go or how long he'd be traveling.

What about Stefan? He'd come here looking for his brother. Was he going to leave without trying to find him?

What about Shaun, Lilly, and the children? He owed it to them to avoid capture by the Circe. Even with Lilly's training, there was no telling how long he could hold out if they questioned him about his friends' whereabouts.

What about Stefan?

What about Shaun and Lilly?

To whom did he feel was the stronger allegiance?

Get the ship fixed . . . then you can worry about it.

His hand slipped as he attempted to turn a valve and he sliced the side of it on the panel.

"Great!" he exclaimed as he looked at the blood dripping down his arm. "Now some other part of me can turn blue."

He found his kit lying on the floor next to his bunk and doctored his hand, sealing the wound shut, then wrapping it with medi-tape. Boone arrived just as he was finishing.

"What happened?" Boone asked.

"I was working too quickly," Ruben replied. "Did you find a shovel?"

"Yes," he said. "It's outside."

Ruben ruffled the boy's dark hair. "Thanks," he said. "What's your mema up to?"

"She was in the garden," Boone replied.

"She stays busy, doesn't she?"

"Yes." Boone looked around at the mess in the cabin.

"Want to help?" Ruben said. "Why don't you put all this stuff away for me while I finish up in the lav."

"Where does it go?"

"Anyplace you can find to put it," Ruben said. "Just as long as it won't move around when I take off."

"Are you still going to take me for a ride?" Boone yelled so Ruben could hear him.

"That's still up to your mema," Ruben yelled back from his place on the lav floor. He finished up with the tool and checked the pressure in the sink. A jet of water flowed out. He needed to top off his tank and flush out the waste, but that would have to wait.

Just like Boone's ride. Maybe someday, when this was all over . . . but not now.

"I'm done," Boone said. "And I found this." He handed Ruben a narrow rod, covered with dried blood.

"Is this what your mema pulled out of me?"

Boone nodded. "It was on the floor."

Ruben's side cramped at the thought. "Ouch," he said. "Let's get started outside."

They moved out into the bright sunlight, and Ruben looked at the impossible job before him. It would take days to dig his ship out of her burrow. The cockpit was buried up to the com, and the rest of the ship had a good amount of earth around it, too.

He didn't dare try his thrusters until he was sure they were clear. If one was bent or broken, he'd wind up with a burnt shell for a ship. And since he'd have to be inside to turn them on, it wasn't worth the risk.

Nothing to do but to start digging.

By the time the sun was high in the sky, his shirt was off and he was thinking longingly of a dip in the stream. Especially since it seemed as if he had made no progress at all.

"How's it coming?" Boone, who had quickly bored of watching him dig, was now alternating between exploring the woods around the clearing and checking on Ruben's progress.

"Just stay where I can see you," Ruben reminded him once more as he went back to the digging.

Water from his ship kept him hydrated, but did nothing to quench his thirst. His quick breakfast had long since been digested, and he longed for some of Tess's cooking.

But going down to the house would only

reawaken the awkwardness of what had happened the previous night.

He still needed to ask Tess about Stefan, but he had not figured out how to bring up that subject. What could he say? *I know you know where my brother is because I saw you with him in a dream?* More than likely she'd laugh at him, after hitting him with one of her pots.

Ky barked, and Ruben slid the blade into his hand automatically, his eyes darting around, checking to see where Boone was. Checking for danger.

Tess came into the clearing, carrying a basket under her arm. Her hair was hidden under a wrap of some sort. Ruben wondered if it was something she had made on her loom.

"I brought you some food," she said without meeting his eyes.

Ruben replaced his blade and wiped the sweat from his face and chest with the borrowed shirt. "You didn't have to," he said as he pitched the shirt aside and walked toward her.

"I did it for Boone," she said, still avoiding his eyes. She placed a hand over her brow to shield it from the sun and scanned the clearing, worry evident on her face until she saw her son. "Boone," she yelled. "Come get something to eat."

Boone ran up to them and dug around in the basket, talking excitedly about the ship and the repairs Ruben had done.

"Boone, take the basket and find some shade," Ruben said. "I'm going to have a talk with your mema."

"No," Tess said. "I have to get back. I have work to do."

"You work too hard," Ruben growled. He grabbed her arm, but she wrenched it away and stood before him.

"That is none of your concern," she spat out.

"Tess," he said as he dropped his hands away in mock surrender. "I just want to apologize." She still wouldn't look at him. Ruben placed a cautious finger under her chin to lift her face up so he could look at her. "Please?"

There were tears forming beneath her dark lashes. But even with the presence of tears he could not help noticing how incredibly pretty her eyes were: dark rims around green-gray irises and lush lashes beneath a delicately arched brow.

He didn't need her tears to know she was sad. Or maybe "without hope" was a better term for it. She seemed . . . resolved.

"You have nothing to apologize for," she murmured so Boone would not hear her. "It is I who should apologize." Her eyes darted down. "I am sorry you were offended."

"What!" Ruben fairly shouted. Boone looked up from the basket and Ky jumped to his feet.

"I hit my hand," Ruben said to Boone, showing him the bandage. Boone seemed satisfied and went back to his lunch.

"How could you think that?" Ruben snapped at Tess. "That's the most ridiculous thing I've ever heard."

"Don't patronize me," Tess retorted as her eyes flashed up and then down again. "I saw the look on your face."

"Could we please talk about this where Boone can't hear us?" Ruben said.

GET UP TO
4 FREE BOOKS!

You can have the best romance delivered to your door for less than what you'd pay in a bookstore or online. Sign up for one of our book clubs today, and we'll send you **FREE* BOOKS** just for trying it out...with no obligation to buy, ever!

HISTORICAL ROMANCE BOOK CLUB

Travel from the Scottish Highlands to the American West, the decadent ballrooms of Regency England to Viking ships. Your shipments will include authors such as CONNIE MASON, SANDRA HILL, CASSIE EDWARDS, JENNIFER ASHLEY, LEIGH GREENWOOD, and many, many more.

LOVE SPELL BOOK CLUB

Bring a little magic into your life with the romances of Love Spell—fun contemporaries, paranormals, time-travels, futuristics, and more. Your shipments will include authors such as LYNSAY SANDS, CJ BARRY, COLLEEN THOMPSON, NINA BANGS, MARJORIE LIU and more.

As a book club member you also receive the following special benefits:

- **30% OFF** all orders through our website & telecenter!
- **Exclusive access** to special discounts!
- **Convenient** home delivery and 10 day examination period to return any books you don't want to keep.

There is no minimum number of books to buy, and you may cancel membership at any time. See back to sign up!

YES! ☐

Sign me up for the **Historical Romance Book Club** and send my TWO FREE BOOKS! If I choose to stay in the club, I will pay only $8.50* each month, a savings of $5.48!

YES! ☐

Sign me up for the **Love Spell Book Club** and send my TWO FREE BOOKS! If I choose to stay in the club, I will pay only $8.50* each month, a savings of $5.48!

NAME: _____

ADDRESS: _____

_____

TELEPHONE: _____

E-MAIL: _____

☐ **I WANT TO PAY BY CREDIT CARD.**

☐ VISA   ☐ MasterCard   ☐ DISCOVER

ACCOUNT #: _____

EXPIRATION DATE: _____

SIGNATURE: _____

Send this card along with $2.00 shipping & handling for each club you wish to join, to:

**Romance Book Clubs
20 Academy Street
Norwalk, CT 06850-4032**

Or fax (must include credit card information!) to: 610.995.9274.
You can also sign up online at www.dorchesterpub.com.

*Plus $2.00 for shipping. Offer open to residents of the U.S. and Canada only. Canadian residents please call 1.800.481.9191 for pricing information.
If under 18, a parent or guardian must sign. Terms, prices and conditions subject to change. Subscription subject to acceptance. Dorchester Publishing reserves the right to reject any order or cancel any subscription.

JOIN NOW!

Begrudgingly she agreed, and they moved into the shadow of the *Shooting Star*.

"How's your ship?" Tess asked, once more avoiding his gaze.

"Remarkably undamaged, considering it was shot down out of the sky." Ruben said. "I fixed the minor problems, but I won't know about structural damage to the thrusters until I get a look underneath. Eli says its fine, but something could be bent or broken that the sensors wouldn't pick up."

"Eli?"

"Encrypted Language Intelligence. It allows the brains of my ship to talk to me. With a voice."

She seemed to know what he was talking about. "You hurt your hand?" she asked.

"It's nothing," he said. "I was in a hurry."

"Oh," she said as she shifted restlessly. Ruben stayed very still. He was afraid she'd run off if he got too close. "Is that a weapon?" she asked, pointing to his blade.

"Yes."

"Why are you wearing it?" Her face appeared panicked for a moment. "Do you think there's danger nearby?"

"Is there?" Ruben asked. "This is your planet. You tell me." A lock of hair had escaped from her careful wrap and dangled enticingly in the exact spot where her neck curved into her shoulder.

"I wouldn't know," she shrugged. "It's not my place to know about such things."

"Tess . . ." he began. What would she do if he touched the stray lock of hair?

"I don't think you're going to have much luck with the digging," Tess said as she looked at the

169

Shooting Star. She stuffed her hair back under the wrap. "Perhaps you could pull it out with the draft horses?" she suggested. "It would be easier, but you would have to get permission from Joah fir—"

"Tess," Ruben interrupted. If only she would look at him. "Who did that to you?"

She crossed her arms defensively over her breasts. "Who did what?"

"Who hurt you?"

Tess looked over her shoulder to check on Boone. "I don't know what you're talking about. And even if I did, it's none of your concern."

"Tess . . ." Ruben ran the back of his hand down the side of her face. Why couldn't he keep his hands off her? Deep down inside he felt that if he could only touch her and maybe hold her, he could make all her pain go away. "I'm sorry I walked in on you. But more important, I'm sorry someone hurt you."

"Why?" she asked. "Why should you care?'

Her question surprised him. But not as much as the realization that he did care.

The sudden thought that things were moving too fast crossed his mind. Why did he care? He who had loved and left more women across the galaxy than he could count? There were a few he thought of fondly—Laylon came to mind—but for the most part, he kept it simple. Perhaps he could keep it simple now.

Ruben shrugged his shoulders and gave her his famous grin. After all, it had never failed him with difficult women. And it seemed as if he had made some progress with Tess. "I just do."

"Don't bother," she said hotly. "You're leaving. So

just go and leave us alone. We've gotten along fine without you and we'll continue to do so."

She spun on her heel and stalked off. "Boone! Time to work on your lessons."

Boone looked up at her, incredulous. "Mema!" he gasped. "I have to help Ben."

"Ben can handle it himself," she said. "Let's go. Now!"

"Tess," Ruben said. "Don't punish him because you're upset with me."

Tess whirled and charged toward Ruben, her eyes blazing.

"Do . . . not . . . tell . . . me . . . how . . . to . . . raise . . . my . . . son." She emphasized each word by poking a finger into the hollow of his slick, bare chest with such vigor that the skin became red and tender before she was done.

She pulled back her hand to continue, but Ruben caught it before the point of her finger could do more damage.

"I'm not your enemy, Tess," he said simply. "I'd like to help you if you'd let me."

"If you want to help us, then leave us alone," she said, her voice barely more than a whisper.

Ruben wondered where her anger had gone. Usually, he admired her spirit, but now she seemed weak, spent . . . resolved.

"For his sake," she said, looking toward Boone, who was watching the two of them with wide eyes. "Please," she added.

Ruben looked over her head and saw the fear on Boone's face. Obviously, the kid was torn between protecting his mother and defending his new friend.

"I'll be leaving as soon as I can get my ship dug out of this mess," Ruben said. "But before I go, there are some things I want to ask you. Things I think you know. If you want me to go, then you'd better be prepared to give me some answers."

He saw panic flit across her eyes for an instant, and then they became guarded and resolved once more.

"I don't know what you're talking about," she said. "I don't know anything." She turned and walked away, grabbed the basket and Boone's hand, and headed back down the trail. Boone looked at Ruben over his shoulder as they disappeared into the trees.

It wasn't until he had returned to his digging that he realized she had not left him a bite to eat.

Chapter Seventeen

"Why do I have to go?" Boone asked as they moved down the trail. His chin had that stubborn tilt to it once more.

"You need to do your lessons."

"But, Mema, Ben needs my help."

"No, he doesn't."

"But he does. I got him a shovel and I picked up his clothes and put them away. I did all kinds of stuff."

"And now you're done."

"Mema! I want to go back." Boone wrenched his hand out of hers. "I want to stay with Ben."

Tess stopped in her tracks. What she dreaded had come to pass. Her heart ached at her son's frustration. She wanted to grab him up and hold him. She wanted to make the hurt he would soon feel pass him by. So many things she wanted to do.

Tess forced her face to remain stern, her tone

impassive. "You can't. You can't stay with Ben. He's leaving." Best to end the relationship now before the hurt got any worse. Best to let Boone go ahead and deal with it. It would be the first of many disappointments in his life. He might as well learn how to deal with them.

"But," Boone protested, "he's going to take me for a ride in his ship."

"He said that?"

Boone looked at the ground. "He said I'd have to ask you first."

"Ftttt," Tess hissed under her breath. Just like that, Ben had made her responsible for disappointing Boone. He knew she would never allow it. How could she risk it, when he had just been shot down in that ship?

"Can I go?" Boone asked. "Please?"

What could she say to a child who had never once asked for anything for himself? And would probably never have much pleasure in his life, if Joah had any say about it.

"Let's see if he gets it dug out first," Tess said. A lot could happen between now and then. Life could change in the blink of an eye. If only it would change for the better.

Maybe Ben would have enough sense just to take off and leave them be.

Was that too much to hope for?

Boone's smile was broad as he went skipping ahead with Ky on his heels. A temporary joy to get him through the next few days. And then when Ben left, she'd deal with the sadness. It would be easier then, when their lives got back to everyday routine.

She couldn't blame Boone for wanting to be with Ben. There was something about him that had tempted her to ignore her chores and pack a basket full of food and go traipsing up the trail. She never would have risked it if Joah had been around. But he had taken off earlier in the day without a word to her.

Was it Ben's careless charm? She recognized that for the stratagem it was. Funny that she did, since she had only been around men who demanded and took without regard for her feelings. But Ben was different. He was used to having his way with women. One smile from him and they probably lined up to do whatever he asked. She definitely wasn't interested in warming his sheets. Nor could she understand why any woman would be.

She had heard it was supposed to be pleasurable. If it was, then why were women made into rapture slaves? Wouldn't they just do it willingly?

She'd never know the answer to that question.

So besides his obvious good looks and the air of mystery that surrounded him, what was it about Ben that made her want to spend time with him, even after the embarrassment of the previous night? She was past fooling herself into thinking it was because she was worried about Boone. She had seen the way Ben behaved with her son. He would not hurt him.

So was that it? Did she like him because of the way he treated Boone? Because he took an obvious interest in her son and didn't mind spending time with him?

He took an interest in you, too.

Tess felt her face flush and blamed it on the heat of the day, even though they were walking in deep shade from the thick forest that encroached on the path.

An image of Ben filled her mind. Shirtless, sweaty, greeting her with a smile. She had found his physical presence overwhelming in the confines of the house. But he was overwhelming outside, too. He was just so . . . male.

For some strange reason, she wanted to touch him. Strange because she didn't want to be touched. That was why she'd jabbed her finger in his chest. She was too weak to stay away from him, and letting her temper flare had kept her hands from caressing his smooth skin just to see what it felt like. It was also an attempt to keep him from touching her. An attempt that he pretty much ignored whenever he stroked her face or played with her hair as if she were *his* property instead of Joah's.

She had imagined what it would be like to touch him when she'd cared for him during those first few days. She had imagined what it would be like to once more have those blue eyes look up at her as they had when she'd fallen on him by the stream. Luckily, Boone had been with her almost every minute, watching and waiting for Ben to wake up, or she would have made a fool of herself.

And then her imaginings had really taken off this morning when she had covertly watched him at his bath. The rippling muscles of his back. The long line of his thigh. The thatch of hair growing on his belly, which trailed down to a place she could not keep her eyes from caressing.

She didn't even know what it was she longed for.

She just knew that in spite of the pain and disgust she'd felt with Joah's son, she wanted something more. Was there something more?

Ben said he wanted to help her, help them. But how could he? Could she trust him? And would she be putting their lives at risk if she did? There had to be a reason he'd been shot down. And she had a feeling it had to do with what she'd seen in the warehouse. She knew without a doubt that was the reason Ben was here.

For Boone's sake, she hoped Ben would just leave.

Boone and Ky were waiting to make the hop with her at the stream. Neither one of them seemed to be in a hurry to go across. She understood why when she saw the wagon in the yard.

Garvin.

Tess stood at the side of the stream, poised between heaven and hell.

Go back! she told herself.

Back to what? To throw herself on the mercy of another man? To exchange one miserable existence for another?

You don't know.

If only she did. If only she could be sure, for Boone's sake. At least she knew that here, no harm would befall him and he would be provided for. Not much of a life, but a life nonetheless.

Are you sure?

Tess shook her head. No doubt Joah would expect her to fix dinner for his friend Garvin. And it had better be a good one or she would suffer.

"I forgot to leave some food for Ben," Tess said to Boone. No need for him to have to witness the upcoming ordeal. Garvin was always careful in front of Joah, but given the chance, he would press her when her owner wasn't watching. But he didn't care at all whether Boone was around. As a matter of fact, he seemed to draw some twisted enjoyment from having her son see him run his hands over her.

"Take it to him," she said, handing Boone the basket. "Looks like I won't have time for your lessons this afternoon."

Boone and Ky took off up the trail, joyous at their reprieve.

Maybe Boone's company would keep Ben occupied for the rest of the day also. For some reason, the thought of Ben and Garvin together in the same house was disturbing.

Joah was waiting for her, of course. Both men sat at the table with an open bottle of wine between them. They had wasted no time getting started.

"Where've ye been?" Joah snapped as soon as she walked into the house. "We've been waiting fer our food," he added.

"With Boone," she said, ignoring Garvin. Why couldn't they have gotten it themselves? There was stew just sitting on the stove. Was it too much work to fill a bowl and eat it?

"Where's the man?" Joah asked, closely watching her as she went to the stove to dip out the stew.

"He went to his ship."

"His what?"

"He said he crashed his starship. He went to fix it."

She heard the harsh whispers as Joah and Garvin stuck their heads together. Joah must have known Ben was an offworlder after the evening they had spent together drinking and telling tales. Surely

Joah had considered that the stories Ben told had taken place on other planets.

"Where is it?" Joah asked her.

"On the knoll." Tess kept her back to them. Her answers were honest. Joah was past wondering if she had seen the crash, although he might wonder how he could have missed it.

The old fool.

"He didn't take any of my tools, did he?" Joah asked suspiciously.

"A shovel," Tess said. "Boone got it for him."

"Is the boy with him, then?"

"Yes." Tess felt her skin crawl as she kept her back to Joah. Would he be angry about Boone spending time with Ben?

"What kind of starship?" Garvin asked. "A big one?"

"I don't know," Tess said. Why did he want to know?

There were more whispers behind her.

What are they up to?

"I'll go see for myself," Garvin said finally.

Tess wasn't sure if she liked that idea. At least Garvin would be out of her hair for a while, which was a good thing. She could barely stand to be in the same room with him. But what did he want with Ben? Surely he didn't mean to harm him.

"Hurry up, girl," Joah said. "A man could starve waiting for ye."

Tess rolled her eyes toward the ceiling. Joah had never been in any jeopardy of starving to death. The man saw to his stomach before he saw to anything else.

"Ye can go after ye eat," Joah said to Garvin.

Hearing this, Tess filled another bowl and turned to carry the bowls to the table.

Garvin was watching her, of course, with his dark eyes. They were black and vacant, bottomless pits. She hated him.

Tess set the bowls down and automatically took a step back out of reach. "Will Master Garvin be staying for the next meal?" she asked with her head down.

"Yes," Garvin said hastily. "Joah and I have a lot of business to discuss."

Tess couldn't imagine what they were always talking about. Joah made the wine; Garvin made the bottles. It seemed pretty straightforward to her.

"I'll start preparations," Tess said. She quickly got her gathering basket and headed toward the garden.

Those two were up to no good, Tess was sure of it. But what did it have to do with Ben? She went to the far end of the garden to dig potatoes and kept a cautious eye on the back of the house. The screech of the door alerted her to Garvin, and she ducked behind a bean vine that trailed up a string trellis.

His black eyes darted around, looking for her, and she held her breath, willing him to be on his way. No such luck. He stepped into the garden and walked between the rows. It was best if he didn't think she was hiding from him. Somehow she knew he'd enjoy the thought, so she stood up and dusted the dirt off her pants.

"The ridge is that way," she said, pointing toward the stream.

"I thought perhaps you could show me," Garvin said.

Tess held the small spade before her, and Garvin stopped. He looked down at the weapon with a smile.

"I have chores to do," Tess said.

"I could think of a few chores you could do for me," Garvin said suggestively.

Tess fought the impulse to gag. Was he attempting to seduce her?

"You know my master doesn't like to share."

"He would never know," Garvin said. "Another bottle of wine and he'll be out for the night." He took a step closer.

Joah came out the door, scratching and stretching, then went to the necessary. Tess's eyes darted after him as she heard the wooden door slam shut.

"You expect me to betray my master?" Tess asked. She pointed toward the ridge. "As I said, the trail is that way."

"Your master would not want me to get lost."

"Just follow the trail."

"I could have him order you to go with me."

The smile that stretched his lips warned her, and a fleeting panic surged through Tess. Go with Garvin up the trail, through the woods? Chances were it would take a long while to reach the clearing if Garvin had his way.

"Master Joah is more concerned about his stomach than about you," Tess said. "He would not want his meal to be late."

The screech and bang of the door announced Joah's approach once more.

"What are ye waiting for?" he asked Garvin.

"I was just telling Tess how much I enjoyed her stew," Garvin said. His dark eyes lingered on her. "I like your hair better when it's down," he said quietly to Tess, his eyes flicking over her wrap. "Try not to disappoint me . . . at dinner."

It was a threat. Tess's eyes flared as she gripped the handle of the spade.

"Don't be giving her any big ideas or she'll think she's better than what she is," Joah said.

"I'll be back soon," Garvin promised her and turned to Joah.

Tess watched them go, the spade still held before her until she saw Garvin hop across the stream and Joah make his way to the winery.

Her knees felt weak, and she let herself drop to the dirt. A sob tore at her throat as she dug her hands into the sun-dried earth and flung the clods away.

How long could she hold Garvin off? How long before he trapped her and had his way with her. How long could she survive here?

Tess swiped her eyes with the back of her hand, not caring that she smeared dirt across her face. At least she had the satisfaction of keeping her hair from Garvin's hateful gaze. No need to mention to the man that it was a mess from her restless night of tossing and turning when her hair was still wet from her bath. At least she had the luxury of wrapping it up and hiding it from Garvin. But that luxury would only last as long as he kept his hands from her wrap. Just as she would only last as long as she could keep his hands from her.

She would hold on as long as Boone needed her. She had to.

Resolved, Tess went back to her digging and

threw a small red potato in her basket. She glanced up toward the ridge.

Ky was up there with Boone, so her son would be safe.

But what about Ben?

Chapter Eighteen

At this rate he'd be an old man before he ever got the *Shooting Star* dug out. Ruben leaned heavily on the shovel and wiped the sweat from his face and chest with the borrowed shirt for what had to be the hundredth time.

The thought of a dip in the stream flashed through his mind as it had countless times during the day. It had been pretty much all he'd thought about as he dug. One more shovelful and he could go to the stream. One more and then he'd go. One more.

Why not go now? It wasn't as if he were accomplishing anything. Why not just go and let the cool, fresh water wash over him?

Then maybe he and Joah could crack open a bottle of wine and discuss using his giant horses to pull him out of this mess.

Ruben decided he liked that plan. "Boone?" he yelled. The kid kept wandering farther and farther away but as long as the big Newf was with him, he should be all right.

There was no answer.

Ruben took a step back from the ship and let his ears absorb the sounds around him. The gentle twitter of birdsong and the slight sway of the treetops was all he heard. With a quick flick of his wrist, his blade was in his hand, and he moved out toward the last place he had seen Boone.

He should have known that the temptation of visiting the other ship's crash site would be too much for the kid to resist. There was no doubt in Ruben's mind that was where Boone was as he moved down the opposite side of the ridge.

"Boone!" he yelled again. He was on another game trail, a narrower one than that coming up from the stream to the clearing. He wondered what kind of wildlife inhabited this planet. He had yet to see anything bigger than his hand, but some creature had made this trail. Obviously, it led to the water source.

Ruben wiped his arm across his mouth. He should have brought some water with him. He had no idea how long it would take him to find Boone. Why was he so thirsty all the time?

"Boone!" He'd better find the boy quick or Tess would likely skin him. And with his luck, he'd turn blue all over. His side was healing well, but from the looks of it, the blue scar was going to be a permanent addition, along with the star on his forehead.

"Here!"

He heard a faint call followed by Ky's bark. Ruben followed the sound and the broken treetops down into a gully. The sound of rushing water became louder, and he saw that the stream curved around the ridge. At least he'd be able to get a drink.

Soon enough the trees opened up into a burned circle, and the charred remains of a Falcon lay half in the stream.

"You haven't seen my cargo bay lying around here anywhere, have you?" he asked Boone as the boy ran up to him.

"Your what?"

"Never mind," Ruben said. He placed his blade back on his wrist and ruffled Boone's dark hair. "I thought I told you to stay close."

"Um, I was. Ky chased—"

"Don't worry about it." Boone grinned up at him. "Did you find anything?"

"Everything's burned up."

Ruben looked around at the charred circle. "Guess it's a good thing that these trees are evergreens," he said. "Of course, the fuel burns itself out pretty quick once it hits the atmosphere."

"Huh?"

"Air."

"Oh," Boone said.

"We might as well look around," Ruben said. "See if we can figure out who did this."

Ky was sniffing around the remnants of a burned-out hull. Ruben recognized the craft as a tech job, a Senate fighter that had been stripped and revamped to fit the personal needs of the pilot. Probably a ship for hire or a bounty hunter. And if it was the latter, had the bounty hunter been looking for him? And if the pilot was after a bounty, why was he shot him down? A bounty would be hard to collect if the hunter got burned up.

There were two charred skeleton in the ruins, but no clues, no reasons, nothing to show why he'd been attacked as soon as he hit the air space above Lavign. Ruben poked hopefully in the rubble with a stick but found nothing beyond what would normally be in a fighter. There was no recognizable insignia on what was left on the uniform, and the com was totally destroyed, so there was no way of tracing or retrieving whatever files had been in the Falcon's intelligence.

A noise caught his attention, strange because the rushing of the stream was so loud. Stranger still because it sounded so out of place in all the primitive wildness of the land.

"That sounds like wind chimes," Ruben said. "Is there another house around here?"

"I don't think so," Boone said.

The sound was coming from upstream. Ruben started toward it, his ears straining. He paused for a moment, suddenly, inexplicably drawn toward the stream. He stooped to scoop up a handful of water, but Ky bumped into him and the water cupped in his hands splashed away.

Ky barked and looked hopefully up at him, his tail wagging.

"What?" Ruben asked the Newf, who promptly moved upstream. Ruben and Boone followed along. The beast seemed to know what had caught their attention.

The tinkling noise was louder. It sounded like glass, as if Ruben were in a tavern and glasses were being piled in a sink. It also sounded as if it were coming from the stream.

The water wasn't as deep here. He could see the

bottom and he splashed into it. The water came to about mid-calf. His legs beneath his boots grew quickly chilled, and he wondered why he had thought he was hot earlier.

"Stay on the bank," he told Boone.

Maybe I should just sit down for a minute.

The thought of immersing himself in the water made him forget why he was here in the first place.

"I will," Boone said. "Mema told me never to get in."

Ky barked again and bounded toward Boone.

"She likes to stay on top of things, doesn't she?" Ruben said.

Wouldn't mind having her on top of me.

Now, that was a random thought. Ruben stole a look at Boone, wondering if the kid could possibly know what he was thinking about his mother.

Boone seemed oblivious.

The sound was stronger now, an eerie noise that seemed to fill Ruben's brain.

Ruben stopped when he realized that Ky had halted also, right above frothy, fernlike foliage covered with blue flowers.

The plant was as big as Ky. It grew out of the bank of the stream and spilled over so that the flowers dangled in the water.

Ruben realized that he had found the source of the sound. He looked closer. The flowers were long, blue tubes and seemed to be . . . crystal? Those that hung in the stream crashed and clattered as the water pulled at them.

Some of the tubes were broken. Ruben pulled one up from the water and saw the ragged edges, as if someone had broken off the top off a bottle.

Strange. The tubes were hollow inside. He checked a whole one growing on the bank and saw that the bottom was sealed and the top was attached to the plant by a stem. He pulled on it and found it difficult to remove, so he used his blade to cut it off.

Ruben held the tube up to the sunlight. It seemed there was a thick liquid inside.

Stranger and stranger. He had never seen anything like it. A plant that grew crystal? Maybe if he looked around enough, he'd find one that sprouted snifters or wineglasses.

Too bad Boone wouldn't get the humor.

"What is it?" Boone asked.

"I'm not sure." Ruben held the tube up to the light once more and shook it. A few bubbles inside slowly rose to the top. Definitely liquid.

A sudden desire to taste the liquid came over him. As if hypnotized, he watched the fluid as it moved in the tube, fascinated by the tiny bubble that traveled the length of it. He grabbed the stem and pulled on it, but it would not come off. Frustrated, he looked around and then felt foolish when he realized that he still had his blade in his hand. One quick snap of his wrist and he neatly sliced the top off the crystal.

It was almost like holding a shot glass. He sniffed at the top.

The next instant, all the air left his body as what felt like a proton blast hit him square in the chest. He fell flat on his back and looked up through the stars circling his head into the huge face of Ky. A tongue the size of his forearm went across his face, and then the Newf moved off him.

"What was that all about?" Ruben said when he

managed to roll to his knees and once again take a breath.

"I don't know," Boone said. He was grinning, his bright green eyes dancing.

The crystal had flown out of his hand, of course. A thick blue liquid formed a puddle on the thick grass that grew along the stream bank. Ruben stretched out a finger to touch it, but Ky stepped on his hand as he reached.

"Get off me, you beast," Ruben yelled.

Ky moved but bared his teeth as Ruben reached toward the puddle once more.

"I don't think he wants you to touch it," Boone said as Ky stationed his huge body between Ruben and the crystal.

"I think I figured that out."

Ruben reached for the crystal. Ky watched him carefully with his big dark eyes but didn't seem to have a problem with him touching the crystal; it was the contents that seemed to disturb him. Ruben slid the crystal into his pocket and sheathed his blade.

"We'd better start back."

Boone nodded in agreement, and they made their way back toward the crash site.

"Have you ever seen a plant like this before?"

"No," Boone said. "But I haven't been many places."

"So where have you been?"

"To the city."

"Where's the city?"

"It's past Master Garvin's. It takes most of the morning to get there."

"How do you get there?"

"In the wagon."

"What do you do when you get there?"

"Master Joah trades for his wine, and Mema sells her weavings."

"Is there a spaceport there?"

"You mean where ships fly in?"

"Yes."

"There is. I saw a ship fly in there once. Master Joah doesn't like the spaceport. He doesn't want off-worlders here."

"Did Master Joah ever think that at one time everyone here was an offworlder?"

Boone laughed. "Me and Mema saw some off-worlders one time."

"You did?" Ruben tried not to let his excitement show in his voice. Would it be this easy, then? To find out about Stefan?

"Yes. We were hiding from Master Garvin in this big house and there were people inside and they were talking to each other. Then this lady in a funny hat came out and then one man fell down and yelled and Ky started barking and Mema and I ran away."

"A lady in a funny hat?"

"Yes," Boone said. He moved his hands around his head. "Poufy with shiny stuff on it."

Ruben dug in his pocket and pulled out the jet crystals. "Like this?"

Recognition spread over Boone's face. "Yes," he said. "Just like that."

They were coming up the ridge behind the *Shooting Star*. Boone's description of what he'd seen was too much like Ruben's dream to be a coincidence.

"The man who fell down and started yelling— what did he look like?"

Boone's green eyes were serious when he turned

them up to Ruben. "He looked like you. We thought it was the same man when we found you in the crash. Mema said it wasn't, though. The other man had long hair like this." Boone brushed his hand to the top of his shoulder. "Who was that man? Do you know him?"

"He's my brother," Ruben said, placing a firm hand on Boone's shoulder. "I came here looking for him."

"The other man called him Stefan."

"That's his name. Is there anything else you can remember?"

Boone screwed his face up in concentration. "There were some men behind the lady. They were holding a circle thing and I think they wanted to put it on your brother."

A curse exploded from Ruben's lips. "A collar," he added. "And don't tell your mema what I just said."

"I won't," Boone promised.

Ruben's dream had been a reality. Stefan was definitely in trouble, and the trouble had happened here on Lavign. But why? What was going on? What did this have to do with his father's assassination?

Ruben slid the jet ornament back into his pocket and heard it chink alongside the crystal vial.

The thought that the two strange objects in his pocket could be related flashed through his mind. In the next moment the idea was gone as Ky came to a stop in front of them with his ears perked toward the clearing on the knoll.

Ruben grabbed Boone and placed a finger to his own lips so the kid would know to stay quiet. He watched Ky carefully to see what the Newf would do as he slipped his blade into his hand.

A low rumble sounded in Ky's throat. Ruben

pointed to a thick clump of ground cover in the woods along the trail, and Boone nodded as he slipped into the cover.

Ruben crept forward, his eyes on the clearing, trying to catch a glimpse of whoever was trespassing on his ship. A shadow caught his eye, and his fingers separated one of the razor-thin sections from his blade.

In the next instant he threw it, and the blade buried itself in the trunk of a tree just a few inches from the ear of a large man who had just walked around from behind the *Shooting Star.*

Ky took off at the same time, growling menacingly at the man, who looked at the blade in astonishment.

"That's Master Garvin," Boone said from behind him as Ruben prepared another blade.

"Do we like him?" Ruben asked as he kept his eyes on the large man.

"Mema doesn't," Boone said. "Are you going to kill him?"

"Depends," Ruben said, keeping his eyes on Garvin. "I'll see what your mema has to say about it."

Garvin's eyes found the two of them and flared for a moment with something that seemed like recognition. He took a step toward them, but Ky held his ground.

"Oy," Garvin said, holding his hands out in front of him. "I came to see if you need any help."

"Sorry about that," Ruben said as he stepped into the clearing with Boone close behind him. "Ky didn't seem to recognize you, so I wasn't sure if you were friend or foe."

Ruben saw immediately that Garvin was sizing him up as he came closer. He seemed puzzled, as if he thought he recognized him, but wasn't sure.

Ruben walked past him, gave him a wry smile, and pulled his blade out of the trunk. The man seemed afraid of Ky, so Ruben let the Newf remain between the two of them as he secured his blade in its sheath.

"You must be the neighbor," Ruben said when he was done retrieving his weapon.

"Garvin," the other man said, his eyes jumping between Ruben and Ky.

"Ben," Ruben replied and stuck out his hand. Garvin seemed surprised at this but finally reached out and they shook hands, each one taking the measure of the other. Ruben placed a hand on Boone's shoulder. "We were just exploring a bit," he said.

Garvin's dark eyes flicked over Ruben once more and then down to Boone. Ky's throat rumbled.

"Boone, why don't you take Ky while I show our new . . . friend . . . here what the problem is," Ruben said, keeping his face open and friendly. He'd had dealings with this type before. Garvin might be showing a friendly facade, but Ruben could tell that the man wasn't here to help.

Help himself is more like it.

"Looks like you've got quite a problem here," Garvin said as they walked around the *Shooting Star*.

"She's buried pretty deep," Ruben said. He propped his boot on the nose of his ship. "Guess I'm lucky to have made it out alive."

"Lucky," Garvin agreed. He peered curiously through the plexi at the cockpit. "What brought you here?"

"I'm a trader," Ruben said. "Thought I might have something you could use."

"You've got cargo in there?"

"No. I lost it," Ruben lied. "Had to jettison my hold before I crashed."

"Too bad," Garvin said. "We don't get many traders on Lavign."

"I can see why," Ruben said.

Garvin seemed to be pondering the hole that the ship was buried in.

Funny that he hasn't asked me why I crashed.

"Maybe we could pull her out with Joah's draft horses," Garvin said.

"Funny," Ruben said. "Tess suggested the same thing."

"Ye've talked to her, then?" Garvin asked. There was no mistaking the possessive flare in his eyes.

Ruben picked up the borrowed shirt and slowly mopped it across his chest. "She saved me," he said, almost casually. "She nursed me back to health."

Garvin's dark eyes went to the puckered blue skin on Ruben's side and then up to the blue star on his forehead. "Like I said," he said slowly, his eyes finally settling on Ruben's. "Lucky."

"Always have been," Ruben said with a wide grin.

"It might run out on ye one day," Garvin said.

"I guess that's a chance I'll have to take," Ruben replied.

Chapter Nineteen

"Boone!" Tess yelled. "Stay out of the way!"

Ruben grabbed Boone up and threw him over his shoulder. Giggles poured out from the boy as Ruben carried him away from the slowly moving starship.

The giant draft horses were doing their job. They were moving the *Shooting Star* out of its burrow with a lot less effort than it had taken to convince Joah to help.

Of course, Ruben had not expected that Tess would be the one working the horses when he finally placed a small bag of credits in front of Joah for the use of his team. Joah had quickly pocketed the bag, then told Tess to take the team up to the knoll before daylight was gone. Then he and Garvin had put their heads together once more.

A sure sign that Ruben should probably watch his back.

Ruben set Boone down and asked Tess as they led the team up the trail, "Does Joah do any work at all around the place?"

"It's not my place to question what he does," Tess retorted hotly.

"You could just leave, you know," Ruben said. "There are a lot of places in the galaxy that frown on slavery."

"There's not exactly a gate at the spaceport for departing slaves," Tess said after checking to make sure Boone was out of earshot. "Don't you think I've thought of that? Besides, after Boone came, there was no way I could leave."

Ruben tried to imagine what it had been like for her. Young, alone, with a baby, trying to survive, the victim of a man's whims.

A lot like the life his mother had led.

"You could go with me."

"And get shot down?" Tess hissed. Boone, who had run ahead, was now running back to them, Ky on his heels as usual.

"That doesn't usually happen," Ruben said. "As a matter of fact, this was the first time."

"Can you guarantee that it was the last time?"

Ruben laughed. "No."

Tess stopped dead in the track. They were walking in single file because the path was narrow and the huge beasts filled the trail. He saw the anger in her face as she shoved one horse to the side so she could look at him.

"My son's life is not to be laughed at." She ground out the words. "I value it more than my own. And I will not allow you to treat it so casually."

Ruben looked at her. Her eyes flashed with anger. He had no doubt that she would have hit him again if she could have reached him. An image of Lilly flashed through his mind. He was actually surprised that he hadn't felt Tess's red hot pincers in his crotch.

"I don't," he said as Boone slid to a stop behind her. "I wouldn't."

"Ftttt," she hissed as she turned, pulling the horse after her. Boone looked between the two of them with curiosity and bounded up the trail.

After Boone came . . .

Boone had been born after Tess came here. How long after? Who was the kid's father?

He was still wondering as he hung Boone upside down by his heels and listened to him howl in laughter while the *Shooting Star* slid to a halt on solid ground. A quick glance underneath showed no visible damage to her thrusters.

Ruben and Boone were both grinning widely when Tess unhooked the draft horses from the cargo bay links.

"I guess you can be on your way now," she said to Ruben with a disapproving look.

"Mema," Boone said, his laughter disappearing quickly Ruben flipped him over so he could stand on his own. "He doesn't have to go yet." He looked up at Ruben. "Do you have to go now?"

"First I've got to make sure she can fly," Ruben said. "Then I need to have a talk with your mema."

"We have nothing to discuss," Tess said. "Come on, Boone."

"Yes, we do," Ruben said. "Boone, go inside the ship. And don't touch anything."

Boone took off as if shot from a proton chamber. He ran inside the *Shooting Star* and hit the hatch on his way by so it slid shut, leaving Ky outside. The Newf seemed surprised but then lay down on the grass beside the ship. Ruben couldn't help grinning after Boone. The kid was smart, and quick besides.

"How dare you!"

He thought he had seen her angry before, but that was nothing compared to the way she was charging at him now.

"How dare you!" Tess screamed as she came at him with fists flying.

Ruben caught her arms and held them out as she landed a few good kicks. He hooked a leg behind hers, and Tess lost her balance. He pushed her up against the side of the *Shooting Star* and pinned her thin frame to it, his hands on her shoulders and his lower body pressed along her hips and thighs.

"Can't you see what you've done?" she cried in fury. "Can't you see how much you will hurt him?

"What are you talking about?" He shoved his body against hers so she couldn't move. Ky jumped to his feet to watch, and Ruben raised an eyebrow at him. The Newf let out a grunt and lay back down.

"Boone! I'm talking about Boone! He worships you, and you're leaving." Ruben relaxed a bit at her words. "You're just making it harder on him."

"You're the one who's in a hurry for me to go!" Ruben growled, but he loosened his hold on her.

"The longer you stay, the more attached he gets!" She looked up at him, tears filling her clear gray-green eyes.

"Come with me," he said. She was so close; he could count the freckles on her nose.

Her lower lip quivered as she looked up at him. Ruben felt a tearing in his gut, a wrench in his heart, and a gathering pressure down low as she tried to move away from him. His hips instinctively pressed against her and once more pinned her to the side of the ship as he quickly lowered his head and caught her quivering lower lip with his own.

He heard her sudden gasp as he kissed her and felt a trembling consume her as her hands pushed without result against his abdomen.

"Come with me," he moaned into her lips. He moved his hands from her shoulders to capture her face as she tried to turn away from him, and then suddenly she was still, as if patiently waiting for him to finish.

Ruben pulled back, his head reeling as he tried to figure out why he'd kissed her, but more importantly, why she had suddenly shut down.

"What are you so scared of, Tess?" he asked. He wiped a tear from her cheek with his knuckle.

"I'm scared for my son," she whispered as she looked down.

He willed her to look at him, but she wouldn't. Why wouldn't she? The same knuckle that had captured her tear tilted her chin up.

"Look at me, Tess."

Her eyes stayed down. He saw the moisture gathered on her long, dark lashes. "May I go now?"

The way she said it, as if he were her master, made more of an impact on him than her fists or her feet had. He stepped back without a word, and she slid away toward the horses, which were patiently waiting in their traces.

"Bring him back to the house before you leave," she said as she gathered up the leads. "Don't make him walk back by himself."

"Tess," Ruben said. "There are some things I need to know."

"I don't know anything," she said and left.

He was still trying to figure out what had just happened as he punched the remote to the hatch.

"Where's Mema?" Boone asked.

"She said you could hang around for a while. And get out of my chair."

Boone slid out of the pilot's seat with a ready grin, and Ruben playfully punched his arm as he settled in. If only his mother could be so agreeable.

"Are you planning to steal my ship?" he teased.

"Are you going to take me for a ride?" Boone asked in return. He was as direct as she was, that was for sure.

"I don't think your mema is going to allow that," Ruben said. "She's afraid I'll crash again."

"Why did you crash?"

"Someone didn't want me flying here."

"Who?"

"I don't know. Maybe it was the people you saw with my brother."

"Did Mema tell you about your brother?"

"We didn't get around to discussing it," Ruben said. "Has she said anything to you about it?"

"No. She said not to talk about it." Boone watched as Ruben punched buttons on the com. "She's always scared of Master Joah."

"Eli, Systems check." Ruben said "Are you scared of Master Joah too?"

"No," Boone said. "He won't hurt me." He moved up next to Ruben, his eyes glued in fascination to the com. "I'm his heir."

Ruben felt as if he had fallen into the icy waters of the stream.

Joah was Boone's father?

Icy, cold rage filled his senses. The com blurred before his eyes as a vision of his hands closing around Joah's neck filled his vision. He would kill him. With his bare hands. He would choke the life out of him. The old man didn't deserve to live. He was an animal. Without thought, Ruben's blade slipped into his hand and he felt the cold press of it as his fingers moved over the sharp edge. Maybe he would skin him first. Was Joah the one who had scarred her? Who else could it be?

The man would surely die before Ruben left this place.

Boone said something, and the words barely penetrated the red haze that surrounded Ruben.

"What?" he said finally, noticing the drop of blood on the end of his finger.

"I said how are you going to fix the engine?"

Ruben blinked as if waking from a long, hard sleep. "The engine?"

"It's broke. She said it was broke."

"She?"

Boone pointed to the com. "Her."

"Eli. Systems report," Ruben barked.

Did it sigh in exasperation? "Engine damage," Eli said. "Hydraulic leak in valve number three."

"Why didn't you report this before?"

"There was no damage before," Eli replied.

"What do you mean, no damage?" Ruben demanded. "You did a check after the crash."

"There was no damage when I did the systems check after the crash," Eli reported.

"Which means that someone has sabotaged the ship since the crash," Ruben said. He jumped up and went to the small corridor between the lav and the cabin. He popped the grid and dropped into the belly of the *Shooting Star*.

"Lights," he commanded, and Eli turned on the lights around the side of the hull.

"What is that?" Boone asked.

"This is where all the mechanics are housed," Ruben explained. "The engine, the pumps, the hydraulics . . ." He found a beacon lying on the floor and was surprised to find that it worked as he shone it up toward Boone, who was lying on the floor and looking down. "If what Eli says is true, that means someone was on my ship and did something to the engine."

"Like the lady in the funny hat?"

"No, not her. That's not the Circe's style," Ruben said. "But maybe someone who was with her."

He moved the beacon over the engine and a curse exploded from his lips.

"I know," Boone piped up. "Don't tell Mema you said that."

Ruben ignored him as he picked up the wrench that was lying on the deck below the engine housing. Someone had obviously used the tool to bash away part of the housing over his number-three valve. A puddle of fluid had collected on the floor and a piece of the valve was lying in it.

"Simple but effective," he said after he swore again, this time quietly enough for Boone not to hear him, he hoped.

"I heard that," Boone said.

"Well, so you know what to do, or what not to do," Ruben said as he took a closer look at the valve.

"Can you fix it?" Boone asked.

"I hope so," Ruben replied. "I'd better, or else your mema is really going to be mad at me." He handed the beacon up to Boone and showed him where to point it.

"Who do you think did it?"

"That, little guy, is the question of the eons," Ruben said.

Who had done it? The same person who had killed his father, framed him for his murder, taken his brother, and shot him down? Ruben found himself hoping so. If someone was out to get him, then he was in serious trouble.

"If it's a girl, why do you call her Eli?" Boone asked.

"What?" Ruben looked up in exasperation, totally at a loss as to what the kid was talking about. He was trying to fit the valve back into place, but the end was damaged and he couldn't get it to go in no matter which way he turned it.

"The lady in your ship," Boone said. "You call her Eli, but Eli is a man's name. I know it because there's a man at the meetinghouse named Eli. And his son is named Eli, too."

"I call it Eli because that's what I call it," Ruben said in exasperation.

"Oh," Boone said. A look of disappointment washed over his face.

"What's wrong?" Ruben asked.

"You don't want to talk to me anymore," Boone

said. "You sound like Master Joah when I ask him a question."

Ruben looked at the tragic face above him and then at the broken piece of machinery in his hand.

His frustration was mounting with each passing moment. It seemed as if the entire universe were conspiring against him, and on top of that he had some kid whining because he didn't like the tone of his voice.

You sounded just like your father . . .

That thought made him feel better. Why should he care what this kid felt? It wasn't as if *he* were the kid's father.

You're the only man who's ever shown any interest in him.

"I need to get out of here," he mumbled to the engine. "And you're not helping."

"Maybe I should go home," Boone said. "Mema will be worried about me."

"Wait," Ruben said as he watched Boone climb to his feet. The kid looked totally defeated. Ruben couldn't let him leave like this. He had to do something. Ruben handed the valve up to Boone. "Do you think Master Joah has any tools we could use to fix this?"

Boone spared a cautious look at Ruben before he closely examined the valve. "Maybe we could scrape the bent side off," he said. "He has this file thing that he uses sometimes."

"Let me see the value," Ruben said, and Boone handed it down. Ruben looked at the end of the valve, then at the slot where it needed to fit.

He grinned up at Boone. This kid was a genius. Maybe he should think about keeping him around.

"Let's try it out," he said as he levered himself out of the hold.

Boone waited for him with a big grin.

"And, Boone?" Ruben said as they walked down the trail. "I want you to take care of your mema for me after I'm gone."

"I will," Boone said.

Chapter Twenty

Tess tried to concentrate on her work but found it difficult with all the things that were troubling her. Boone had yet to arrive. Ben was leaving. Garvin had taken every opportunity to press her, and Joah made no effort to stop him. She had hurried through her evening chores to escape Garvin but dared not go to bed until she knew Boone was safely back.

She dared not go to bed until Ky was back.

Joah and Garvin were talking together. Never a good thing, as far as she was concerned. She heard bits and pieces of their conversation as she worked the treadle on her loom with bare feet and moved the shuttle back and forth.

"Offworlders."

Her foot moved, and a gentle whoosh sounded as the threads shifted into place.

"Credits."

She slid the shuttle holding the long pieces of fabric that she had torn and tied together to make the outer layer for her coat.

"Upstream."

Whoosh.

"Bounty."

Whoosh.

"Tomorrow."

Tess stopped. What could they possibly be talking about? She had assumed they were hatching a plan to transport the wine off-world on Ben's ship, but the conversation had taken a suspicious turn.

What was upstream?

A bounty for what?

What was going to happen tomorrow?

Tess froze, the shuttle poised in her hand, her ears straining, hoping to catch something that would tell her what the two men were planning.

All she heard was the heavy clink of glass as more wine was poured, and the sound of their raised voices as they disputed something. They were well into their third bottle by now. Surely they would go back to the winery soon.

Where was Boone? She had thought him safe with Ben, but what if whoever shot Ben down came looking for him again?

A feeling of panic started deep in her chest. She never should have left her son. What was she thinking?

In the other room, it was strangely silent now. Tess went to the door. The night air crackled with heat and humidity, and the sky held heavy, dark clouds. A slight breeze lifted the tail of the old nightgown she was wearing. The rushing of the stream filled the air with noise, but beyond, in the mountains, she was sure she heard thunder, and a quick flash of light assured her that her ears had not been mistaken.

When would the rain come down the mountain? She longed for it as if it would quench a never-ending thirst. If only the rain would come.

"What are ye looking at?"

Garvin. Her flesh crawled as he stepped up behind her, close, pressing her.

"I'm waiting for Boone," she said and stepped out onto the porch to put some distance between them. She wrapped her arms around her body protectively and wished that she had not changed out of her clothes.

Garvin followed. "Ye worry over the boy too much. Ye will smother him and make him weak."

"That is none of your concern," Tess said, stepping away once again.

"It will be soon enough," Garvin said. "Do ye think yer master is going to live forever?"

Tess turned to look at him. She could feel his dark eyes appraising her, but they were lost in the darkness, making it impossible to gauge his intent. A chill chased down her spine, whether caused by his words or the quickening wind, she did not know.

"What are you planning?" she dared to ask.

"My future—and yours," he said. "Joah has no son to leave his holdings to."

"He has Boone," Tess said. "He has a grandson."

"The son of a slave?" Garvin spat out the word in disgust. "Can ye even prove that the boy's of Joah's blood?"

With a shriek, Tess went after him. She dug her

nails into his face and drew blood. Garvin was surprised by her attack, but reacted quickly with a backhanded blow that knocked her into the yard.

Dazed but alert enough to know that he would not stop there, Tess scrambled to her knees and rose to unsteady feet, just to have the breath knocked from her body as Garvin grabbed her from behind and threw her over onto her back.

He straddled her, and she fought against him, swinging her fists. He caught her hands easily and pinned them over her head.

"Get off!" she screamed.

"No one can hear ye," Garvin said. "Joah is no longer with us, and there's no one else to come."

"You killed him?"

"He didn't feel it. Everyone will assume he just drank too much tonight. It was time for him to go on. Past time."

"Ben!" Tess screamed. *"Ben!"* But she knew there was no way he could hear her on the knoll.

"He's not coming," Garvin said. "I made sure he'll be busy working on his ship all night."

Tess stopped her struggles as his words registered. She looked up at Garvin with a feeling of dread. The look on his face froze her blood.

"What did you do?" she said.

"That's none of your business," Garvin said. "The important thing is that the offworlder will be occupied all night, while I'll be getting to know my new possession."

"No!" Tess screamed as Garvin ripped open the front of her gown. She felt his hands on her breasts and she bucked against him. *"Boone!"* Garvin tore at

her gown further, and the worn fabric ripped as he pulled it away from her.

Boone . . .

In the next instant, Garvin's heavy body was miraculously gone. Tess crawled away as she heard Ky's growls followed by shouting.

"Mema!"

"Boone!"

She grabbed her son and tried to pull her gown together as the two of them turned to watch Garvin and Ben fight in the darkness. Ky was in it too, but as he attempted to get at Garvin he was also attacking Ben.

"Ky!" Tess called out. "Get off!"

The next instant she was blinded by a blast. The three who were fighting went still.

"Ben?" Tess called.

The pile of bodies moved.

"Ky?" Boone said.

Garvin shoved the bodies away and clambered to his feet with a weapon in his hand.

Tess stared at him in shock. She had one hand holding her gown closed and the other on Boone's shoulder. "What . . . where . . ."

"Not everyone on this planet is opposed to technology," Garvin said. "I found this on the offworlder's ship and thought I might have a need for it."

"Are they dead?" Boone asked.

Garvin looked down at the two bodies of man and dog sprawled on the ground, then up at the lights flashing around the mountain. The sight of them seemed to change his mind about something. "I hope not," he said. "It won't fit in the plan. The witch wants him alive for some reason. It don't matter about the beast." Garvin walked toward them. I think it's best if I wait to enjoy you. I take the boy with me instead."

"*No!*" Tess pulled Boone to her.

"They're coming for *him*," Garvin said, nodding at Ben. "And I need to make sure he's where he's supposed to be." He sounded as if he were explaining a problem to a confused child. He kept the weapon aimed at Tess as he jerked Boone away from her. "You make sure he's at his ship at sunrise tomorrow and just maybe you'll see your son again."

"Don't take him," Tess cried. "Please." Boone's eyes were wide with fear, but he did not cry out.

"You come to me willingly," Garvin said. "And just maybe I'll let him stick around long enough to work for my sons." He pulled Boone after him. "Our sons."

He swung his arm and hit Tess on the side of her head with the hand that held the weapon. Stars exploded as she fell to the ground, but she fought against them. She felt her cheek against the hard ground and tried to get to her feet. Through the haze that filled her eyes, she saw Garvin carry off her son.

And as she slid into the darkness, she felt the rain on her face.

Chapter Twenty-one

Waking up and not knowing where he was or what had happened to him was becoming a bad habit. And having raindrops pelt his face wasn't helping matters. Perhaps the fact that Ky lay across him had something to do with why he couldn't move his legs.

"Geroff," Ruben growled and shoved. Ky let out a low growl but did not move. Ruben struggled to a sitting position and managed to get his legs out from under the Newf.

Lucky for both of them that the blaster had been set on stun. Had Garvin shot them intentionally, or was he just too stupid to know better? What else had the bastard done on the *Shooting Star*? So far, Ruben could add thievery and sabotage to his list. Was there more?

"Tess?"

Garvin had been all over her. And Boone had seen it. They had hurried down the trail with the threat of

rain on their heels and the hope that they could repair the ship's valve.

They'd found Tess fighting off Gavin as she lay on
the ground with her clothes half ripped off.

Ky had gone on the attack as soon as they jumped
the stream.

And Ruben had been right behind, the urge to kill
overpowering him for the second time that day.

He would have, too. His hands had been around
Garvin's neck when the man pulled a blaster from
what seemed to be thin air and hit both his attackers
with a stun.

Garvin must have made himself at home on the
Shooting Star to find the blaster.

"Tess?" Ruben called out again. He blinked
against the blinding rain as Ky lumbered to his feet.

Ruben managed to fight his way to a standing position and turned to find Tess lying some distance
away on the ground.

He tried to run, but all he could do was stagger.
He fell to his knees next to her.

"Tess?"

She lay on her side. Blood mixed with rain poured
from a wound under her hair. Her clothes hung in
tatters, leaving her breasts and stomach exposed.

Ruben checked her pulse. She was alive.

Where was Boone?

"Boone?" Ruben called out. He squinted into the
heavy darkness but could see no sign of Garvin or
the boy.

"Ky!" Ruben bellowed. "Find Boone!"

The Newf already had his head down and was
sniffing the ground. Ruben gathered Tess into his
arms and carried her to the house. He placed her on

the bed that he had used, pulled a blanket over her, and ran back out into the night.

"Beacon," he said. It was raining harder now, pelting his skin. "I had a beacon." Where was it? He had dropped it as soon as he'd seen Garvin on Tess. He ran back toward the stream and found the beacon accidentally when he kicked it.

Broken.

He had to have light. He had to find Boone.

Thunder rumbled overhead, followed by a flash of lightning.

The yard was barren, empty except for Ky, who was making ever-widening circles in the darkness.

Ruben ran back into the house. There had to be a beacon somewhere. He ran into the kitchen and found Joah slumped over the table.

"Wake up!" Ruben shouted.

Joah didn't stir.

Ruben grabbed his shoulders and shook. Joah's head lolled back. His lips were blue. Ruben looked closely and quickly realized that the man was dead.

Dead.

Why?

How?

He needed to find Boone.

He found a beacon in the storage room and ran back out into the rain.

Ruben searched the grounds. He searched the winery. He searched the shed while the heifer bellowed in protest and the chickens cackled their disdain. He searched the vineyards, and called Boone's name until his voice no longer worked. Ky searched, too, on his own, and then followed Ruben as he ran through the pasture and around the giant draft horses, which had taken shelter under a sprawling tree.

There was no sign of Boone, and even as he searched again, Ruben knew what had happened.

Garvin had taken him.

But where? And why?

Exhausted and soaked through, he went back to the house. Ky refused to follow. He kept his nose to the ground and moved into the darkness.

Joah was still sprawled over the table, and Ruben took a moment to place the old man's body on his bed. He felt no sympathy for him whatsoever. Joah deserved to die. Ruben would have killed the old man himself.

He had bigger things to worry about now.

Tess.

She had not moved. Ruben went back to the kitchen and filled a bowl with water from the pump.

He realized he was shivering and pulled off his shirt. He grabbed a towel from the storage room and went back to Tess.

He wiped the blood from her face and hair. She stirred a bit, her lips moving, and he realized that her teeth were chattering.

Ruben flipped back the blanket and made short work of removing what was left of her gown.

"Bastard," he spat out.

Feel free to curse. Boone's not here.

He wrapped her up in another blanket and sat down on the bed with Tess in his arms. He leaned against the wall and held her close against him, giving her warmth even though he was freezing himself.

Ruben closed his eyes and listened to the rain pounding on the roof.

"Boone," he said. "Please, if You're there, protect Boone." It was the first time he had ever prayed. Shaun had always said he believed there was a higher being watching over them. For once in his life, Ruben hoped there was. He didn't know what else to do.

He realized that Tess was awake. Her hand clutched the edge of the blanket so tightly that her knuckles were white.

"He took him," she said. "Garvin."

"I know." His arms tightened around her, pulling her close.

"You have to be at your ship at dawn. He said they want you alive."

They . . . the Circe.

"Will he give Boone back?"

"I have to be willing. I have to go to him willingly."

Become Garvin's slave . . .

"Joah is dead," he told her.

Murdered?

"I know. I'm glad," she said without a hint of emotion.

"I should have killed Garvin when I first saw him."

He imagined the scene. His blade burying itself in Garvin's heart instead of the tree. He could have done it. It would have been easy. He should have.

"You're not a killer."

"I could be. I will be because I will kill him."

If it's the last thing I do before they take me.

"Why? Why do they want you? Who is it? Why is this happening?"

I don't want to betray my friends.

"Tess. You have to tell me something first."

"I saw your brother," she said as if reading his

mind. "I should have told you right off, but I was scared. I was afraid for Boone. I was afraid of Joah, and I was afraid of Garvin. I was mostly afraid of the woman with the evil eyes. I still see her in my dreams." Her voice broke. "I'm tired of being afraid. If it weren't for Boone—"

"Don't say that, Tess. Don't even think it. We'll figure a way out of this."

"Who are they?" She pushed herself out of his arms and settled on the mattress to look at him. "What do they want?"

"They want my friends."

"What?"

He told her. He told her about Shaun and Lilly. He told her about the Circe. He told her about Stefan and he told her about the trouble he was in. He told her all of it except where Shaun and Lilly were. That was one thing he had sworn never to tell anyone.

"The Circe can read minds?"

"Yes. They can control people also. The collar you saw—they use it to control a person's body. It takes away the will."

"I never told you I saw a collar. I did, but . . . how did you know? Did Boone tell you?" She sat facing him on the bed with the blanket held tightly under her chin.

"I knew before he told me. I saw it in a dream."

"You saw in a dream what I saw? When? How?"

"The first time was twelve solar days ago. I was in cryo and on my way to see my friends. I dreamed about Stefan being in trouble. I thought I had the dream because of the bounty on my head, but then Lilly saw the same vision in my mind."

"It was twelve days ago that I saw it happen," Tess

218

said. "Do you think you could have seen everything I saw? At the same time? Is that possible?"

"Twelve solars ago I would have said no. But now, I just don't know."

"When you talked to me that day by the stream—the day we found you—you asked if I knew your brother. You knew that I had seen him."

"Lilly thinks there was some kind of link that made me see what Stefan was seeing. She thinks there was some sort of conduit between me and Stefan."

"Do you think they took your brother just to get to you?"

"Yes, but it was a gamble on their part. I hadn't seen Stefan in fifteen years. I don't even know if he'll remember me."

"And yet you came when you found out he was in danger." Her gray-green eyes stared intently at him. "You're here," she whispered.

I'm here . . .

"So I guess it worked," he said in disgust. "I should have stayed away."

"But you didn't. You came for your brother."

"Yes, but I can't sacrifice Zander and Elle for Stefan. I can't do that."

"What about Boone?" Her voice cracked on her son's name, but she quickly pulled herself together. "What are you going to do? What are we going to do?'

What am I going to do?

Ruben stood, tired of sitting, tired of talking, tired of feeling inadequate, foolish, used, abused. What was he going to do? He paced the room, and Tess watched him move, her eyes following him as he prowled around.

"I don't think Garvin will hurt him. He needs him as bait."

Are you saying that for yourself or Tess?

He had to get Boone back. He had to keep Garvin from taking Tess. He had to save Stefan, and he had to protect Zander and Elle.

What am I going to do?

He couldn't do it all.

Save the children. You have to save the children. Sacrifice Tess?

No!

Sacrifice Stef?

He might already be dead.

But what if he isn't?

Stef for Boone? Stef for Zander and Elle?

No!

How long can you hold out against the Circe?

Sacrifice yourself . . .

The bang of a door made them both jump.

"Boone!" Tess said, jumping from the bed.

"Wait," Ruben cautioned. His blade slid into his hand and he turned expectantly toward the main room.

It was Ky. He was drenched. He walked into the middle of the main room and shook the water off his body, spraying everything around him. Tess moved beside Ruben as he sheathed his blade, and they both watched the Newf go into Boone's room and return with the quilt from his bed.

Ky dropped the quilt in the middle of the floor and with his customary three turns lay down on it facing the door.

"He can't find his scent in the rain," Tess said.

"How did you get him?" Ruben asked. "Where did he come from?"

"He just showed up one day. He had been beaten pretty badly and somehow he managed to drag himself up into our yard. I guess he came down the same trail that you did."

"How long ago?"

"Going on four years. It was right before Boone turned three. Ky's stayed by his side since the day he showed up."

"My father had Newfs. Amanor is the only planet I've ever seen them on. And I've been to a lot of planets."

"Maybe he came with your brother."

"Or my half-brother, Dyson."

"Dyson?"

"He was here, too. I saw him in my dream. Maybe it wasn't his first time here."

"The man with the missing finger? Yes, I saw him," she confirmed.

"But what is he doing here? What does Lavign have to offer someone like Dyson?'

"I don't know."

Ruben scrubbed his hands through his damp hair, which made the spiky locks stand up on end. "How long until dawn?"

"A while, I think," Tess said.

Ruben looked in bemusement at the damp tendrils of dark hair that hung about her shoulders. He couldn't help himself. He picked up a lock that curled at the end and rubbed it between his fingers.

"Maybe we should try to get some sleep," he said as he looked into her eyes.

"I know what you're planning to do," Tess said, suddenly understanding the sadness in his gaze.

"You're going to kill yourself. After you get Boone back and kill Garvin, you're going to kill yourself so they won't get your friends." Her eyes, bright and clear beneath the dark lashes looked right into his soul.

How was it that she knew him so well? How did she know what he was thinking at almost the same time he did?

"Tess," he said. "When it happens, you have to get Boone and run. I know Ky will protect you. But you have to get as far away from here as you can. I'm going to kill as many of them as I can, but this blade is the only weapon I have, and I don't know how long I can last against blasters."

"Why are you doing this? Why don't you just leave now?"

He grinned at her. "Well, for one thing, my ship is busted." He pulled the valve from one of his many pockets. "But even if it wasn't, I couldn't just leave Boone." His grin left as quickly as it had come, and he caressed the length of her hair with the back of his hand. "I couldn't leave you."

She smiled at him. Her smile was sweet and charming and took his breath away.

"Tess," he said quietly, simply.

The blanket that she had held so tightly suddenly slid to the floor.

"You don't have to," he said as his eyes drank in the sight of her.

"I want to," she murmured. "I want you." She stepped into his arms and they circled around her, carefully, cautiously, giving her room to escape if she chose.

"I won't hurt you."

"I know." Her face, usually so full of hopelessness, now held nothing but trust. She must be scared for herself, terrified for her son, possibly even worried about him. But all he saw was trust.

He'd never seen it before. At least not on a woman's face. And he suddenly realized that this was what Shaun and Lilly had. This was what he'd been missing his entire life without knowing it. This was what he wanted more than anything, and what all his trading and dealing and credits stashed away could not bring him. This was what he needed.

Tess.

Her face turned toward his, her lips parted. His mouth joined hers, and the sudden desperate thought that he needed to survive the morning came over him. One time would not be enough. One night with Tess would not satisfy his need. He had thought himself ready to die gallantly for his friends because he had nothing to lose but his life. And not much to show for it.

But now he had everything he'd ever wanted wrapped up in his arms. And a little boy depending on him also.

"Tess," he sighed as she answered him with her kiss, and her hands swept over the skin of his back, brushed lightly against his scar, and then settled on his hips, right above the waist of his pants.

Ruben's hands roamed her back and then lower, squeezing and kneading the skin. She moved against him, and all thoughts but one left his mind.

He lifted her by her hips, and her long legs wrapped around him and settled against the place that had taken over for his brain.

"Tess," he gasped.

"Hurry," she said and fumbled with the clasp of his pants. Her hands seemed to be driving both of them into a frenzy, and she tossed her head back as his lips moved down her neck. "Please."

Somehow he stumbled toward the bed. Somehow he found it and fell forward, catching both of them just before he landed on top of her.

"Please," she cried out. She moved her legs up and slid his pants down as he braced his arms over her. Her gray-green eyes looked up into his, and he felt himself being pulled inside their depths as he moved into her and she cried out again.

His eyes were deep blue pools of cool, clear water and she was drowning.

How could this be? How could she suddenly know that this was what she wanted? She had been taught how to perform this act and found it loathsome. But suddenly she knew that this was where the rapture part of it came in. Her mind, once stubbornly closed against her tutors and owner, was suddenly and beautifully opened.

And it was all because of Ben. Only Ben. There would be no other. Only this man. This time. This night.

And she saw in his mind that he felt it, too. She saw the other lovers he'd had in the past fall away from his thoughts until only she remained. She saw his past, all of it, and she knew that his wandering soul had found a home at last, with her. She did not understand how she knew it, but she did. She saw realization dawn in his bright blue eyes, and realized that he knew what she was thinking at the same time she was thinking it.

Then as the physical need overcame the mental, she stopped thinking at all. And when the stars burst in her head, she saw that they were as blue as his eyes. Even though she had been carried away she was able to place her fingertips to the star-shaped scar on his forehead and was not surprised to see that the stars in his mind looked the same.

Chapter Twenty-two

"Where do you come from?" They were twisted together, legs and arms tangled, skin against skin. Somehow he had taken off the rest of his clothes. He couldn't remember when or how. Tess's head lay on his chest, her ear pressed against the place where his heart thumped a steady rhythm.

"I don't remember," she said. "I don't remember anything before being sold to the slave trader. My first memory is of leaving what I think was an orphanage. I don't even know what planet I was on."

"Strange," Ruben said.

"Why?"

"It's almost as if you were reading my mind."

"I know."

"How could that be?" His fingers traced a lazy pattern over her shoulder. "Has it ever happened before?"

"No. I thought it was because . . . we were making love."

"It was," he said. "Tess, please believe me when I tell you I've never felt connected to anyone in this way before. I've never experienced anything like this before."

"Me either. Of course, you probably have a lot more history to draw on than I do."

"You did see everything," he laughed. What did it matter if she knew everything about him? He wanted her to know. He wanted to tell her. But since there was no time for that . . .

Tess felt the movement deep in his chest as laughter flowed out. How could he laugh when he would be dead in just a few hours?

The same way that she could joke about his past. It was easier to pretend that none of this was happening. Pretend that Boone was safely asleep in his bed and there was no fear or death coming with the dawn. Pretend that the love they'd just discovered was going to last forever and they had all the time in the world to talk about their futures and their pasts.

But that wasn't true.

As if reading her sudden panic, he spoke again. "Will Boone be sorry that his father is dead?"

"Boone doesn't remember his father."

"I thought Joah—"

"It was Joah's son." She pushed herself up. "It was in this bed. Joah bought me from a slave trader saying he wanted me to be housekeeper, but when I got here I knew he had bought me for his son. No other woman would have had him. He was too evil, too mean. He would just grab me and drag me in here night after night."

Ruben picked up her hand, linking his fingers through hers.

"He hurt you." The fingertips of his free hand grazed one of the puckered scars on her breasts.

"He did," she said dismissively. What he had done to her was part of the past and best forgotten. "But he stopped when it was obvious that I was with child. He couldn't bear to look at me. It was almost as if I were parading his sin in his face. He never said a word when Boone was born, never acknowledged him. He died when some casks fell on him in the winery. Boone was nearly two. And that was when Joah started drinking."

"Boone is the image of you."

Tess smiled, feeling as if a great weight had been lifted from her shoulders. "Joah and I never talked about Boone. We never talked about his son. We never talked about anything. Boone just became a part of our lives. I still did my chores and I cared for my son. Joah never gave him anything. He never acknowledged him. He never even held him."

"This place will be Boone's," Ruben said. "You can survive here."

She looked at him, and he was amazed to see that her eyes were more gray now than green. Was it because of the dim light in the room?

"You're just saying that to justify your going off and dying," Tess said. "You think that if you kill Garvin, we'll be able to take care of ourselves."

"What am I supposed to do? I can't let the Circe know about Shaun's children. You don't know what they're capable of. You don't know what they'll do to that innocent little boy and girl."

"Would it make a difference if I told you that we need you? Boone and I?"

Ruben got up. He snatched his pants from the floor and quickly pulled them on. He sat down on the edge of the bed and put on his boots. He strapped his blade into place and then looked around the room distractedly and realized that he had left his shirt in the storage room.

"My friends will show up eventually. There's a beacon on the *Shooting Star* and Shaun will trace it. He knew where I was heading." He felt the creak of the bedsprings as Tess moved.

"I'll leave a message with Eli," he began.

"Eli?"

"My ship." He couldn't stand to look at her. He felt as if he were betraying her. But what else could he do? "I'll ask my friends to take you and Boone to Oasis. They'll take care of you. They'll keep you safe. I have enough credits that you'll never have to worry about anything. You'll never have to work again."

"Ben—"

He grinned. A heart-stopping, heartbreaking grin. "Everyone calls me Ruben," he said and despite the ache he felt, he turned to look at her. "I made it up from my given name, Rubikhan Benjamin. A personal insult to my father, making a mockery of my name. My mother was the only one who ever called me Ben. And Stef."

"Ruben?" She tried the name.

He dropped a kiss on the top of her head. "I like Ben. Especially when you say it."

"Where are you going?" she asked as he turned to leave.

He pulled the valve from his pocket. "I'm going to fix my ship. Boone had an idea, and I'm going to see if it will work."

"And if it does?"

"Then I guess we'll just have to see what happens. Maybe I'll get lucky again."

"I'm going with you."

"I wouldn't have it any other way," he said. Was he being selfish, wanting to spend his last few hours alive with her? Or should he keep her here where she might at least be safe?

He took her arm as she went by with a sheet wrapped about her. "You have to promise that you'll do exactly what I say, Tess. I'm going to do everything I can to make sure you and Boone are safe before—"

"I know," she said.

Ky followed them as they went into the winery for tools. The rain had lightened to a fine mist accompanied by a heavy bank of clouds. A thick fog settled over the ground, making it almost impossible to see from one building to the next. The beacon cut a thin path through the mist as they made their way along.

"Going to be a bleak morning," Ruben said. Ky was more of a shadow than a body as he trotted in front of them.

"We have a bit of time."

He grabbed what he thought he might need, and they made the trek back to the *Shooting Star*.

"Where do you think Gravin took Boone?" Tess asked when they had arrived at the ship.

"To wherever the credits are." He dropped into the hold and showed Tess where to shine the beacon.

"I think Garvin is a big coward. He should have just taken me and left you and Boone out of it."

"He's always wanted me," Tess said as she watched him work. "I guess this was the only way he could think of to get me."

"Like I said. A coward." He grinned up at her. "But your son is a genius."

"Really?"

"He's a natural." Ruben lifted himself through the hold and went into his cabin to grab a shirt before he entered the cockpit. "Eli. Systems check." He sat down in his chair as he pulled the blue thermal over his head. The only light was the soft glow from the com.

"Running," Eli said.

They waited. Even in the dim light, Tess saw that his eyes seemed bluer now that he wore the shirt. Or was it her perspective that had changed? Was everything more beautiful now? Even the fog had a mystical, ethereal beauty as it shifted silently on the other side of the plexi.

"All systems fine. Should I power up?" Eli asked.

Tess lifted an eyebrow at the com. Her eyes seemed greener now.

"Yes." Ruben smiled at her.

"Destination?" Eli asked.

"Geopoll," he said. "Scan east of our location."

"Scanning."

The image came up, complete with what both Ruben and Tess recognized as the buildings of the farm.

"There," Ruben said and punched in the coordinates where the pasture was located.

"What are you doing?" Tess asked.

"Eli, this is Tess," Ruben said. He grabbed her hand and pulled her beside him. "Say something to it."

"Greetings, Eli," Tess said with a confused look on her face.

"Greetings, Tess."

"Record and identify," Ruben said.

"Greetings, Eli," Tess's voice sounded from the com.

"Tess will be giving you orders also," Ruben explained.

Eli did not respond.

"Eli, confirm voice command," Ruben said.

"Confirmed," Eli said in a somewhat huffy tone.

Tess laughed. "I think she's jealous."

"She'll get over it," Ruben said. "Eli, you will also recognize Boone. Tess will identify."

"Confirmed," Eli said.

"Yeah, she's jealous. She's using her official vocabulary."

"She has another one?"

"Don't ask," he said.

"Eli, when Tess gives the command, you will take the ship to these coordinates."

"Comfirmed."

"Do you mind sharing your plan with me?" Tess said.

Ruben pulled Tess into his lap and placed his remote in her hand. "When we get Boone back, I want you to grab him and run into the ship. This remote opens the hatch. All you've got to do is tell Eli to get you out of here, and the ship will fly you to the pasture. As soon as you get there, you need to hide. I don't think they'll come after you if they have me, but you'd best get as far away from the ship and the farm as you can."

"And then what?'

"Wait for Shaun. You'll know him when you see him. You'll know by his eyes."

"Why can't the ship just fly us to another place?" Tess asked. She had watched him closely, hung on every word he said. "All of us."

Ruben ignored the last part. "You can't autopilot going in or out of the planet's atmosphere. Once you're up, Eli can fly around the planet, but she can't take you off the planet. It takes a pilot to do that."

"You're a pilot."

"I think Boone will be able to figure out a lot of it," Ruben went on. He looked through the plexi and saw nothing but a vast gray cloud.

"You expect my six-year-old son to fly your ship?"

"Like I said, he's a genius." He grinned as if he were the one responsible for Boone being so smart.

"Ben—" Tess began.

"It's all I got, Tess." His face was serious again, his blue eyes piercing. "I don't have any weapons on board; I used them up when I was attacked. I don't know what kind of firepower Dyson has."

"So you think Dyson is behind all of it?"

"From what you saw and what's happened since, I think so. I just don't know why."

"So that's it. I grab Boone and fly away while you stay here?"

"I've got this," he said and showed her his blade. "It's enough to take care of Garvin. And maybe, if I'm lucky, I can get Dyson, too. I've got ten chances if I get lucky enough."

"You depend a lot on luck. Has it always been that way?"

"The way I look at it, luck brought me here to you.

233

On an entire planet I crash-landed right on top of you. Is that luck or what?"

"It could be fate."

"Whatever it is, I'm glad it happened, Tess. I'm glad I got to know you and Boone. I wouldn't have missed it for anything."

"Even your life?"

He touched her cheek. "You're worth dying for," he said in a husky voice.

Tess bit her lip to keep it from trembling. She felt the tears gather behind her eyes and willed them away.

He grinned at her.

"Ftttt," she said, shaking her head before he kissed her.

She laid her head against his shoulder as his arms tightened around her. "So what do we do now?"

"We wait."

And with his arms wrapped tightly around her, they watched through the fog for the coming of dawn.

Chapter Twenty-three

She slept for a while. He was glad of it. It gave him time just to look at her. The curve of her cheek, the soft parting of her lips, the slight upward turn of her nose, the delicate sweep of her brow, and the wild disarray of her hair.

There wasn't enough time. At one time he'd thought he had all the time in the universe. He had no obligations, no one waiting for him, no responsibilities, nothing calling to him except his friendship with Shaun. He had wandered about; fleeing one place, hanging around another if there was fun to be had or a credit to pick up. If anyone grew attached, he would be on his way.

He didn't want any attachments. They always led to disappointment. And why suffer disappointment if you didn't have to?

But now time was running out.

Even with the heavy swirl of the fog, he could sense the brightening of the dawn.

"Tess." Ruben's lips brushed her temple. "It's time."

"Boone." She was instantly awake, instantly aware.

"Where's the remote?"

She showed him. It was still in her hand. She looked at him with wide eyes that showed deeper green instead of the lighter gray of the night before.

"You grab Boone and get in the ship," he said. "Don't wait for me. Don't even look for me. Just go. Do you understand?"

She nodded, words failing her.

Not enough time.

He kissed her then. Hard, demanding, pouring everything he wanted to say, needed to say, into it the kiss. They were both breathless when they finally broke apart.

There were no words.

"Let's go," he said.

He led her from the ship, their hands linked as he opened the hatch. Ky stood right outside, his head turned toward the trail down the opposite side of the knoll.

"Can you see anything?" Tess asked as Ruben stepped out into the fog, his blade in his hand.

"Stay behind me," he said. "Be ready to move."

A low growl rumbled in Ky's throat. Ruben placed a steadying hand on the Newf's massive head as they walked out of the shadow of the *Shooting Star*.

The fog blanketed the knoll, giving the area a surreal, dreamlike quality. Each footstep parted the mist, causing it to swirl around them. The silence was oppressive, almost suffocating.

He felt Tess behind him, heard her silent intake of breath as Ky growled once more.

"Stay," Ruben said as Ky continued to growl.

A twig snapped. It was hard to tell where, but Ky kept looking toward the trail on the back side of the knoll.

Shapes were becoming discernible as the invisible sky lightened. The heavy, dark shadows of trees and undergrowth came into view as the fog seemed to lift a bit. Or maybe it was just the coming of dawn that made it seem so.

"Mema!" Boone's voice seemed eerie, disjointed, as if it were coming from another place and time.

"Boone!" Tess jumped to run to her son, but Ruben stopped her with an outstretched arm.

"Remember what I said," he whispered, and she nodded, catching her lip with her teeth to keep from calling out again.

"Hello, Brother," someone called out.

Dyson.

"Only half-brother, Dyson," he called back. "The worse half."

"You don't know how much it breaks my heart to hear you say that, Ben."

It was now easier to see, but the fog still distorted sounds. He relied on Ky to keep him turned in the right direction.

"Ben," Dyson continued. "Rumor has it that you don't use that name anymore. That you've changed your name. Our dearly departed father would be heartbroken if he knew."

Was his half-brother moving around? Was he trying to throw him off?"

"One thing hasn't changed, Dyson," Ruben called back, his eyes constantly scanning, looking for Garvin. Looking for Boone. "You're still a useless git."

Tess was as still as death behind him. Without looking, he knew that she was also searching for Boone.

"If I didn't know any better, Brother"—the word *brother* was more of a snarl—"I'd think you were jealous."

"That's always been your excuse, Dyson. You don't know any better."

Keep him talking. Look for Boone.

"Imagine my surprise when I saw that you were the one who had crashed here," Dyson said. Apparently, he couldn't come up with a snappy comeback for Ruben's insult.

"Imagine my surprise when I got shot down," Ruben said. "I guess I have you to thank for that."

"It was like a special gift," Dyson said. "You . . . here . . . things couldn't have worked out better if I'd planned it."

Ky turned his head to the right.

"Why are you here Dyson?"

Tess touched Ruben's arm, and he nodded. He knew what was happening. He separated a piece off his blade with his fingertips.

"You'll find out soon enough," Dyson said. "After you tell my friend all she wants to know, I'll answer your questions."

An eerie noise sounded above them. Almost like a starship. Could it be? It was impossible to tell with the heavy fog. It might not even be above them because of the distortion of noise and distance.

Did Dyson have that much firepower on-planet? A ship had shot Ruben down. There could very easily be another one.

"I've heard you've been hanging around with some trash," Ruben said as the form of Dyson suddenly stepped into view. He was bigger now, soft around the edges, but the hateful look on his face was the same.

"Are they the reason our father was killed?" Ruben asked.

Something was moving behind them, coming up the trail.

"Oh, you would be the one to know that," Dyson said. "After all, you're the one who killed him. You and your brother."

"Yeah, I've been meaning to talk to you about Stefan—"

In the next moment several things happened at once, the strangest of which was the heifer charging up the trail through the fog, bellowing at all of them as if they had set her tail on fire.

As they all stared at her in open-mouthed shock Ruben caught sight of Garvin, stumbling from his hiding place to get out of the heifer's way. He was holding Boone in front of him with his hand over the boy's mouth, but his chest was an easy target Ruben flung his blade, hitting the big man directly in the heart.

Garvin looked up in surprise and then down at the narrow sliver that protruded from his chest.

"Boone!" Tess screamed and took off at a run toward her son at the exact same time that Ky jumped forward in an explosion of fur and gnashing teeth.

Garvin crumpled, and Boone jumped away.

Ky charged Dyson at the same time that Dyson threw an object toward Ruben.

Stun grenade!

"*Tess!*" Ruben shouted. The grenade landed between them. "Take cover!"

There was no way he could get to her in time. As he dove toward the edge of the knoll, hoping that his roll would take him far enough away from the blast so he would not be knocked unconscious, the most amazing thing of all happened. A ship broke though the fog, fanning the clouds away with its exhaust. Just as Ruben landed and twisted himself into a protective position, just before the grenade went off, he could have sworn he saw the insignia of Oasis.

Chapter Twenty-four

"I think he's coming around now." He heard a woman speaking. He felt the light brush of her hand in his hair. Tess?

"About time," a male voice growled. A very familiar male voice. "Why does he have a blue star on his head?"

"I don't know," the feminine voice said. "It probably happened when he crashed."

"But it's blue!"

"It's not like he's all blue. I think it has something to do with the way the wound healed."

Ruben blinked, opened his eyes, and saw two very familiar and concerned faces looking down at him.

"Shaun?" He must be dreaming or hallucinating or something. "Lilly?" Or maybe it was the Circe, trying to trick him. "What are you doing here?"

"Saving your ass," Shaun said as he moved his eye shields back into place. He wore two blasters on each hip and held a proton rifle in the crook of his arm. A huge blade was stuck in his belt. "Who's trying to kill you?" he barked. "Why do you have a blue star on your head?" That was definitely Shaun.

Ruben sat up and shook his head to clear it, then rubbed his hand across the blue star.

"Where's Tess?" He looked around. He was on the ground at the edge of the knoll. The grass had been flattened by a blast pattern. "Boone?" Ruben jumped to his feet and wobbled before Shaun grabbed his arm to keep him upright.

"There's no one here but a very dead guy and a giant black beast," Shaun said.

"Ky," Ruben said through the haze that was his brain. "Is he alive?"

"He's alive," Lilly said. "He's over there." She was also armed. She had a blaster at her hip and a pair of blades stuck in her belt.

"I found this in the body." Shaun said as he handed Ruben the sliver from his blade.

Ruben checked the blade for blood and found that Shaun had cleaned it for him. He attached it to the rest and slid it back on his wrist. He was somewhat amazed that he still had it after the blast.

"So why are you here again?" Ruben asked as it finally sank into his frazzled brain that he was, indeed, talking to his friends.

"Zander," Lilly said. "He had another one of his spells."

"What?"

"His voice got kind of weird again, and he told us that you had crashed and that we had to come help you," Shaun said. "And Elle just sat there and agreed with everything he said and told us to hurry. So here we are. Guess it's a good thing I still have your beacon."

"What?" Ruben looked at them closely. "When did this happen?"

"Five solar days ago. Right after dinner."

"But that's when I crashed."

"We figured that out when we saw the ship." Shaun jerked his head toward the *Shooting Star*. "What happened to the cargo bay?"

"I dropped it."

"On something, I hope?"

"Yes." He pointed down the opposite side of the knoll. "You'll find what's left of what I dropped it on down that way."

Shaun gave an obligatory look toward the back of the knoll and then pulled the remote from one of his many pockets. "I found this, too." He handed it to Ruben, who looked at it as if he'd never seen it before.

"Zander saw my crash?" Ruben asked. "Like before? In his head?"

"We don't know for sure," Shaun said. "But we were worried about you, so we decided to come and see if you needed any help."

"You left the children?"

"Michael is with them," Shaun said.

"Who are Tess and Boone?" Lilly asked.

"He took them," Ruben said as he looked at the remote. It was all coming back to him.

"Who took them?" Shaun growled.

"Dyson," Ruben said.

"Your half-brother?" Shaun asked. "The one you don't like?"

Ruben nodded, then looked at Lilly. "Tess knows about the children."

"*Our* children?" Lilly asked quickly, her face filled with panic. "Who is Tess? Are they safe?"

"Oasis is five days from here, Lilly," Shaun said. "No one can get to them there."

"The Circe are here," Ruben said flatly.

A combined look of fear and dread crossed their faces as Shaun and Lilly exchanged a desperate look.

"Maybe you should start at the beginning," Shaun said.

"Where's your ship?" Ruben asked.

"We landed it in a field on a farm down the trail." Shaun looked at him.

"Let's go."

"What about the Circe?" Lilly asked.

"It was just like I saw in my dream."

"With Stefan?" she asked. "The Circe are on this planet?"

"There was one on my ship." Ruben found the ornament in his pocket along with the crystal vial from the plant and dropped both of them in her hand.

"What is this?" Shaun asked as he picked up the vial.

"Another mystery," Ruben said. "I found that upstream growing on a plant."

"On a plant?" Shaun asked incredulously. He sniffed the open end of the vial.

"There was a liquid inside also," Ruben went on. "And I found that on my ship," he said, referring to the ornament that Lilly held in her palm. "Obviously, a Circe was on the *Shooting Star* at some point after I crashed."

"How bad was it?" Lilly asked. "I see your scar,

and I'm amazed that such a serious injury would heal so quickly. You've healed almost like the Circe, except there is no scarring with our wounds. Why is it blue?"

"I don't know," Ruben said. He flipped up his shirt to show them the wound on his abdomen and back. "I got this also. Impaled myself on a piece of the co-seat."

"Ouch," Shaun said.

"I practically crashed on top of Tess and Boone. They were here when it happened. Tess patched me up and left me in the ship. She was afraid of the repercussions, since they don't take kindly to offworlders here. I woke up sometime later and found my way down the trail, then fell into the stream. I would have died except Ky pulled me out." Ruben looked around for Ky and upon seeing the Newf, went to where he lay, followed by Shaun and Lilly. "Joah, Tess's master, wanted to throw me back in, but she wouldn't let him. He even beat her for defying him. She saved me."

"He what?" Lilly asked incredulously. "Who is Joah?"

"He was Tess's master. She's a slave. Or was a slave. Joah is dead. Killed by him." He flipped a thumb over his shoulder toward Garvin's lifeless body. "He wanted Tess for himself and took her son Boone to lure me here. Tess would get Boone back if she went willingly with Garvin. And I was supposed to be a bonus prize for Dyson and the Circe. I'm pretty sure they offered him a reward."

"I can understand why the Circe would be anxious to get their hands on you," Shaun said. "But why are they here in the first place?"

"That, my friend, is the question I want answered also." Ruben rubbed his hand over Ky's head, and the Newf blearily opened his dark eyes. "Where's Boone?" he asked, and Ky lumbered to his feet, shook his immense frame, and put his nose to the ground.

"You love them," Lilly said as they watched Ky. "Tess and Boone."

Ruben kept his eyes on Ky as the Newf sniffed around in the grass. He purposely kept his eyes from his friends.

You love them.

Well, yeah, what was not to love? He thought of Boone. The kid was cute, he was smart, he was funny, he had potential.

Tess . . .

The night he had just spent with Tess curled into his mind. The feel of her skin, the touch of her hand, the sudden drop of her defenses as she came to him in the same stubborn manner that she used to push him away. The clarity of her gray-green eyes beneath the sudden dip of her dark lashes. The silky texture of her hair as it hung in wild abandon around her shoulders.

The way she put him in his place yet made him feel strong and worthy at the same time, because in spite of all her protests to the contrary, she needed him.

And the kid, too.

They had to be terrified. Tess knew what the Circe were capable of.

If anything happened to them . . .

Ruben realized that his hands were clenched into fists so tight that the skin around his knuckles had turned white.

"Yes, I do love her," he said quietly as he gazed out over the thick forest and dense underbrush that now hid Tess and Boone.

He held great affection for Shaun and Lilly. He adored Elle and Zander. He respected Michael. He had loved his mother, even though his memories were filled more with disappointment than fondness. He had never had much of a chance to develop a relationship with his brother.

But he loved Tess. He had never known that such powerful emotion existed. Even after witnessing the relationship between Shaun and Lilly, he still considered it more a quirk of fate or destiny or something . . . but love?

Lilly placed a gentle hand on his shoulder.

"If you love her," she said, "then we should rescue her."

"Don't you want to get back to Oasis?" Ruben asked. "To Elle and Zander?"

"They will be fine," Shaun said, placing his hand on Ruben's other shoulder. "We came to help you. And if we take care of the problem here, then we may head off a problem on Oasis."

Ky found a scent and took off down the trail.

"Should we follow?" Shaun asked. "Or should we fly?"

Ruben looked off toward the mountain. The forest was dense. They would have to use infrared to track, and there was no guarantee that they would be able to find a place to land, which meant they would not be able to sneak up on Dyson.

"We ride," Ruben said.

"My ship or yours?" Shaun asked as he casually laid the rifle over his shoulder and crooked his arm over the stock.

"Tess's."

Chapter Twenty-five

Somehow the world was upside down. From her position, all she could see were plate-size hooves splashing hock deep in the stream. The sound of the rushing torrent filled her ears as droplets of water hit her face and dangling arms, stinging the exposed skin with a burning sensation.

"Boone!" Tess gasped. It was hard to breathe as she was sprawled over the back of a draft horse with her hands bound in front of her.

No answer. She raised her head and called out again, only to be pushed back down by a heavy hand in the middle of her back. She couldn't hear anything, and her hair had fallen from its twist and covered her eyes. Each step that the horse took was a jolt to her insides as the animal was moving in a forceful trot.

Tess twisted around to see what was in front of her. Through the rising mist she saw another set of legs and another rider. She craned her neck the other way and saw the same behind her.

Where was Boone?

The forest seemed to be denser than what she was used to around the farm. She could not feel the sun on her back, yet it had to be there, somewhere, above her.

Or was the fog still heavy? Shouldn't it have burned off by now?

How long had she been unconscious?

She tried to figure out what time it was. The last thing she remembered was running for Boone and then being flung through the air, her momentum carrying her toward Boone, who had looked at her with an expression of sheer terror.

Where was Boone? If only she could see or hear something that would let her know he was alive.

He had to be alive. She swung around again, trying to see something, anything, and the hand shoved her down again.

"Quiet!" someone barked at her.

Tess resisted the urge to scream in frustration. If they would just tell her about Boone . . .

What about Ben? Was he alive? The Circe wanted him alive. Was he with them?

The witches want Ben.

What were they going to do with her? With Boone? With Ben?

Tess decided that not knowing was worse than whatever might come. She had to know about Boone. She swung her arms under the horse, grabbed the wide girth that held the saddle in place, and pulled with all her might, kicking her legs upward as she yanked.

She was rewarded with a quick flip that landed her flat on her back in the stream. The shock of the cold felt as if a million needles had penetrated her skin, and the force of the water was so strong that she feared she would not be able to find her footing with her hands tied. How deep was the water? She was completely immersed, and the force of impact had knocked all the air from her body. She needed to breathe.

But then again, what did it matter if she ever drew another breath? Why not let the stream carry her away? Carry her down past the knoll, past the farm, past Garvin's, past the town, and on to the unseen ocean. Just float away and leave it all behind.

The agitated movement of the horse's giant hooves brought her back to awareness. She was in immediate danger of being struck in the head and drowning, and then what good would she be to her son?

Hands pulled her upright from the stream. Water poured off her as she mopped her face and pushed her hair back with her bound hands, taking a deep gulp of air. She shivered uncontrollably as her eyes darted hastily over the group surrounding her.

There . . . Boone . . . staring at her with wide green eyes from the back of a draft horse.

"Boone," she gasped and stumbled toward him, only to fall flat on her face once more in the water.

Someone had tripped her.

"Enough," someone said as she was once again hauled up, this time by her hair. "She'll be worthless if she can't speak."

Tess spat out the water that seemed to be creeping into every pore of her body. She felt as if she were floating outside of herself, observing the action as if she were sitting on a cloud, hovering just above the stream.

She recognized Dyson right away, with his missing finger. It looked as if it had been torn away.

Someone unseen was still holding on to her. His hand was wrapped in her hair so tightly that she couldn't move her neck. Two other men stood close by, waiting for her to make another move.

"Boone?" she said again.

"I'm fine, Mema," he said. He was holding tightly to the back of a man's shirt. The man he was riding with seemed stiff and awkward on the back of the horse. No wonder Boone was holding on so tight.

Her eyes trailed up and saw shoulder-length hair surrounding a very familiar face.

"Stefan?" she blurted out.

He ignored her, staring straight ahead with eyes as blue as Ben's.

Then she realized that there was a light blinking right below his chin.

The collar.

"Put her back," Dyson said, and the man holding her lifted her dripping body as if she weighed nothing and threw her on the back of a horse.

At least she could sit up now, she noted as one of the men climbed on before her. But she was freezing cold and her skin felt clammy, as if she were coming down with a fever. With stiff fingers, she grabbed the back of his shirt so she wouldn't slide off again. She feared they would knock her out if she caused any more trouble.

She pasted on what she hoped was a confident smile for Boone as they fell into line. Stefan's mount nosed in right behind Dyson's as if the man was controlling his actions.

He is.

Ben had told her about the collar and how whoever wore it had no more control over his own actions than a puppet. No wonder he was so desperate to find his brother.

Tess stole a look around the broad back of her captor. Boone seemed fine. But how much longer would he remain that way?

Where was Dyson taking them? How much further? What would happen when they got there?

Where was Ben?

He'll come for us.

Tess wasn't so sure that Ben's coming for them would be a good thing. Even if he was alive and was able, he had nothing to barter with now. Sure, he could exchange his life for theirs, but what guarantee did they have that Dyson would honor such a bargain? Garvin, who apparently had been in league with Dyson, was dead, and he had been the only one who cared whether she lived or died.

The fog was fading, and the late morning sunlight was bleeding through the treetops that grew close together overhead. Tess was still shivering but she kept her distance from the body in front of her. They were steadily climbing now, into the mountains. She had never been this far up before. She had never even been beyond the knoll.

She couldn't help being curious. She looked around, but there was not much to see, just thick woods that grew all the way down to the banks of the stream. She figured they were riding in the middle of the stream that flowed by the farm. She guessed that they were traveling along the streambed to cover their tracks. Or maybe the woods were so dense that there was no trail and this was the easiest way to get wherever they were going.

Why was Dyson here? Why had he been in the warehouse in the city? Why was Ben's brother a prisoner? What were the Circe witches doing on Lavign? What was going on, and how had she and Boone landed in the middle of it?

"Where are you taking us?" Tess asked.

Everyone ignored her. She peered around her captor's back and saw Boone looking back toward her.

"What do you want with us?" Tess said, this time louder.

And still they ignored her.

"Let us go!" Tess demanded.

"Shut her up," Dyson said without turning around.

She was instantly surrounded by the two other riders, while the man she was riding with turned to her with a determined look on his face.

Tess held up her hands in surrender. "I'll be quiet," she said to the three intent faces.

"Make sure that you do," her companion growled. "Or talking will be the last thing on your mind."

She nodded, as always more worried about Boone than herself. She knew she would be no use to him if they hurt her.

They continued on, the animals splashing through the stream as they steadily climbed. The banks on either side were higher now, as if the stream had cut a deep slice into the earth.

Tess became aware of another sound. She couldn't place how long it had been since she'd first heard it.

Perhaps she heard it now because she was concentrating on their surroundings instead of trying to figure out what was happening.

It was a tinkling sound, not unlike a set of wind chimes that Garvin had once given her in his quest to win her. The chimes had consisted of several thin blue glass tubes tied to a piece of wood, and they had made a pleasant sound when the wind caught them. She had hung them in the breezeway behind the house, but the first big thunderstorm that came through had shattered the glass.

It was that same sound she heard now, over the rushing of the stream.

Her eyes scanned the area around the trees. Nothing there. Not even a movement in the leaves to indicate a breeze.

She cast her gaze to ground level. The earth on either side of them was as high as the riders' heads, and the stream bank was covered with a frothy fernlike plant that grew among the tree roots and down the banks into the stream. The ferns were full of cobalt blue flowers that looked like long tubes.

Tess peered closer as the bank closed in on them a bit, almost brushing their legs as they rode. A fern dragged against the side of the horse she was riding, and the tinkling noise was unmistakable. It was coming from the fern, or possibly the flowers.

"Careful there," the rider behind them said. "Don't want to mess up the profits."

Tess heard a shattering sound as the fern fronds bounced back into place and a trail of bright blue liquid marred the clear water of the stream. Her eyes followed it as it dissipated.

She understood then. It all made perfect sense. The flowers were crystal. The bright blue color matched the shade of Ben's scar. The crystals broke, and the fluid inside poured into the stream. Ben had fallen into the stream with open wounds. She had pulled what seemed to be shards of glass from the wounds as they healed. She wondered what the blue liquid would do to a person's system if it was ingested regularly.

No wonder the water tasted so bitter. No wonder it had such an effect on the heifer. No wonder she herself hated the taste of it and forbade Boone to drink it, or even play in it.

And she knew without a doubt that she had seen this bright blue color before. It had marred the lips of the Qazar addict she had seen in the city.

Just before she'd seen Garvin outside the warehouse.

Just before she and Boone had gone into the warehouse and seen Dyson and his partners.

Dyson was harvesting Qazar from Lavign. This was the source of the drug. How easy had it been for him? There was no planetary defense system, so he could come and go at will.

His ships were the source of the lights she saw constantly around the mountains. She had thought it lightning but it was Dyson coming in and going off the planet.

But how had Garvin been a part of it? What had his role been?

If her hands had not been tied, she would have smacked her forehead. Garvin had made the glass bottles used by the vineyard. He'd blown them from the sand that gathered in a crook of the stream on his property. Somehow he must have hidden the Qazar inside the bottles.

But how were the Circe witches involved? What did this have to do with the assassination of Ben's father? What was Stefan's involvement?

Tess stared at the back of Dyson's head as if trying to pry the answers out. She kept her eyes upon him as she looked over her captor's shoulder.

Dyson stopped his draft horse and turned in his saddle, his eyes scanning behind him. They settled finally on Tess, and he looked at her as if seeing her for the first time.

Tess stared back at him, willing him to say or do something that would let her know what was going to happen to her and Boone.

But all he did was stare hard at her and frown before moving on again.

A chill went down her spine that had nothing to do with the fact that she was still soaking wet.

Somehow Dyson knew that she had figured it all out. She had seen it in his mind just as clearly as she could see the broad back in front of her.

And if she didn't figure a way out of this mess, she and Boone were going to die.

Ben . . .

Chapter Twenty-six

Shaun was not happy about Ruben's proposed choice of transport. And that was putting it mildly.

"This is not one of your kick-down-the-door-and-start-shooting situations," Ruben patiently explained to him as Lilly made friends with one of the gentle giants. "They are expecting us."

"If they're expecting us, why bother sneaking up on them?" Shaun argued.

"Because they won't expect *this*," Ruben said as he checked the charge in the blaster Shaun had handed him and strapped the weapon securely at his hips.

"If they've got a Circe with them, they'll know exactly what we're doing." Shaun said. "I think I should just fly in and blast them, and then you can sneak in and get your woman."

"His woman?" Lilly said, shooting Shaun a look that plainly said he was in trouble. "She has a name."

"Tess." Shaun said, humbly correct now. "And what's wrong with blasting them?"

"Have you been bored lately?" Lilly asked. "Ever since we got on the ship, you've been dying to shoot something."

Shaun grinned sheepishly. "Well—"

"I'd quit while I was ahead if I were you," Ruben said. "And no blasting. You might hit Tess or Boone."

"I'm just not so sure about riding these things," Shaun said. "It looks . . . painful."

"I've seen you ride before," Ruben said as he handed the reins to his friend.

"I have ridden," Shaun said. "Just nothing this wide. And not without a saddle. I'm not sure I can stretch that far."

"You can," Lilly said as she gracefully swung up onto the draft horse. "Or you could if you'd do your meditations like I've asked you to."

"Maybe you should use some of your persuasion techniques on him," Ruben said as he mounted his draft horse and tried to discreetly arrange himself with some degree of comfort against the animal's backbone. Shaun laughed at his friend and then frowned after using the fence rail to climb on behind Lilly.

"Don't tempt her," Shaun said. "She's aching for a fight, same as me."

"Being a recluse is a disadvantage at times," Lilly said as they moved out. "Sometimes we think you're having all the fun."

"Yeah," Ruben said. "This is fun."

Lilly looked over at him as they rode side by side. "We'll get them back," she said.

"Can you see it?" Ruben asked hopefully.

"You know I can't see the future," Lilly said. "But I will know when we're getting close to them."

"That's good enough for me," Ruben said. His mount took the stream in one hop and Lilly and Shaun's followed.

They rode the trail up to the knoll and then down the opposite side. They rode past the wreckage of the Falcon and Shaun let out with an appreciative whistle.

"What?" Shaun asked when Ruben gave him a pain-filled look.

"I was teaching Boone how to do that."

"Me too," Shaun said. "With Zander . . . and Elle, of course."

The responsibilities of fatherhood. It was not something he had thought about much. But with Tess it was a package deal.

Teaching Boone to whistle. Watching the kid's eyes light up as he explored the *Shooting Star*. Seeing how devoted Ky was to him.

Animals sensed things about people. No matter what kind of a bastard his father had been, there was goodness in Boone. He was bright and funny and the image of his mother.

What kind of father would Ruben make? Would Tess think he was good enough to raise her son?

He had to be better than what Boone had experienced so far.

What was he thinking? He was just assuming that Tess would have him.

She had you last night.

When she thought he was going to be dead in a few hours. . . . Ruben rolled his eyes and shook his head. He'd better save her before he thought about the future.

And what if he went to all the trouble of saving her and she still wouldn't have him?

A grin split his face. She'd have him. He would convince her. After all, he hadn't survived all these years of smuggling just on his good looks. Convincing her would be just the beginning of the pleasure they would share.

"What are you grinning at?" Shaun asked.

"Just thinking," Ruben said.

"There's Ky," Lilly noted.

Ky sat by the stream as if waiting for them to show up. Ruben dismounted and went to the Newf.

"Which way did they go?" he asked as he rubbed the large head. Ky got to his feet and snuffed the earth down to the stream and then looked up hopefully at Ruben.

"Looks like they went into the stream," Shaun said. He pointed to the ground. The earth was churned up by the tracks of men.

"I don't see any footprints that look small enough to be Tess or Boone's," Ruben said as he examined the tracks.

"They were probably carried," Lilly pointed out.

"Knocked unconscious by the blast," Shaun added.

Ruben looked over at the opposite bank. "Nothing there," he said.

"In the stream," Shaun said.

Ruben looked at the rushing water. The sound was hypnotizing, and he felt tempted, once again, to drink, to immerse himself in the stream and let it carry him away.

"The stream," he said as if in a trance.

Ky let out a gentle woof, bringing Ruben back to the present. He looked around and saw Lilly and Shaun watching him with puzzled looks.

"Let's go," he said. He swung himself back on his horse and urged the animal into the stream. Lilly and Shaun followed, but Ky clung to the bank.

Ky hates the stream.

What was it about the stream? Why did it call to him so strongly?

Without thought, Ruben's hand went to his pocket for the crystal vial. It wasn't there. He had given it to Shaun.

Ky hated the vial, too. He had stopped Ruben from touching the liquid inside. What did the Newf know?

The liquid goes into the stream when the vials break.

Ruben touched the scar on his forehead. The liquid was blue. His scar was blue. The stream was the connection.

But what was the liquid?

And what did Dyson have to do with it?

They rode on in silence. Ky stayed close to them when possible. When the forest got too dense, he would either jump to the opposite side or else wend his way through the trees until he could rejoin them.

"Why doesn't he just get in the water?" Shaun asked as they saw Ky waiting for them upstream on the bank.

"He hates it," Ruben said.

"Strange," Shaun said. "I've never seen a breed like that."

"He's a Newf," Ruben said. "My father always had them. It's the first time I've ever seen one off Amanor."

"Where did he come from?"

"Tess said he just showed up one day. Came down the trail from the knoll. He was hurt, and she nursed him and he attached himself to Boone."

"So maybe he came from Amanor," Lilly said. "With Dyson."

"We were thinking the same thing. But the big question is why? What does Lavign have to offer someone like Dyson?"

"What is that?" Shaun asked, as he pointed down to one of the crystal-covered plants. "Is that the plant you were talking about?"

"Yes."

"Stop," Shaun told Lilly and slid off the draft horse. He pulled a knife from his belt, cut a flower from the plant, and held it up to the dappled sunlight that filtered through the treetops. He slid his shields up on his forehead to take a closer look.

"What is it?" Lilly asked.

"Strange," Shaun murmured. He seemed hypnotized by the liquid as it moved back and forth in the vial. He used his knife to knock the end off the vial.

"Careful," Ruben said. He looked at Ky, who was watching from the bank above with great interest.

Shaun sniffed the vial and then touched his finger to the end of it. A droplet of cobalt blue liquid balanced on the end of his finger as if it were a small sapphire.

"Don't," Lilly said as Shaun slowly raised his finger to his lips.

"I wouldn't," Ruben said.

Their words had no effect on Shaun. It was as if they had not spoken. His tongue darted out and tasted the liquid, and a smile spread over his face. He lifted the vial to drink, but it was jerked from his hand as if attached to a wire. The liquid poured out into the stream and quickly disappeared in the water.

"Are you insane?" Lilly asked incredulously. She had moved the vial with her mind.

Shaun grinned at her and then turned to get another vial.

"No," Lilly said. Her face was set, and Ruben knew she was attempting to control Shaun with her mind.

What was in that vial?

And then suddenly he knew. Qazar. Addicts had blue lips. They ingested it orally. The liquid was the same bright blue.

It was in the stream. That was why he was always so tempted by the water. The drug was known to be highly addictive, but when diffused in the stream it must lose some of its strength.

Shaun had tasted it in its purest form. And he wanted more.

Lilly was trying to stop him, using her strongest weapon, her mind. But Shaun's mind too was a weapon.

Shaun dropped the knife as if it burned him. He looked over his shoulder at Lilly, calmly fished it out of the water, and turned back to the Qazar, all the time wearing that same stupid smile.

"Shaun," Lilly said. She slid from her mount, splashed through the stream, and placed herself between Shaun and the plant. "What are you doing?" She tried to touch his face, but he flung her arms away.

"Shaun!" she said desperately and reached for him again.

Shaun shoved her, and she stumbled back against the stream bank. His smile was bizarre, as if he were possessed.

Or wearing a collar.

Ruben had seen enough. He launched his body from the back of his mount, hitting Shaun in the side. They tumbled into the water as Ruben reached for the hand holding the knife. He felt it slip from Shaun's grip as they went under.

Ruben knew he had to react quickly. Shaun was physically stronger than he was. He just hoped the Qazar had addled his friend's brain enough that he could get the upper hand.

Ruben came up for air but kept his hands on Shaun's neck, holding him under.

"What are you doing?" Lilly screamed. She came up beside him.

"It's Qazar," Ruben yelled. Shaun was scrabbling at his hands and he didn't know how long he could hold him. Ruben dug his knee into Shaun's abdomen for added force. "Can you reach him?"

Lilly plunged her hands into the water and grabbed Shaun's head. His clear gray eyes looked up at them with a look Ruben had never seen before and hoped never to see again. There was no doubt in his mind that Shaun would kill both of them if he could reach them.

Lilly tightened her grip, willing her mind into Shaun's, trying desperately to reach him.

Bubbles flew to the surface from Shaun's mouth. He was running out of air. Suddenly he stopped struggling. Ruben looked closely at his friend. The pale gray eyes were still open, and he looked up at them expectantly.

"He's back," Lilly gasped.

"Are you sure?"

"Yes." She leaned back. "Let him up before he drowns."

Ruben let go of Shaun's neck but kept his knee in place as Shaun slowly sat up.

"Qazar?" Shaun gasped. He looked at Ruben. "Did you know?"

"Not until you tasted it and started acting insane." He moved off Shaun and staggered back against the stream bank. "That must be why Dyson is here. He's the source of the drug."

Shaun looked almost longingly at the plant. "I want more," he said simply as he sat in the middle of the stream. "It's the most amazing thing I've ever felt. As if I could conquer the universe."

"You *can* conquer the universe, you big idiot," Ruben said. "If you wanted to."

"Well, that made me want to," Shaun said. He looked at Lilly. "Did I hurt you?"

Lilly shook her head. Ruben realized she was fighting tears, and he turned away as Shaun found his feet and took her into his arms.

Ruben picked up Shaun's knife and gave him and Lilly a moment's privacy before he handed it back. "We need to move," he said. "I wouldn't put it past Dyson to kill Tess and Boone if he's messed up in this."

Shaun nodded grimly. Ruben wondered what kind of battle was raging inside his friend's mind and body. It couldn't be easy. If someone with the mental powers of Shaun was affected by Qazar, no wonder the rest of the universe was quickly becoming addicted.

"So now we know what your half-brother is up to," Lilly said as they continued on their way, soaking wet and shivering with cold. "But what do the Circe have to do with it?"

"That's easy," Shaun said. "What do the Circe want more than anything else?"

"You mean besides you and Lilly?" Ruben asked.

"Yes," Shaun said.

"Power," Lilly said.

"And if you have something that everyone in the universe wants . . ." Shaun said.

"You've got the power," Ruben finished for him.

He looked grimly upstream. They were starting the climb. How far ahead of them was Dyson? How long before they caught up? Were Tess and Boone still alive? They had to be.

Hang on, Tess . . . Boone . . . I'm coming.

Chapter Twenty-seven

They left the streambed. The climb was too difficult for the horses with their thick, heavy legs. The animals had been bred for pulling large loads, not climbing. The stream was now a series of falls, each one tumbling into the next, with sharp rocks sticking up at odd angles. They must be getting close to the stream's source. Tess could no longer see blue sky over the thick treetops. Instead there was the massive gray shadow of the mountain.

Tess held on tighter now, her bound hands wrapped tightly in the fabric of the shirt of the man she rode with. The close contact disgusted her, but falling off was a worse option. She was still damp, her skin steaming now in the heat of the day.

Watching Stefan's careless riding unnerved her. She kept imagining her son falling off the back of the horse and landing on a rock, struck instantly dead, or being washed downstream while Dyson watched with an evil grin. How horrible it must be for Stefan to be under someone else's control. She knew exactly how it felt, but at least she had the luxury of being able to care for herself.

You're a slave no longer.

It was funny how the thought suddenly occurred to her. With everything else that had happened in the past day and night, she hadn't even realized that Joah's death meant she was no longer his slave. And Garvin's death meant she no longer had to fear him either. She grieved for neither one.

"I'll die a free woman," she said.

"Quiet," her escort barked.

Tess rolled her eyes. Who would hear them? They were deep in the mountains. There were no settlers here. There wasn't even any obvious wildlife about, except for the occasional bird flitting in the tree branches. Dyson's operations must have run all the local animals off.

The trail wound back and forth and constantly upward as it followed the path of the stream. Tess noticed that the Qazar grew thicker here. Everywhere she looked she could see the frothy ferns, but most of them were devoid of the blue crystals.

They've been harvesting, she observed. She did not speak the words out loud, but she did wonder once again if Dyson knew that she had figured things out on her own.

Tess watched in apprehension as first Dyson's and then Stefan's mount scrambled up a particularly steep pitch of the trail and then trotted out of sight. She held on with every bit of strength she possessed as the horse she was on followed suit.

They were in a clearing now, an enormous area that had at one time been covered with long grass; that was long gone, trampled by the heavy traffic. Off to one side was a fighter ship covered by a huge sheet of some unknown material. Tess reasoned that the covering was camouflage to disguise the ship from above. On the opposite end of the clearing was a huge cave with an overhang that sheltered two starships, one much larger than the other. On top of the overhang was a huge weapon with a man beside it. The man waved down to the men on horseback, then went back to his watch.

Boone stood safely on the ground. Stefan had put him down and now stood beside him as if waiting to hear what he was supposed to do next. Tess slid off the draft horse and ran to her son, not giving a thought to whether she should have asked permission.

Boone threw his arms around her neck as she fell to her knees in front of him.

"Mema," he said. "Are you hurt?"

"No," Tess cried. "What about you? What did Garvin do to you? Where did he take you? Did he hurt you?" It was hard to hold on to him with her hands bound, but she managed to assure herself that he was unhurt.

"He's dead now," Boone said. "He didn't hurt me, but I'm glad he's dead."

Tess fought back tears as she smiled at her son's sweet face. He should not have seen death at such a young age. Especially such a violent one. But she had to admit, she was glad Garvin was dead.

"Mema—where's Ben?" His deep green eyes were wide with fear, but his voice did not betray him.

"I don't know," Tess said.

"Is he dead too?"

"I hope not," Tess said. "I don't think so."

"I don't think so either," Boone said. He leaned in and whispered in her ear, "I think he's coming for us."

"Me too," Tess said with a nervous smile.

"Master Garvin said that Master Joah was dead and we were going to belong to him. That's why I'm glad Ben killed him."

"Master Joah is dead," Tess said. "Garvin killed him."

"Mema," Boone said. "You're free now. You don't have a master anymore."

Tess looked at her bound hands. So far, freedom was disappointing.

Except for last night.

There was no reason for Ben to come. Not for her and not for Boone. Not even for Stefan. He could just get in his ship and fly off. His friends and their children would be safe. She knew about the children, but he had not mentioned which planet they were on, just that they were well hidden. There was no need to rescue her to keep what he'd told her secret. The witches had probably figured it all out anyway. They couldn't expect the couple not to have children.

So Ben could leave, knowing that his friends were safe. And he wouldn't have to sacrifice himself. Why should he? He barely knew her, and he admitted that he did not know his brother.

But he wouldn't do that . . .

But he should. He should just go. Tess looked back

down the mountain as if expecting to see the *Shoot-ing Star* take off at any moment.

If Ben left, there would be no reason for Dyson to keep her and Boone alive. None whatsoever.

"Mema," Boone said. "I have to go . . ."

Tess looked around for a convenient spot. They were close to the edge of the clearing. The men seemed oblivious to their prisoners as they went about unsaddling the draft horses and moving barrels to the cave.

Dyson was nowhere to be seen, and Stefan had not moved from his spot.

"Just go behind a tree," Tess said as she kept an eye on the comings and goings around the cave.

Boone moved to the edge of the clearing, and Stefan immediately followed him.

"He just has to go," Tess said, but Stefan ignored her. Tess grabbed his arm, and he looked down at her hand and then at her face as if expecting her to say something.

"Go ahead, Boone," Tess said as she smiled at Stefan. "Stefan won't bother you."

"What's wrong with him?" Boone whispered. "Why is he like that?"

"It's because of the thing around his neck," Tess said quietly. "Go on."

She looked carefully at Stefan as she held on to his arm. He didn't move, just looked at her as if waiting for her command.

He was so much like his brother. She knew exactly what Ben must have looked like at the same age. Except for the long hair, they were identical, with their high, hollow cheekbones and perfectly straight noses.

Identical in every way, except Stefan seemed so young and so lost. Had Ben been the same, or had he used his dazzling charm for protection?

Tess looked into Stefan's amazingly blue eyes and blinked.

Help me. . . . You can help me.

It was as if he were speaking to her, inside her mind.

"What?" Tess said, looking closely at Stefan.

You're one of them. You can help me.

His face never changed, but his eyes conveyed the desperation of his message. She heard him as clearly as if he'd shouted to her.

"Where's the boy?" Dyson demanded as he came toward them.

"Here," Boone said. He stepped back into the clearing.

"You were supposed to watch him," Dyson said to Stefan.

"He had to go," Tess said.

Dyson looked at Tess, then at Stefan, whose face still held the same blank expression.

"What did he say to you?" Dyson asked.

"Nothing," Tess said. And even though she knew the answer, she asked, "What's wrong with him? What is that thing around his neck?"

Dyson's mouth stretched into an evil grin.

She watched him carefully. His eyes were a watery blue, his frame huge and somewhat flabby, as if he were accustomed to overindulgence instead of hard work. His hair was a pale golden blond, probably at one time beautiful and silky but now thinning on top.

He had the same father as Ben and Stefan, yet Tess

saw no resemblance whatsoever. They all must take after their mothers.

Just like Boone.

"You'll find out soon enough," Dyson said. "As a matter of fact, we have a collar waiting here for our missing brother. As soon as he arrives, you'll see up close what it does to the man who wears it."

"What makes you think he'll come?"

"He'll come," Dyson said. "He always does the honorable thing. Even when he ran off, he did it because it was more honorable than killing our beloved father." Dyson laughed, a short barking sound that sent a shiver down Tess's back. "Of course, it might just be that he's a coward. I guess we'll find out soon enough."

"What are you going to do with us?" Tess asked as Dyson herded her and Boone toward the cave.

"Garvin told me what an excellent slave you were," Dyson said. "And since he's dead and we were partners . . . I guess that means you now belong to me."

I'd rather die . . .

"Partners in what?" Tess kept up the pace, trying desperately to keep out of Dyson's reach. Boone trotted at her heels, quietly absorbing the conversation, and Stefan trailed after all of them.

Tess's mind scrambled. Servitude was nothing to her, but she couldn't let it happen to Boone. Somehow she had to make sure that he got away.

"My export business," Dyson replied as he waved his arm in a wide sweep to encompass the clearing and everything within it. "He provided the containers I use to ship my product." Tess's attention was caught once again by the deformity of his hand. What had happened to his smallest finger?

"What is your product?" Tess asked. She knew the answer but wanted to hear him say it. She needed to keep Dyson talking. She needed time to get Boone away.

"The most desired substance in the universe," Dyson said. They entered the cave. "You don't know how close you came to discovering my secret that day in the city."

"What do you mean?" Tess asked.

"Oh, I know it was you that day in the warehouse," Dyson said. "I know because I recognized my Newf."

"Ky?" Boone asked.

Dyson laughed. "Is that what you call him?" He shook his head. "I never had a name for him. I just brought him along because I thought he'd be handy in case someone came poking around. He was handy, all right." Dyson held up his mangled hand. "The stupid git took my finger off the first time I had to teach him a lesson."

"He bit your finger off because you were beating him?" Tess asked.

"Yes, he did," Dyson said. "And when I get my hands on him, I'll make sure he never bites me or anything else again."

"No wonder Ben hates you so much," Tess said.

"It's always been mutual," Dyson muttered. "Stay here." He turned to Stefan. "Make sure they stay here," he commanded and walked off.

Tess watched as Dyson walked up the ramp into the smaller starship. The larger one was in the process of being loaded with barrels. She assumed that the one Dyson went into was for his own personal use so he wouldn't be caught with his . . . product.

The cave was damp and musty, and she briskly rubbed her arms as a chill once more set in. At least Boone was dry. He stood by her side, curiously watching the goings-on. How much of this had he figured out? Did he even know what Qazar was, what it did?

"Boone," she said when she was sure no one could hear them, "when we get a chance, I want you to run away."

"And leave you?"

"Yes."

"I can't leave you," he said. "I have to take care of you. Ben told me to always take care of you."

Tess's heart ached as she looked down into Boone's earnest face. "You have to find Ben and show him where we are." She placed her hand on the back of his head as he looked up at her. "Do you think you could do that? Hide in the woods and then follow the stream and find Ben. That would be the best way to help me."

"I can," he said. "I'll bring Ky, too." He said it vehemently, his face full of hatred for Dyson. As small as he'd been when Ky showed up, he remembered how close to death the Newf had been.

Tess spared a look at Stefan. He was standing silent, his face blank, but his eyes were watching.

Tess glanced at the collar. How hard would it be to remove it? Could she just take it off? Then all three of them could escape.

His eyes implored her.

What? What should I do? she thought.

Help me.

What was happening? It was almost as if she could read his mind. Was it because of the collar?

Dyson reappeared, followed by a woman wearing dark robes and an ornate hat.

A Circe. Tess recognized the woman from the warehouse. What was her part in all of this?

The woman turned her wicked, pale eyes upon Tess and she felt fear building inside her. She had to save Boone before it was too late. She had to get him away from the evil.

What should she do?

As if in answer, a barrel fell from the ramp leading into the ship and burst open, scattering shards of blue glass and liquid cobalt on the earth. The man who had been carrying it looked down in shock and horror.

"Run," Tess hissed at Boone as Dyson and the Circe turned toward the sound. Tess threw her shoulder into Stefan and knocked him to the ground as Boone took off.

Her hands searched Stefan's neck, seeking the collar, trying to find the connection, the clasp. She knew his first order was to stop Boone. If only she could stop him and get the collar off.

"Where's the boy?" Dyson roared. "Find him!"

"Run, Boone!" Tess shouted as her fingers grappled with the collar. Stefan struggled beneath her, his desire to follow orders overriding his wish to escape. She couldn't find the end of the collar, and her fingers tangled in his hair.

The next thing she knew, a hand was once again wrapped in her hair and she was pulled to her feet by Dyson.

"Where is your son?" he ground out between clenched teeth.

"Gone," she said. "Safe."

He shook her as if he wanted to kill her.

"Find him!" Dyson yelled to his men.

"Where is the boy?" a voice hissed in her ears. An evil voice that brought a slithering chill to Tess's spine. "It was foolish of you to send him away. Very foolish."

Dyson shoved Tess away, and she caught herself to keep from falling into the woman's dark robes. She straightened up and found that she was face to face with the Circe witch. The woman's eyes widened and her nostrils flared in obvious distaste as she looked at Tess.

At the sound of someone in pain Tess turned from the woman. Dyson was viciously kicking Stefan, who still lay on the ground.

"Stop!" Tess cried out and ran to block the next kick. "You'll kill him."

"Eventually," Dyson said as he attempted to shove her away.

"No!"

Dyson stopped in mid-swing and looked at Tess in confusion.

Tess stood her ground between Dyson and Stefan. She heard shouts from the clearing. They were still searching for Boone. With any luck, he had gotten away. He was small, he was fast, and he could hide if he had to.

Run!

Then an icy feeling came over her. She felt as if she were slowly being immersed in the stream. Her will started to fade away as if she had no control over it whatsoever. A dark shadow filled her mind, coiling and uncoiling as if a snake had entered her brain.

The Circe witch came up to her and stopped, her face a mere breath from her own.

"Who are you?" the woman asked.

And for the life of her, Tess could not tell her.

Chapter Twenty-eight

Shaun was struggling. Ruben heard Lilly talking to him as they rode behind. Everywhere they looked, there was Qazar. How long would the effects of the drug last? Would he crave it for the rest of his life?

The way was getting more difficult also. And it occurred to Ruben that since this was most likely the way Dyson had come, the route would be watched. But surely his half-brother would expect him to come in from the air.

How much farther?

Ky was beside them again. He plowed through the underbrush with his nose to the ground. They had to be going the right way. The Newf seemed determined.

"I need to walk," Shaun growled. "I can't stand this any longer."

Ruben turned to study his friend. His eyes seemed haunted, and Lilly looked worried.

"I think we should go on foot," Ruben agreed. "We can walk parallel to the stream. Maybe that will give us a chance to sneak up on them."

"Good idea," Shaun said. He was already on the bank. "Let's go." He held his rifle crooked in his arm and looked impatiently up the mountain. Ruben turned the animals downstream and sent them back home with a slap on the rump. He joined Ky, Shaun, and Lilly on the bank.

Watch him . . . so I can search.

Lilly had come into his mind.

"This way," Ruben said, pointing away from the stream. "We'll stay close enough to hear it."

Ky plowed on ahead, his head turned toward the mountain. He seemed to know where he was going, so Ruben let him lead the way.

Their steps were accompanied by an occasional tinkling sound. Qazar. They were disturbing the plant with their strides. Shaun muttered a string of curses as they walked. "Is there anyplace this stuff doesn't grow?"

"Try the litany," Lilly said. "Repeat it."

My mind is my own. Ruben knew it well.

"I'm tired of repeating it," Shaun barked. He wiped a hand across his mouth and scanned the ground with his eyes. "How much longer?"

Shaun was weakening. As long as Lilly had maintained contact with his mind, he'd been able to resist, but now she had to search for the Circe and it would take every bit of her concentration to find the witch.

Ruben had to do something. If he couldn't count on Shaun, they were in big trouble.

"What?" Shaun barked when he realized Ruben was looking at him.

Ruben punched him. A quick right to the jaw. Shaun's head flew back, and his hand went to the blood that poured from his lip.

"Why the hell did you hit me?"

"Because you're acting like an idiot and I need your mind to be on the mission."

"The mission?"

"You heard me. The mission."

Shaun's fist clenched, and Ruben got ready for a blow but he kept on talking. "Quit thinking about what you want and start thinking about a scared woman and her son. Think about my brother and remember what it felt like when you wore the collar. Think about how you'd feel if it were Lilly and the children up there. Then get mad as hell and take it out on Dyson and whoever else is mixed up in this disaster."

Ruben was vaguely aware that Ky was barking somewhere in the distance, but he ignored the sound as he kept his eyes on Shaun. He had to reach him.

Shaun relaxed his hand and looked around as if he were just waking up from a deep sleep.

"I think I like that idea," Shaun said and placed his hand on Ruben's shoulder.

"We'll get you through this," Ruben said, returning the gesture and giving Shaun's shoulder a squeeze. "But we've got to find Tess and Boone first."

"I'm over it," Shaun said. "I just had to quit thinking about it."

"Someone's coming," Lilly said. She stood up the trail a bit with her blaster in her hand.

Ruben drew his weapon, and they all took shelter behind the trees.

He peered around his cover and saw Ky bounding

toward him with his tail wagging. And behind him was Boone.

"Boone!" Ruben yelled.

Boone charged right for him and threw himself at Ruben. Ruben gathered the boy in his arms and lifted him into a hug, holding on tightly, as if to make sure he was really there.

"Are you all right? Where's Tess?"

"Up there," Boone said. "With the bad man."

"How far?"

"Far. I ran away. Mema told me to find you. They looked for me, but I hid and then ran when they weren't watching."

"Can you take us back?"

"Yes. I can." Boone wrapped his arms around Ruben's neck. "I told her you'd come for us."

Ruben gave a casual sniff. Were those tears threatening to leak out of his eyes? When had this kid become so important to him?

"Who are those people?" Boone asked as he finally realized that Shaun and Lilly were there watching them.

"These are my friends," Ruben said. "This is Lilly and this is Shaun."

"Hello, Boone," Lilly said with her gentle smile. "We're here to help Ruben."

"Who is Ruben?" Boone asked.

Shaun laughed. "Good question," he said. He still looked a bit haggard around the eyes, but he sounded normal. "Who is Ruben?"

"They call me Ben," Ruben explained.

Lilly grinned at him.

"What?" Ruben said.

"Your mother called you Ben," she said.

"How did you know that?" Shaun asked Lilly. "Did you tell her?" he asked Ruben.

"She found it out on one of her trips."

"What else do you know about him that you haven't told me?" Shaun said.

"If you're feeling so nosy why don't you just look for yourself?" Ruben suggested.

"Boone," Lilly said, ignoring the two of them. "Tell us what you saw."

Boone screwed his face up in concentration. "I saw three starships. Two in a cave and one like the one that crashed, with a big sheet on top of it."

"A Falcon?" Shaun asked.

"There were lots of men and they were putting barrels in one of the ships. And on top of the cave there was a big gun."

"Proton cannon," Shaun said, and Ruben nodded.

"Boone," Lilly said. "Did you see a woman there? A woman wearing a funny hat?"

Boone shook his head. "I don't remember one."

The three adults looked at each other. The presence of a Circe would definitely make a difference in how they entered the camp.

"Boone, Lilly is going to touch your head right here on the side," Ruben said. "And when she does, she'll be able to see everything that you saw."

"Will it hurt?"

"I promise it won't," Ruben said. "She does it to me all the time."

"It might tickle a bit," Lilly said with her gentle smile. "Why don't you lean your head against Ben?"

Boone put his head on Ruben's shoulder, and Lilly touched his temple with her fingers.

"You are very brave," she said to Boone. Then she

described what she saw in his mind. "It's like he said. Three ships, proton cannon, a huge clearing, lots of men loading barrels." She looked at Ruben. "Stefan is there. He has a collar. Tess is with him . . . confusion . . . he ran . . ." Lilly closed her eyes. "I'm going back a bit . . . yes . . . a Circe. He just got a glimpse of her before he ran." She took her fingers from Boone's temple. "You did what your mema said. You ran and you hid. You were quiet when they were close to finding you."

"Then I ran some more until I heard Ky barking." He looked at Ruben. "The bad man beat Ky, and Ky bit his finger off."

"I knew there was a reason why I liked Ky so much," Ruben said. The Newf wagged his giant tail at the mention of his name. Ruben lowered Boone to the ground. "Although I'm surprised he didn't die from biting Dyson."

"He almost did die," Boone reminded him.

"So we've got a proton cannon, a Falcon, a whole bunch of bad guys, and a witch," Shaun said. He looked at the group. "I like the odds."

"We need a plan," Lilly said.

"Wait until dark," Shaun said. "We'll have the advantage. You can use my eyes."

Boone made a face, but the adults continued with their plans.

"If they're loading ships, they might take off before dark," Ruben said.

"Or maybe some of them will take off, and that will even the odds a bit," Shaun commented. "Besides, do you think they would go to all this trouble to lure you here and then just leave? They want you, my friend."

"He's right," Lilly said. "I think this might have something to do with your father's death. You've always thought Dyson was the one responsible."

"Maybe our father found out what he was up to."

"That's a distinct possibility," Shaun said. "And the Circe would jump at the chance to take control of Amanor."

"Kill the leader, take over the army. Sounds like something they would do," Ruben said. "Then they get Stefan under their power and frame me. Easy to do since I've been conveniently missing all these years—"

"And a renowned smuggler," Shaun interrupted.

Ruben ignored him. "They can blame the entire thing on me. It looks like revenge for all the wrongs my father heaped on my mother's people."

"How does it feel to be an assassin and a drug smuggler?" Lilly asked.

"Depends on how big the reward is now," Ruben said.

"A million, last time we heard," Shaun said.

"Then I guess it feels pretty good."

"Ben?" Boone said. "How come he's going to give you his eyes?"

Shaun laughed. "Let's see how you handle this," he said. Ruben grinned ruefully at him. Shaun seemed to enjoy watching his attempts at fatherhood.

Ruben knelt next to Boone. "Shaun is special, just like Lilly. He can see what's inside people's heads. And both of them can talk to you inside your head so no one else can hear." He hoped his explanation didn't sound too confusing to a kid who had been raised on a backward planet. "But Shaun is even more special because he can see in the dark. Then he can show us what he sees so we can have the same image."

"Can you do that, too?" Boone asked.

"No," Ruben said. "I can't. Sometimes I wish I could."

"He has different things he's special at," Lilly said. "He's a very good pilot."

Boone's hand touched the blade on Ruben's wrist. "He's good with this, too. He killed Garvin with it. It happened really fast."

"I wish you hadn't had to see that. Killing someone is not something to be proud of."

"You had to," Boone said. "You were trying to save me."

Lilly smiled wistfully at him over Boone's head.

"Are you going to kill more men to get my mema back?"

Ruben looked at Lilly, who nodded.

You can't protect him from this. He's a part of it.

"Probably. But only because I know they want to kill us."

"Will they?"

"Yes, if we let them. That is why you have to do what I say and stay where I tell you. And just like your mema said, you might have to run away. Can I count on you to do that?"

"Yes." Boone's face was earnest. "I will."

"Show us where your mema is," Ruben said.

"I don't suppose anybody thought to bring any food with them," Shaun asked as they wound their way through the forest. "I'm suddenly starving."

Chapter Twenty-nine

"You know your son is going to die out there," the witch said. "Poor little thing, all alone, looking for his mother." Her tone was one of satisfaction instead of sympathy. She looked into Tess's eyes. "He'll probably get eaten by a wild animal."

Tess saw what would happen. Boone's body being mangled and dragged, clenched in the jaws of a horrible beast that shook him and then tore off his limbs and ate them while Boone screamed for her to come and save him.

She screamed. The sound echoed in the back of the cave where the witch had taken her. She fell on her knees and screamed until she was hoarse. The vision of Boone being torn apart was so real, that she had to believe it was true.

Yet how could it be?

She found herself lying on the cold dirt floor of the cave. She could feel the earth, worn smooth and packed hard, and yet just a moment ago she had been in the forest, witnessing her son's horrible death.

It was the witch doing it. She had planted the vision in her mind.

But it seems so real.

I can make it worse if you want.

Flames . . . horrible leaping flames . . . and Boone in the middle of them . . . he was on fire.

Mema . . . save me, please, Mema, why won't you help me?

"Nooooo," Tess moaned. She knew it was not real. She dug her fingertips into the earth because she knew that the cave was reality. As long as she held on to reality, Boone would be safe. Boone had escaped from this place. He might even be with Ben by now. He had to be with Ben.

"Who are you?" the witch asked again.

"I told you," Tess cried. "I'm Tess. I'm a slave. I don't know anything."

"You lie," the witch said.

The earth became flames. Tess's hands, which had been gripping the earth, were now on fire, and the skin flamed and fell away, leaving bleeding, oozing stumps.

"Who are you?"

Tess looked at her hands, once again whole.

"Why are you doing this?" she gasped out as she fought to catch her breath.

"Because I want to know who you are."

"Why?" Tess cried. "I'm just a slave, nothing more."

The flames came again. Burning her alive. She felt her skin blister and fall away and she looked down at her body and saw nothing but burning, oozing tissue. She ought to be dead, yet she was alive and she was screaming.

"Shut her up," Dyson said. "The noise is unnerving the men."

Tess lay panting on the ground.

"This does not concern them," the witch said. "They are paid to work. They are not paid to worry about her."

"So what's the problem," Dyson said. "She's just a slave."

"No, she isn't." The witch ground the words out.

Tess knew Dyson was staring at her. She closed her eyes and turned her face away. He knelt next to her and fingered a strand of her hair. "So there's more to you than meets the eye," he said casually.

His knees creaked as he stood. "Just don't mark her up," he said. "Or I'll have no use for her."

The witch hissed in disgust.

"Are you watching for him?" she asked.

"Yes," Dyson said. "We're watching the sky and the stream."

He was still staring at Tess. "If she's got a secret, why don't you just look inside her mind to find it?"

"I did, you fool," the witch spat out. "She's hiding it. And she's hiding it well."

What am I hiding?

"I did learn something interesting," the witch continued. "How strange that she would know of it."

The voices faded. Dyson and the witch had walked away. Tess allowed herself to curl up for a moment, willing her mind to once again get a grip on reality.

She had known when the witch entered her mind.

She had felt her slithering about inside as if she were a snake. She hated it. She hated the Circe.

Yet consciously she was not hiding anything. She had nothing to hide, except what she knew about Ben's friends, and the witch had pounced on that fact the moment she'd entered her mind. Tess had not consciously tried to hide what she knew. She wouldn't even know how.

So why was the witch so certain that she was hiding something else? Why would the life of a slave be of interest to her? All she knew was work and worry and a few brief moments of joy.

Let Boone be safe . . . let Boone be safe . . . let Boone be safe . . .

Tess opened her eyes, her breathing once again normal. From where she lay, she could see the length of the cave beneath the bellies of the two starships. The loading was still in progress, she saw barrels going up the ramp and legs coming back down.

If only they would just let her lie here. Just take their Qazar, take the men and go. Just let her die.

Let me die.

As long as Boone was safe.

How could she be sure Boone was safe? She hoped he was. He was smart enough to make his way back down the mountain. He should be able to find home.

What then? What would happen to him if Ben wasn't out there? If only she knew that Ben had him. If she could be sure . . .

The vision of the wild animal tearing at her son was fresh in her mind. Ben's telling of how evil the Circe were was not even close to the reality of it.

She saw the robes of the woman next to the legs of

Dyson. They were standing at the mouth of the cave. Tess pushed herself up to a sitting position.

Her wrists were raw and bleeding from the strip that bound her hands. She'd fought the binding when the witch was torturing her. If only she could get it off, she might be able to get away.

Tess looked around. Stefan stood between the two ships. She saw his boots between the landing gear.

If only she could get to him. If she could get the collar off, then maybe they could both get away.

If only . . .

Her life was pleasant compared to what Stefan must be suffering. It was one thing to be at the mercy of others, but to have your own will taken away, to not even be able to take a step without having someone else wish it . . .

Stefan . . . what are you thinking? What are you feeling? If only I could help you.

Tess was amazed to see him turn and walk toward the back of the cave. She stole a quick glance under the ship and saw that Dyson and the Circe had moved out into the daylight. The men loading the Qazar passed between where they stood and the front of the cave.

Dyson must have sent Stefan back to watch her.

Stefan walked around the ship and looked at her. His blue eyes, so much like Ben's, seemed to pierce right through her, looking into her mind.

Tess held out her bound hands, hoping against hope that he would do something.

Stefan looked around. There were some crates stacked between the ships. He picked up a set of shears from the top of one and without a word walked over to Tess and snipped the strip that held her hands.

Tess looked up at him in disbelief.

"How?" she whispered. The collar still blinked around his neck. She saw what looked like a latch at one side of it. Her hands and fingers felt numb and she fumbled a bit, but suddenly the latch popped and the collar was in her hands.

"Why did you do that?" she asked, still whispering.

Stefan blinked as if suddenly coming awake. "You told me to," he said, keeping his voice low. He looked at her as if seeing her for the first time. "You're one of them." He pulled her to her feet, and she quickly realized that he was as tall as his brother.

"One of who?"

"The witches," he said. "Or else you could not command me."

Tess felt her jaw drop open in shock.

"You know my brother," he said. "Ben."

"Yes."

Why does he think I'm a witch?

"I saw him with you. Down there."

I had commanded him?

His speech was jerky and disjointed, as if he were having trouble getting the words to coordinate with his thoughts.

"How long have you worn the collar?" Tess said.

"How long?" His eyes became distant. "Since the first day here. Since Dyson tricked me."

"The warehouse?" Tess asked. "I saw you."

"That day," he said. "Since that day."

"We've got to get out of here," she said.

Stefan looked around. Did he even know where he was?

"I can fly," he said, looking at the ship. Tess wasn't sure whether he was talking about himself or the ship. He seemed lost. Her heart swelled for him. His mother had died when he was a bit younger than Boone was now. His brother had deserted him, although she couldn't blame Ben for that. He had been nothing more than a boy himself.

They were born into richness and greatness, yet they had nothing.

"There's a big gun on top of the cave," she said, hoping he was talking about the ship. "They would just shoot us down."

She ducked and looked under the ship. Would the witch know that she was free?

Stefan thinks I'm a Circe witch.

Dyson and the woman were still outside. How long before she and Stefan were discovered?

She shouldn't have looked. She shouldn't have thought about it. As if reading Tess's mind, the Circe turned and looked at her with those evil eyes.

"Run," Tess said to Stefan. They took off down behind the ship toward the front of the cave while the witch and Dyson came up on the other side, between the two starships.

It was foolish to think they would succeed, but they had to try. They made a break for the ravine that ran alongside the clearing.

Tess heard the curt snap of the blaster at almost the same instant that Stefan yelled and plowed into her from behind. She fell face first into the ground with the solid weight of his body lying across her.

She tried to push up. He was too heavy. Tess dragged herself forward, out from under Stefan's weight, and climbed to her feet.

Dyson and the witch stood behind them, each wearing a look of great satisfaction.

"Stefan?" Tess looked in horror at the blast wound in his back as Dyson prodded his side with one foot.

Stefan moaned, and Dyson flipped him over and peered intently at his face. A grimace of pain flashed across Stefan's handsome features. Tess let out the breath she was holding. He was alive.

"Guess I won't miss the brothers' reunion after all," Dyson said. "I still have that to look forward to." He motioned some of his men over. "Put them on the ship," he said.

Two men gathered up Stefan and another grabbed Tess and shoved her toward the cave.

She jerked loose. "Get your hands off me," she snarled. She had been shoved, grabbed, hauled, mentally tortured, nearly drowned, and struck more times than she could count. Her patience had reached its limit. The man obeyed, holding his hands back as if he'd been burned.

"Do you understand now?" the witch said to Dyson as she gazed at Tess with her pale, evil eyes.

"Look at her," Dyson said. "How can it be?"

"That is what I mean to find out."

Tess stared at Dyson and the Circe. Behind them, the two men carried Stefan onto the smaller ship.

How bad is he hurt? Will he die? It could just as easily have been me lying there with the skin burned off my back.

He saved me.

Tess knew Dyson and the Circe were talking about her, but she didn't care.

"Remember not to mark her up," Dyson reminded the Circe. "I have need of her."

"I have no concern for your needs," the Circe said.

"Without her, we have nothing to bargain with,"

Dyson reminded her. "He will not just walk into our trap. He needs a reason to come."

"We have the brother," the Circe said. "He came for him."

"Stefan might not live long enough," Dyson said, without any discernible regret. "Remember that we need at least one of the brothers to take the blame."

"So you can take power," she finished for him. "I know the plan well." She directed her evil gaze upon Tess. "She can wait until we leave this place," the Circe said finally. "Then we will have time. Plenty of time." Her words were a threat, and her icy gaze cut through Tess's anger and resolve.

Tess felt her feet jerk forward, and she took a step toward the ship. She righted herself and steeled herself to fight the will of the witch, but a sudden image, a reminder of what was in store for her if she did not cooperate, flashed before her.

And the fact that Stefan might be dying called out to her. She had to help him. He had saved her from the blast.

Tess went into the ship of her own free will.

They had thrown Stefan facedown on a bunk. She heard the hatch slide shut behind her as she went to him.

"Stefan?" she said gently as she sat down beside him. She pushed the long, golden brown hair from his face.

His blue eyes fluttered, and she bent over to look at him.

"It . . . didn't . . ."

"Shhh," she said.

"How bad?"

Tess looked at the wound on his back. The blast

had burned through his clothing, leaving a mark bigger than her fist. The skin was blackened and oozing with blood. It had to be excruciatingly painful, and it was impossible for her to determine the extent of the damage. She knew nothing about the weapon. She knew it could stun; she had seen evidence of that with Ben the night before in his fight with Garvin.

But this was much worse.

"Bad," Tess said. "You have to hang on. Your brother is coming."

He tried to smile. It looked just like Ben's.

"I came here . . . to . . . be like him," he said. "I knew . . . he had a rep . . . for smuggling . . . I wanted . . . I didn't know it was Qazar."

"I know," Tess said. He seemed so young compared to Ben. There were nine years between them Ben had told her. Clearly, Stefan idolized the brother who had abandoned him. "I heard you, remember?"

"That day . . . I almost got away . . ." His eyes closed for a moment. Tess caught her breath, and then they opened again. "It was a trap . . . for Ben."

"He knew that," Tess assured Stefan. "He'll be ready."

"He came," Stefan sighed. "He came anyway." His eyes shifted to her face. "He came for you."

"No. He came for you. He didn't know me."

"You . . . brought him here."

"No. He came for you."

"I thought they were all . . . bad." His eyes seemed distant. "But you are . . . good." The eyes closed.

"Stefan!" Tess shook his arm.

He can't be dead. He can't.

She was rewarded with a sharp intake of breath. He was alive. But how long would he stay that way?

Chapter Thirty

Dusk had fallen. The forest had turned to shadow, the earth now silent and the trees without movement. Even the creatures that normally stirred in the night were quiet, and the damp air held a taste of apprehension.

Dyson was waiting for him to come, Ruben knew. The area in front of the cave was brightly lit from above, and there were guards stationed around the perimeter of the clearing. Maybe his half-brother expected him to just stroll in.

Don't count on it, Lilly said in Ruben's mind.

So he thinks you're just going to stroll in, Shaun said.

Ruben found it strange to have a conversation with his friends without saying a word. He could hear Shaun and Lilly talking to him, inside his head, and they knew his responses.

They lay on their bellies in the dense underbrush, Ruben, Shaun, Lilly, Boone, and Ky, all quietly watching and waiting. They had carefully snaked their way in to a point where they could observe the camp.

I'll take out the gun, Shaun said. They all looked up at the proton cannon that hung ominously over the clearing.

I'll find Stefan and Tess, Lilly said. They gazed toward the cave.

I'll take care of Dyson. Ruben made it a conscious thought, and an image of his blade buried in his half-brother's throat entered his mind.

Looks good to me, Shaun said. *Take out anyone you run into between here and there.*

Boone lay beside Ruben, his eyes wide as he looked toward the clearing. He had not made a sound since they'd crept forward.

"I want you to go back to your hiding place," Ruben whispered in his ear. "Take Ky with you."

"I want to help."

"You have helped," Ruben said quietly. "Now you have to hide so your mema doesn't kill me."

Boone grinned at the joke and quietly moved down to the hiding place they had agreed upon before scouting the camp. Ky followed, but he stopped a few times to look toward the clearing as if he wanted to be a part of the attack.

When full dark had settled, when the creatures of the night finally began their song and when the stars pricked the sky overhead, they moved. They had no idea how many they would face. They did not know where Tess or Stefan were being kept, and since there was an unseen Circe present, they decided that Lilly would not begin her search until the battle had begun.

Ruben and Lilly moved in opposite directions as

Shaun headed through the woods toward a fall of rocks alongside the cave. Ruben watched him circle behind the Falcon, which appeared to be poised and waiting for takeoff. Whoever the pilot was meant to be was a mystery, as the ship seemed to be empty.

Shaun's target was the proton cannon mounted on top of the cave. He approached without being spotted, using his mind to distract the guards until he reached the side of the clearing where the mountain met the earth, and then he began his climb.

I'm climbing now. Shaun showed Ruben the clearing from his vantage point. Ruben had never before experienced Shaun's extraordinary night vision. He saw every outline clearly, as if illuminated by the light of day.

Our turn, Lilly said in his mind.

Ruben slid his blade into his hand and slipped behind the first guard. He clamped a hand over his mouth and felt his blade slip into the soft and vulnerable skin under the neck.

Blood spurted onto the thick moss that carpeted the forest floor as Ruben quietly lowered the dying man to the ground. He wiped the blade on the man's shirt and moved on without a backward glance. He couldn't feel sorry for his victim. Whoever he was, he was responsible for killing people with Qazar. He deserved no better than what he had received.

Just like Garvin.

Ruben moved on to the next guard. He hoped Lilly was having similar luck. He knew she could move much more quietly than he through the forest. He also knew that she was well versed in the use of a blade. He did not know if she had killed before. He knew her to be capable of it, especially if it meant the safety of her children.

His kill total was three before he heard a noise from above. A rock fell from above the cave, and the man he was sneaking up on turned his head in that direction. Ruben froze in place, daring not to breathe, until he saw a body fall from the top of the cave.

It isn't Shaun, Lilly assured him. He didn't have time to answer. The guard had seen him and fired his weapon.

Their attack had been discovered. He heard the fire of blasters. Everything went dark, and he realized that Shaun had taken out the beacon.

He heard men yelling and knew that Shaun was picking them off with his proton rifle as they ran out of the cave. They'd thought they had the advantage of darkness. Ruben spared a moment to be grateful that his friend wasn't firing the cannon.

They still didn't know where Tess or Stefan were.

One of the guards came charging toward him, firing his blaster. Ruben dove away from the shot and felt the sting of bark as it flew into the air, scored from the tree trunk by the blaster. He rolled to one knee and flung his blade.

And missed. He heard the heavy thunk as the blade buried itself in a tree.

Why hadn't he separated it? Ruben cursed himself for a fool as he covered his head and flattened himself against a tree to avoid another blaster shot.

"Dyson wants him alive," a voice said above him.

Ruben looked up and saw another man standing over him. Where had he come from?

"Get up," the man said.

As Ruben slowly rose, he felt the blaster at his hip.

He was so used to the blade that he had forgotten about his other weapon. The second man fell from Shaun's shot in the same instant that Ruben drew his blaster and shot his original target.

Lilly? Ruben asked in his mind as he retrieved his blade and turned toward the cave.

She's searching . . .

Tess knew that Stefan had sustained internal injuries. He was dying before her eyes.

"Please," she said. "Just hang on a little bit longer." She wiped the sweat from his face with a cloth she had found in the lav and pushed his damp hair back. His eyes, which had seemed amazingly blue earlier, now were pale and lifeless as he stared at the wall behind her. She would have thought him dead except for the occasional tremor that shook his body.

"Don't die, Stefan," she continued. "Ben is coming."

Was he? She had no idea how long they had been locked in this cabin, but she was sure the day had to be waning. Her stomach told her so, if nothing else.

If only she didn't feel so isolated. If only she had some clue as to what was going on outside. If only she knew that Boone was safe.

If only she knew without a doubt that Ben was coming for them. For her.

Why should he?

Because there was something between them, some sort of connection. Ben had told her he'd never felt connected in that way before. That had to mean something. She hadn't imagined the beauty of their lovemaking the night before.

Or was she just trying to convince herself of a love that didn't really exist?

She'd never thought she would want a man in the way she wanted Ben. She had never known a man like him. He was willing to lay down his life for his friends. He was ready to sacrifice himself so Boone would be safe. He had come to Lavign looking for a brother he didn't even know.

He would come.

But what then? Could he save them? Would Dyson let her go in exchange for Ben's cooperation? What if he didn't? What would happen to Boone?

What if by some miracle they were able to get away? *Tess . . .*

Even as a free woman, her life was not her own. She should have let Joah roll Ben back into the stream. She never should have helped him the night she crashed. She shouldn't have chased the heifer up the knoll that night.

If he had died you never would have known what it was like . . .

Even if they couldn't get away, she would be content if she knew Boone would be safe. Was that assurance too much to ask for?

Tess . . .

What was that persistent voice in her mind? Why was the Circe haunting her like this? Wasn't it enough that she was a prisoner? She would be at the witch's mercy soon enough.

Ben sent me to find you.

"It's a trick," Tess said out loud. "I won't help you find him."

I'm Lilly.

"Lilly? Ben's friend?"

I'm here to help you.

"What? How?"

Open your mind.

Tess looked around the cabin in disbelief. Could it possibly be the Lilly that Ben had told her about? Had his friends somehow miraculously arrived on Lavign?

Open your mind.

"Boone?" She was terrified to ask. Terrified of the answer.

Safe . . . look.

A moment of panic overwhelmed Tess. What if it was a trick? What if it wasn't? There was only one way to find out.

Tess closed her eyes and willed her pounding heart to slow down. She took a long, deep breath and concentrated with all her might on Boone. Her ears picked up noises. Something happening outside. Confusion. Shouting. Men running. Was that blaster fire?

Concentrate.

The shallow sound of Stefan's breathing joined with her own and the two mingled into one sound, calming and soothing as if time itself were slowly fading away. She heard the beat of her heart. She heard the blood flowing through her veins.

A vision formed in her head, gently filtering in as if carried on a butterfly's wings. Boone and Ky, lying side by side in the darkness, peering through the underbrush at the clearing. Then she saw Ben and another man with strange pale eyes the same color as the witch's. But his gaze held no evil or malice. She did not recognize him.

Shaun, the voice said, identifying the strange man. *We're all here to help you.*

"Where's Boone?" Tess asked.

Safe. Just think it. I can hear your thoughts . . . and . . .

An explosion shuddered the ship. Stefan moaned.

Can you get out?

No . . . we're locked in . . . Stefan is hurt.

I see him.

Someone is coming. Tess looked at the door. It wasn't that she heard anything, she just felt it.

The hatch slid open and the Circe witch entered, her eyes venomous.

"Who are you communicating with?" she demanded.

Tess shook her head in denial and immediately fell to the floor as flames once more consumed her.

My mind is my own. No other may possess it. I will keep my mind and use it to overcome my enemies.

The words came unbidden to her and Tess saw the witch's eyes widen in shock and surprise at the same moment that the flames went away.

The witch struck Tess with the back of her hand. The blow turned her head and made her stumble against the wall.

"The man wants me to leave you unmarked," the witch said. "But he will soon learn that it is my desires that matter, not his." The Circe turned her head and stared at Stefan, whose eyes had flickered open at the commotion.

He arched off the bed and screamed wildly in a hoarse voice.

"Stop!" Tess yelled at the woman.

The witch laughed at her. Tess felt the anger well up inside her. This had to stop. She launched her body at the woman, her hands curled into claws.

Tess had the thought that if she could just get to

the witch's eyes, the madness would stop. Scratch out her pale, evil eyes. Tess plowed into her, and they fell in a tangle of robes and flailing arms against the wall. The Circe's hat fell off and her hair flew out in a wild snarl of streaked gray and black.

Tess's nails dug into the Circe's cheek. She shrieked in rage. Tess could feel her gathering her power, but before the witch had a chance to strike out, Tess grabbed her head and slammed her against the wall.

"Who . . ." The evil eyes glared at her before the witch lost consciousness and slid to the floor.

"Lilly?" Tess said the name out loud, hoping that Lilly would communicate with her.

Nothing. She turned and saw Stefan sitting on the edge of the bunk, looking at Tess in shock as he held his arms against his abdomen.

"How did you . . ." he gasped.

"We need to get out of here," Tess said as she went to him. "Can you walk?"

"It depends," he said weakly as he flung an arm over Tess's shoulder. "Where are we . . . going?"

"We're going to find your brother."

Stefan flashed a grin that was so much like Ben's, it made her heart skip a beat. "I knew he'd . . . come for you," he said as they stumbled toward the hatch. "I would."

Chapter Thirty-one

Ruben surveyed the scene. How many men did Dyson have working for him? Three ships could haul quite a few mercenaries.

How many of them were willing to die? Apparently, quite a few. Greed did that to a man. Yet Ruben had never flown a cargo he was willing to give his life for.

Where was Tess? There had been no word from Lilly. Nothing from Shaun either. He had no way of knowing what was happening to them if they didn't communicate.

His eyes, now accustomed to the darkness, kept a careful watch on the cave opening. The soft glow of stationary lights on the starships gave the effect of green neon within.

Got her.

It was Lilly's voice in his head.

We've been discovered, Ruben responded.

Where's the Circe? Shaun asked.

She's fighting Tess, Lilly told them.

Ruben grinned. He was worried, but he was glad Tess was fighting her captor. If she could get away, with Stefan, then they could just blow the cave and everyone in it into vapor.

I like that idea, Shaun put in.

Stefan is hurt, Lilly added.

"What the . . ." Ruben turned with blaster ready to fire at the sound of crashing in the underbrush.

Ky lumbered up, with Boone behind him.

"I told you to stay put," Ruben said. He grabbed Boone and pulled him down beside him.

"The noise stopped, so I thought it was safe to come out," Boone said in explanation. "Is it over?" He peered toward the clearing.

"No."

"Have you found—"

"Your mama's alive," Ruben said. "Lilly spoke to her."

"Are you mad at me?" Boone asked.

"Yes."

Ha ha, came Shaun's laughter in his head.

"Shut up," Ruben mumbled at Shaun.

Something's happening, Lilly, alerted them.

"Whatever happens, you stay here. You do not move. You do not get up. You don't follow me and you don't follow Ky," Ruben ordered. Boone nodded.

Maybe he'd been too rough on the kid. He seemed really scared. His eyes were huge in his face.

Don't back down, Shaun advised.

"Did I ask you for advice?" Ruben said.

"Are you talking to your friends?" Boone asked.

"Yes."

"It sounds funny," Boone said.

"That's because they're driving me crazy." He looked at Boone, who was crouched next to him in the underbrush. The kid was imitating him. His body was positioned exactly the way he held his, and he even held a sharp rock in his hand at the ready, in the same manner that Ruben held his blade. All that was missing was a blaster.

Impulsively, Ruben threw the arm that held the blaster around Boone and pulled him close. "I don't want anything to happen to you," he said. "When this is all over, I'm taking you and your mema away from here."

"You are?" Boone's voice was muffled against his chest.

"It your mema will let me," he said.

"She will," Boone assured him.

Get ready.

Ruben turned toward the cave. The big starship was firing her engines.

"I've always admired stubborn women," Dyson said as he placed the blaster against the side of Tess's face. "My mother was one. She never took no for an answer."

"Since she was the first wife of a king, she probably wasn't used to hearing it," Tess said.

Stefan grinned. His face was pale, and he was making a gallant effort to stay on his feet.

"I see that my dear half-brother has filled you in on our family history," Dyson said. He motioned them forward. "His reputation in the seedier taverns of the galaxy doesn't include his penchant for pillow talk."

"Maybe he just told me because I'm special." Tess lifted her chin a notch. "I didn't need him to tell me about you, however. I figured that part out on my own."

"Just let her go, Dyson," Stefan said. "You've got me."

"No," Dyson said. "I want his last thought before he's executed for the assassination of our father to be that I have his woman."

"Why?" Tess asked. "What difference do I make?"

"You don't make a difference," Dyson said. "It's just brotherly competition."

They moved to the front of the cave. Dyson held the blaster in Tess's face. Stefan, barely able to walk, was covered by one of Dyson's men. From what Tess could see, most of Dyson's men had fallen, taken out by the gun on top of the cave.

The ship loaded with Qazar fired her engines.

"We'll be leaving soon," Dyson said. "All of us."

"Don't forget about your friend," Tess said. "I'd hate for her to get left behind."

"Did I remember to thank you for taking care of her for me? If she's not on board, there's nothing I can do about that." Dyson laughed. "Oops."

"Greetings, Brother," Dyson yelled from the cave front. He held Tess in front of him, using her as a shield. Stefan stood on the opposite side with a blaster aimed at the back of his head.

"Mema!" Boone cried from somewhere nearby.

Tess's heart leaped into her throat. "Boone," she sighed. He was safe. And when this was over, she would personally kill Ben for bringing him into the middle of a battle.

Dyson shoved the point of the blaster into her cheek. "Should we take him with us?"

"No."

"I think I will," Dyson replied, breathing in her face.

Tess ground her heel into his foot. "Leave him be," she said between gritted teeth.

"Fine with me," Dyson said. He jerked her off balance. "He can starve to death, for all I care."

"You're about to die, Dyson," Stefan said.

"No, you are."

Tess strained her eyes to see between the shapes and shadows that edged the clearing. Boone was out there somewhere. Please let him be safe.

Something moved. Something huge. Something coming toward them.

Be ready.

Ben walked into the circle of light before the cave with Ky at his side. His blaster rested on his hip, and his blade was once more in its sheath on his wrist. He stopped walking when he reached the light, and gave Tess a reassuring look before turning his eyes on Stefan, who looked as if he had reached the end of his strength.

"How are you, Stef?" he said.

"Alive," Stefan said. His voice was weak, but he remained standing. Tess flicked her eyes to him.

Hang on. She reached out to him with her mind.

"How touching," Dyson said. "And baby brother thought you didn't care."

A low growl rumbled in Ky's throat.

"Thanks for bringing my Newf," Dyson said.

"He was hungry," Ben said.

Dyson made a face.

"If you wanted a reunion, Dyson," Ben said dryly,

"you could have just sent me an invitation. That way we wouldn't have had so much"—he moved his hand to encompass the bodies lying on the ground—"trouble."

How could he stand there looking so calm? Tess thought. It was almost as if he did this kind of thing every day.

"Throw down your weapons," Dyson said.

Ben lifted his blaster from his hip with his fingertips and dropped it on the ground.

"Blade too," Dyson said.

With a flick of his wrist, Ben slid the blade into his hand.

Dyson ducked behind Tess and rammed the blaster harder into her cheek. "On the ground, just so we're clear."

Ben's eyes blazed as he casually moved his hand and the tip of the blade buried itself in the ground right in front of Dyson's shoe. Dyson jumped back a step, taking Tess with him. If she hadn't been so terrified of Dyson, she would have laughed.

Stefan did laugh, and jerked when Dyson's man jammed his blaster against the back of his head.

"Tell your friend up there to throw down his weapon," Dyson said.

Ben grinned as a proton rifle landed on the ground in front of Dyson.

"Does he have any more?" Dyson asked.

A blaster landed next to the rifle. Tess felt Dyson stiffen and noticed that he rolled his eyes upward, but since they were still standing within the shelter of the cave, he couldn't see anything.

"Tell him to come down," Dyson said.

"You tell him," Ben said.

Dyson moved his blaster from Tess's cheek to Stefan's. "I don't need him if I've got you."

"You don't have me yet," Ben said, his face suddenly deadly serious. "Kill either one of them, and I swear you'll never get off this planet."

Ky's growl rumbled louder.

"Tell him," Dyson said.

Ben looked up. "Want to join the party?" he asked.

Tess gasped when a large man landed with catlike grace next to Ben. How could he jump down that far and not get hurt? The man, who wore eye shields, moved next to Ben, casually folded his arms, and smiled at her.

"Show-off," Ben said.

"You're just jealous," the man said. He gave Tess an appraising look. "She's pretty," he said. "I approve."

Tess couldn't help smiling shyly at Ben's friend.

Shaun. Tess felt the love in Lilly's mind as the name formed in hers.

"Aren't you—?" Dyson began as he looked at the man next to Ben. Then he grinned broadly. "Looks like I'm going to cash in on two rewards this trip."

"Do you know what he's talking about?" Shaun asked Ben.

"Don't have a clue," Ben said. "So what's the plan, Dyson? Are we just supposed to walk onto your ship and let you fly us away?"

"Something like that," Dyson said.

"Let Tess go," Ben said. "Stefan too."

"I'd like it better if everyone went on my ship," Dyson said. "Including your friend."

"You always were a spoiled little git," Ben said. "Always wanted things your way."

"Usually got my way, too," Dyson said. His eyes strayed to the blade.

"You never got over that, did you?" Ben said. "You couldn't stand it that our dear father gave me that blade."

"He never gave me anything," Dyson said. "Beyond what was required."

"So you killed him?" Ben said.

"I killed him because he found out what I was doing. I killed my brother because he had our father's ear. I never could stand him." Dyson looked at Stefan. "Unlike some, I did not worship my older brothers."

"What exactly are you doing?" Ben asked. "Plotting to take over the universe?"

Dyson smiled. "As a matter of fact, I am. What good is an army if all it does is train? I've got the Qazar craze going strong, which has weakened the Senate Protectorate. Most of their fighters are out hunting for drug runners. I've got you to take the blame for our father's death. And I've got very strong allies."

As if on cue, the Circe witch walked up beside them. Tess noticed that she had put her hat back on. She also noticed with some satisfaction that the woman seemed a bit disheveled.

"There's someone else," the witch said. "His woman." She inclined her head toward Shaun. Her eyes glittered maliciously. "We shall take their children also."

"Get her out here where I can see her," Dyson said.

"Good thing you woke up," Tess said to the Circe. "He was planning on leaving you."

"Quiet," Dyson barked.

"You would betray me?" the Circe said, looking at Dyson in disgust.

Dyson yelped in pain.

Stefan dropped to the ground like a stone.

Tess threw her shoulder into Dyson and he stumbled against his man.

"Stupid bitch," Dyson yelled as he fought to remain upright.

"It wasn't me," the witch screamed back. She was already running for the ship.

"Tess! Get down!" Ben yelled.

A blaster went off over Tess's head as she dove toward Stefan and covered him with her body.

She heard the heavy thunk of someone hitting the ground and heard Ky growling viciously. A loud whine filled the air.

"Get your beast out of the way!" Shaun yelled.

"*Ky!*" Tess yelled. There was so much confusion, she couldn't see what was happening. Finally she realized that Ky's jaws were clamped around Dyson's leg. Dyson kicked frantically as he scrambled to climb into the starship, which was shaking with the force of its engines.

"*Ky!*" Boone yelled. Tess turned, frantically looking for her son.

Dyson fired his blaster at Ky, but the Newf was already bounding away, running as hard as he could toward Boone, who was racing toward the cave.

"*Ky!*" Boone screamed.

"*Get down!*" someone yelled.

The cave filled with unbearable heat as the starship lifted from the ground. Tess ducked her head against Stefan's neck as she felt flames licking at her boots. She heard a voice screaming and realized that she was the one making the sound.

She felt the incredible pressure of the vertical blast, and then the pressure was gone.

"Tess!" Strong arms pulled her away from Stefan. She felt herself enfolded against a wide chest as the ringing in her ears slowly faded away.

"Boone," she sobbed as Ben opened one arm and enclosed her son between the two of them.

"Are you all right?" Ben asked. His blue eyes stared down at her, brimming with something she didn't quite recognize. Then he kissed her, crushing her against him as if he were afraid she would slip from his grasp.

"I can't breathe," Boone said from between them. Tess laughed through her tears as they parted, each one laying a hand on Boone's head.

"We've got to go," Shaun said as he pulled on Ben's shoulder.

"What is it?" Ben said.

"They know where the children are," Lilly said. "She got it out of my mind in the middle of the battle."

"The Falcon," Ben said. Shaun was already running for it. He grabbed Tess by the shoulders and kissed her again. "I love you," he said and took off after Shaun before she had a chance to say a word.

Tess watched with her fingertips held to her lips as the Falcon's engines roared to life.

"I love you, too," she said as the ship blasted from the earth.

Chapter Thirty-two

"Stefan?" Lilly knelt next to him.

"Is he dead?" Tess asked as she joined her. Boone and Ky stood in the clearing, Boone's eyes scanning the night sky.

"No," Lilly said. "I basically knocked him out," she explained. "He was barely hanging on anyway, and I thought it might be safer for him if he was unconscious."

"You did all that?" Tess asked. "You were the one who made Dyson yell, weren't you?"

"Yes," Lilly said. "Unfortunately, I had to let my defenses down and the Circe was able to see inside my mind also." She looked toward the sky. Her worry was evident.

"Ben and Shaun will get them," Tess said.

Lilly turned to her and smiled gently.

She's so beautiful, Tess thought. The witch's gray

eyes were evil and lifeless, but Lilly's sparkled like pale amethysts. Lovely, kind, compassionate . . .

Stefan was right. Not all the Circe were evil.

Lilly looked at Tess, as if trying to see something in her mind. "Where do you come from?" she asked.

"I don't know," Tess said. "I have no memory before eight years ago."

"She's like you," Stefan said. Both women looked down at him.

"He keeps saying that," Tess said.

"Shhhh," Lilly said to Stefan. "I'm going to help you."

Stefan nodded and even seemed to relax a bit. Tess wondered how his back was faring.

Lilly pulled up Stefan's shirt, exposing a lean torso and chiseled muscles, just like Ben's. She placed one hand on the other and moved both hands over Stefan's abdomen. She stopped when she reached the spot that corresponded with the wound on his back.

Lilly placed her hands on Stefan's skin, and his muscles constricted against the slight pressure. She closed her eyes.

Tess held her breath as she watched. Lilly's hands seemed to glow with a strange light. She kept her hands pressed against him, and Tess noticed that her brow was furrowed as if she were in deep concentration.

"I need your help," Lilly said.

"What should I do?"

Lilly took her hands. "Put them here." She placed Tess's hands next to hers on Stefan's abdomen. "His liver is damaged," she said.

Stefan gasped.

"I need you to visualize what a healthy organ should look like," Lilly continued.

"What are we doing?"

"Healing him."

"Why . . . I can't."

"You can," Lilly said. Her voice sounded perfectly calm, perfectly reasonable. "You have the power inside you. I need you to join your power with mine. I'm weak right now. And I'm afraid he doesn't have much time."

"You can," Stefan said. "You're one of them."

Tess looked at him and wondered if maybe both he and Lilly were crazy. He was so pale now. His eyes seemed almost gray, instead of the bright blue they had been earlier.

"You can do it," Lilly said. "You just have to picture it in your mind, and then desire it."

Tess nodded.

"I'll help you," Lilly said. "Just follow me."

Tess shut her eyes. She felt Stefan's skin beneath her hands. It was cold and clammy. She tried to see beyond the skin.

See it.

Yes. She did. She saw the organ. It was torn, bleeding.

See it whole now.

Tess imagined it as it should be. Healthy. Whole. Vital. Working. She willed it with all her might. Through her closed eyes she saw a glow. She felt Stefan's muscles jump beneath her hands. She heard him gasp out.

She felt her hands tingle. She felt her hair rise up around her as if lightning had just danced through the air.

And then she slid into darkness.

* * *

The Falcon screamed into the night sky at full power with Ruben's steady hand on the control.

"Anything?" he said.

Shaun had his shields up, his eyes glued to the com. His jaw was set in a way that Ruben recognized. "Nothing yet," he said.

"It's not like we're competing with other traffic," Ruben said. "We should be the only two ships in the sky."

"What's the range on this thing?"

"Short," Ruben said. "It's not made for deep-space travel."

"We've got to get them before they hit a hyperport."

Ruben punched up the computer. "Let's see if we can cut them off."

He set the coordinates and the Falcon blazed through the stratosphere and into the space beyond. They flashed by the moon, finally risen in the night sky.

"You should have stayed behind," Shaun said. He kept his eyes on the com, knowing that Ruben had his on the plexi, scanning the sky, working together as was their custom. "With your brother."

"There's nothing I can do for him now," Ruben said.

"You could be with him."

"And let you have all the fun?"

"There," Shaun said, jabbing a finger on the com. A blip showed on the circular screen.

"Visual," Ruben said, his eyes automatically turning in the direction where he knew the ship would be. "Did we check to see if we had any weapons?"

Shaun flipped a switch. "We're packing."

"Range in five, four, three, two, one," Ruben said.

Shaun flipped the switch down and they watched in satisfaction as a missile tore away from the Falcon.

The starship made an evasive maneuver, but not quickly enough to avoid the hit. The missile sheared through the cargo bay, and pieces of it chunked away.

"We got their escape pods," Ruben said as he watched the pods cascade away.

"Firing," Shaun said and launched another missile. "Switching to guns."

He took the stick in hand and fired the guns mounted beneath the Falcon as Ruben turned the ship toward the pods that were falling though space. An explosion shook them, and Ruben looked up to see that the second missile had taken out the main body of the ship.

"She's finished," he said.

"Got one," Shaun said.

An alarm sounded, shrieking in the cockpit.

"Shrapnel?" Shaun asked.

"Fuel," Ruben said as he tapped his finger against a gauge. "We burned it all getting here. We've got to turn around to get back."

"Some of them got away," Shaun said in disgust as Ruben turned the Falcon back toward Lavign.

"Maybe they were empty," Ruben said.

Shaun pressed his hands to his temples and closed his eyes. Ruben knew he was searching with his mind.

"I can't tell," Shaun said after a few moments. "Either she's not there or she's blocking. Or maybe she's just too far away."

"Or we got her," Ruben said.

"Yeah," Shaun said. "We got her." He didn't

sound convinced, but there was nothing else they could do.

"Thanks for coming," Ruben said finally as they soared back into orbit over Lavign. "We would all be dead right now if not for you and Lilly."

"Family," Shaun said simply.

"Family," Ruben said in agreement. He had one now.

Tess, Boone, Ky, and a brother whom he had neglected. Responsibilities . . .

"So how hard is it to be a farmer?"

Chapter Thirty-three

"Mema. Wake up," Boone said.

Tess's eyelids fluttered. She felt so warm, so comfortable, she didn't want to move.

"Mema." Boone pushed her arm, and she felt Ky's hot breath on her face.

She opened her eyes to find Boone and Ky staring down at her with concern in their eyes.

"What happened?" she asked.

"You fixed Stefan," Boone said. "Then you fell asleep."

Tess sat up quickly, then immediately regretted it as she became dizzy.

"Are you sick?" Boone asked.

Tess put her hands over her eyes until the spinning stopped. "No," she said as she reached out to Boone. "Come here," she added and pulled him to her.

"Ben's not back yet," he said.

Tess looked over his head as she tried to get her

bearings. She was lying next to a fire and was covered with a blanket. Stefan lay on the other side, breathing steadily. Tess was relieved to see that his skin seemed to have some color in it.

"Where's Lilly?" she asked.

"There," Boone said, pointing toward the side of the cave. Lilly sat with her back against the wall and her eyes closed in deep concentration.

"I helped her build the fire," Boone continued.

"You did a good job," Tess said. She stood up slowly and made her way over to Lilly.

"Can you . . . speak . . . to them?" she asked.

Lilly opened her eyes and smiled. "They're coming back. We should see them soon."

"Stefan?"

"He's resting," Lilly said. "When I get my strength back, I'll heal the wound on his back."

"How come—"

"You were able to do that?" Lilly finished for her. "You're a Circe."

"I'm not! Wouldn't I know? Shouldn't I have eyes like yours?"

"I don't know the answers or the reasons, but we can look into your mind and find them."

"I have no memories," Tess said.

"Your memories are still there," Lilly explained. "They're just blocked from your view. We can find them."

"But my eyes?"

"'The eyes show the power.' Or so the saying goes. But now I think that it might not be true. Maybe evolution has taken over again. Nature finds ways to protect itself."

"I don't understand," Tess said.

"Look," Boone said. He pointed skyward and the women gazed up to see the Falcon hovering over them as it descended gently to the earth.

Boone ran toward it, practically standing underneath the ship as it came down. Ky danced around him, barking at the sky.

"Boone," Tess said. "Back up."

"He's made for the stars," Lilly said as the women walked toward the landed spaceship.

The hatch slid back on top, and Tess was relieved to see Ben and Shaun both climb out, although they both seemed a bit weary.

"What happened?" Tess asked.

"We took care of it," Ruben said as he wrapped his arms around her. Beside them Shaun did the same with Lilly. "Are you sure you're all right?" Ruben asked as she melted against him.

"I love you," Tess said.

"I love you." He pulled back and looked down at her. "We're leaving this place," he said. "If you want to."

"You mean you'd stay here?" she asked in wonder.

"Do you want to?"

Tess looked at Boone, who was clambering onto the Falcon. "No," she said. "My son wants to see the stars."

"How about you? Do you want to see the stars?"

Tess touched her fingertip to the blue star that scarred his forehead. "This star will be enough for me," she said.

They put Stefan on the smaller starship. He didn't stir when they lifted him.

"I told him to sleep for a while," Lilly explained. "Rest is the best cure."

The men gathered all the bodies they could find into the back of the cave. Ruben flew the starship out into the clearing, Shaun moved the Falcon in, and when they were all safely on board the starship, he fired a proton blast at the roof of the cave. They all watched through the plexi as the cave fell in, burying the bodies and the Falcon.

"What about the Qazar?" Tess asked.

"I'll notify the Senate in a roundabout way where the source is," Shaun said. "They can decide what to do about it."

"Are we going into space now?" Boone asked excitedly. He stood next to Ruben.

"No," Ruben said. "We're going back to the farm."

"The farm," Boone said, his voice full of disappointment. "I thought we were leaving."

"We will." Ruben said. "But not on this ship."

"We're going on the *Shooting Star*?" Boone asked.

"The best way to travel," Ruben said.

Shaun rolled his eyes. "Mine's better," he said. "It has beds. Enough for everyone."

Boone replied with a jaw-popping yawn. "Does it have lavs?" he asked sleepily.

"Yes," Shaun said. "Why?"

"You'll see," Ruben said with a grin.

"There's a body on the bed," Shaun said as he looked around the primitive house. Lilly had gone immediately to the loom with a million questions for Tess.

"That's Joah," Ruben explained.

Boone had fallen asleep before they landed. Ruben

carried him into his room and laid him carefully on his bed. Ky trailed in after him with Ruben's quilt in his mouth.

"We should bury Joah," Tess said as she took the quilt from Ky and placed it over Boone. Ky did his three turns and lay down on the floor next to the bed.

"Tomorrow," Ruben said. He pulled Tess to him. "Tonight all I want to do is sleep."

"Just sleep?" Tess teased.

Ruben lifted an eyebrow at her. "Tempting as you are," he yawned, "sleep sounds a lot better. As long as you're with me, that is."

"Help me move him," Shaun yelled.

"I'd better get some clean sheets," Tess said.

Ruben took her arm. "I promise this is the last time you'll ever have to change sheets," he said. "Or do any other chores."

"I don't mind the work," Tess said. "Working with and for someone you love is no chore."

Ruben dropped a kiss on her forehead. "I do like the way you cook," he said. "I'd hate to give that up."

"Maybe I should teach you how."

"No. I don't think so," he said as he went to help Shaun.

They bundled Joah's body in a blanket and carried him out to the winery. Shaun eyed the bottles stacked against the wall.

"Don't," Ruben said as his friend pulled one out to examine it closer. "They've all got Qazar in them."

"How?" Shaun held the bottle up to the light to examine the liquid within.

"Joah used the stream to irrigate," Ruben said.

"I guess we should torch it all, then," Shaun said wearily.

Ruben rubbed his eyes. He felt as if he would drop where he stood. Yet he was also consumed with a great sense of relief. Just one day ago he had stood in this very spot and prepared himself to meet his death.

Now he had an entire lifetime to look forward to.

"I was pretty foolish up there today," Shaun said. "I don't know what happened to me."

"It's hypnotic," Ruben said. "The same thing happened to me, only with the water. I drank it and couldn't get enough of it. Even now, I hear it out there and all I can think about is going to the stream."

"Then it's a good thing you're leaving."

"Yes, it is."

The two men paused as they walked out into the darkness. "The people of this planet shun technology," Ruben said. "They think it's evil. But a different evil found them."

"It's not *things* that make people good or bad," Shaun said. "It's greed. That's one truth you can never escape. You'll find it everywhere."

"Even on Oasis?"

"Even on Oasis."

They turned toward the house. Soft light shone from the window, beckoning them.

"Look," Shaun said. Ruben looked toward the pasture and smiled to see the giant draft horses resting under the tree.

"Are you as sore as I am?" Shaun asked.

"Yes, I am," Ruben laughed. "I've already told Tess there will be nothing but sleep tonight. Poor thing. I'm sure she's in there crying her eyes out in disappointment."

"You have a lot to learn about women, my friend,"

Shaun muttered as they stepped onto the back porch. "Where's the lav?"

Ruben laughed and pointed down the path. "Wherever you want to make it," he said as he went inside.

"You have to be kidding."

Tess was waiting for him in the bed. She opened the sheets and smiled sweetly as he pulled off his clothes and finally, gratefully slid between them.

"Was it my imagination, or were you walking kind of funny?" she asked as she settled her head on his shoulder.

"We rode the draft horses," he said as he pulled her nude body up against his.

"Dyson had some, too," she yawned. "I wonder what happened to them."

"We turned them out," he said. "We came across them in a pen when we were gathering up the bodies."

"Good."

"And you had saddles."

"I guess that would make a difference."

"Tess?"

"Mmm?"

"I love you."

"I love you . . . too."

"Lilly!" Shaun's shout outside sounded aggravated. "We're sleeping on the ship!"

"I guess he doesn't care for the necessary," Tess said contentedly against Ruben's shoulder.

Ruben didn't hear her. He was fast asleep.

Chapter Thirty-four

Sunlight streamed through the window. Mouth-watering smells drifted into his consciousness, along with the sound of happy chatter.

Contentment. Ruben stretched luxuriously under the sheets, and then grimaced in pain. "Ouch," he said, his hand automatically going to his groin. "From now on, it's the *Shooting Star* or walking."

"That leaves out several other means of transportation," Tess said from the doorway.

"Is he up yet?" Shaun yelled from somewhere in the house.

"Shaun's anxious to get home," Tess said. "They're worried about the children."

Ruben rolled up on his side and, with the sheet wrapped loosely about his waist, propped his head up on his elbow. "Give a man a planet to run and he thinks he can boss everybody around." He patted the mattress. "My sheets are cold. Why don't you warm them up for me?"

Tess grinned at him and pulled the door shut behind her. "Your breakfast will be cold," she said.

"Warm breakfast or warm sheets," he said, returning her grin. "That's an easy choice."

He reached for her arm and pulled her to him, welcoming her with a kiss. "You washed your hair," he said as he inhaled the fragrance.

"I took a shower," she said.

"On Shaun's ship? How is Stefan?"

"Still asleep. Lilly wants to go ahead and put him into . . . cryo?" She looked up at him questioningly and he nodded. "But I thought you might want to talk to him first."

"I do." He dropped a kiss on her nose. "We have a lot of catching up to do."

"You've got time," she said.

"I want to spend it all with you."

Shaun beat on the door. "Get up!"

"I am up," Ruben yelled back as he flashed a devilish grin at Tess.

Tess giggled.

"Don't make me come in there," Shaun growled.

"We'd better go," Tess said. She quickly slid out of Ruben's reach, tossing his clothes at him as she opened the door.

"I will kill you," he said to Shaun, who glared at him with satisfaction on his face.

Everyone was gathered in the kitchen. Boone's smile was as wide as his plate.

"Shaun let me sit in his chair on the ship," he announced happily. "And I did preflight with him."

"We thought Boone and Ky could go with us," Lilly said. "Since your ship is so—"

"Cozy?" Ruben suggested. Lilly knew better than to make fun of the *Shooting Star*. After all it had saved her life a few times.

"Did you ever fix that co-seat?" Shaun asked.

"I will now," Ruben said. "It just about killed me." He lifted his shirt to show them the wound.

"The Qazar in the water made it blue," Lilly said, coming to the same conclusion as Ruben.

"I think it froze his wounds, too," Tess said. "They healed remarkably fast, and I pulled chunks from them that looked like solid blue ice."

"It wasn't the Qazar that healed him so fast," Lilly said. "It was you."

"What do you mean?" Ruben asked as he swallowed a bite of his breakfast.

"Lilly thinks I'm a Circe," Tess said.

"But her eyes," Ruben said. He looked at Tess. "What color *are* your eyes? They keep changing."

"They look green today," Boone said. "They're always greener when she's happy."

"Not everyone on Circe has gray eyes," Lilly said.

"The ones with the power do," Shaun said.

"Maybe not," Lilly said. "Maybe they just think that the only ones with power have gray eyes. I could look into your mind, if you want," she said to Tess.

"Find my memories?" Tess said. She looked at Ruben. "What if they're bad? What if I've done something I'd rather not know about?"

"That won't make a difference," Ruben said. "Don't you want to know how you got here? Who did this to you?"

"I don't know." She looked at Boone. "I guess I'm just scared. What if I was like that woman?"

"I promise you weren't," Lilly said. "I doubt that you or anyone else realized that you had any powers. I'm fairly certain that if you were born on Circe, you were immediately dismissed as a failed breeding plan and consigned to servitude."

"They do that?"

"They do all kinds of things," Shaun said. "The bitches."

"Shaun," Lilly said as Boone grinned.

"Sorry," Shaun said. "Don't repeat that," he said to Boone.

"He already knows," Ruben sighed, and Tess gave him a stern look.

"Maybe we should wait until we get to Oasis," Tess said.

"Dreading it won't make it any easier," Ruben said.

Tess sighed deeply. "Boone," she said. "Go sit with Stefan. He should be waking up soon."

"I want to—"

"Boone," Ruben said. "Go."

The stubborn set of the boy's chin was so much like Tess's that Ruben had to smile, although he made sure Boone didn't see it.

"What should I do?" Tess asked Lilly.

Lilly led them into the main room and sat down in the middle of the floor. "Sit," she said.

Tess sat down opposite her. To Ruben and Shaun's amazement, she placed her ankles on her knees in the same position that Lilly took.

"Ruben, you might want to stay close," Lilly said. "Sit behind her."

He sat down behind her and slid his legs up

around hers, grimacing in pain as he stretched his limbs into the same position they'd been in when he rode the draft horses the day before. Tess leaned back against his chest, and he wrapped his arms around her.

"Just open your mind," Lilly said.

Tess closed her eyes and felt the gentle touch of Lilly's fingers at her temples.

Open your mind.

Images flashed before her. The day past, the night with Ben, watching him bathe, his taunting as she cooked. Nursing him, Joah beating her as she sought to save Ben. The crash.

Days passed by in reverse order, quicker than she could count. She relived Boone's birth and the joy he'd brought her. Then she saw the agony that had led up to it.

It's over . . . it will never happen again.

She was in a strange place. She didn't remember it. Hands held her down and she was branded on her shoulder. She was a prisoner in a damp, dreary place. She cried.

A battle took place. Fire came from the sky. She was in the middle of it. She was lost. She couldn't find anyone to help her. A man dressed in black picked her up and put her on a spacecraft with some other children. She looked for a boy but couldn't find him.

Then she was happy. She was by the sea. She played in the waves with a boy . . . her brother . . . while a woman with dark hair and a man with extraordinary green eyes watched them with smiles on their faces.

The days spun past, happy days. Joyful days. Carefree days until she was nothing more than a babe in her mother's arms. A mother who looked at her with pale gray eyes and a happy smile on her face.

Tess's eyes flew open. "My mother was a Circe?"

Lilly nodded. "Do you remember?"

She did. The memories overwhelmed her. Her body shook as they poured into her mind. "My parents were part of a rebellion," she said. "They escaped and formed a secret society on Circe. They were discovered and killed. Everyone was killed." Sobs overtook her. "The children that survived had their memories erased and were sold into slavery."

"Bitches," Shaun repeated. "We should wipe out the entire planet."

"I wonder if it's still going on," Lilly said. "I wonder if there's anyone left."

"Wouldn't you know?" Ruben asked. He held Tess close as she fought for control of her emotions.

"I've never been there. I did all my training on the Senate planet," Lilly said. "And I'm sure if there is a rebellion, it's not information that is allowed to get out. It would suggest they don't have total control."

"And we all know how they feel about power," Shaun said.

"At least that explains my dream," Ruben said. "I wondered how I could have witnessed what happened to Stefan in my vision."

"It was Tess," Lilly said.

"But how?" Tess said. "I don't understand."

"It's because you were destined to find each other," Lilly said. "Just like we were." Shaun took her hand. "The understanding will come later. I'll teach you."

"I have powers?" Tess asked.

"Some," Lilly said. "You're definitely a healer. We'll figure it out."

"On Oasis," Shaun said.

"Mema?" Boone said. "Stefan is awake."

Ruben groaned as he stood. "Never again," he said as he limped after Boone.

"Lilly said Tess is a healer," Shaun said. "And Lilly healed me."

"Shut. Up," Ruben said.

Lilly stopped Tess as she went to follow him. "Are you all right?" she asked.

Tess smiled at her. "I've got a lot to think about," she said.

"It's five days to Oasis," Lilly said. "That should be plenty of time for both of you."

"Thank you," Tess said. "For everything."

"Thank you," Lilly said. "For loving him. I'm sure it won't be easy at times."

"It's the easiest thing I've ever done."

"How are you, Brother?" Ruben asked. He pulled a stool up beside Stefan's bunk and sat down.

"I'm fine. Thanks to Tess and Lilly."

"Tess said that you protected her," Ruben said. "You took the shot."

"She saved me," Stefan said. "I couldn't let Dyson hurt her. Did you get him?"

"I don't know," Ruben said. "We got his ship, but some of the pods got away."

"So I guess we're still wanted for the assassination of our father?"

"No. It just so happens that my friend Shaun carries a lot of influence with the Senate. He'll get the charges dropped."

"What does he do?"

"He's the ruler of Oasis."

Stefan seemed impressed. "Oasis was on our father's list. You know, universal domination and all."

"Stef," Ruben took a deep breath. How was he supposed to make up for the last ten years? "I'm sorry . . . about leaving you—"

"You did what you had to do," Stefan said quickly.

"I was selfish."

"I was five."

"But—"

"I'm just sorry that I got you into this mess," Stefan interrupted. "I almost got you killed."

"I'm not sorry," Ruben said. "I never would have met Tess if not for this."

"So I guess this means she's going to be my sister?"

"I guess it does." Ruben grinned.

"You know, we never had a sister."

"Our father had nothing but sons?"

"As far as I know. He didn't claim any daughters."

"He was a bastard."

"Yes, he was."

"How did he die?"

"Dyson cut his throat. He wanted it to look like you did it with your blade."

"He always hated me for that."

"You deserved the blade. It came from our mother's dowry."

They were silent a moment, both lost in memories of their mother.

"So what happens now?" Ruben asked. "On Amanor?"

"I guess the rest of them will fight it out for control. I know I don't want the throne."

"Neither do I."

"So can I go with you for a while?" Stefan asked. "I'm a pretty good pilot."

"It's in your blood," Ruben said.

"Are you looking for a partner?"

"Not me. I'm retiring," Ruben said. He was amazed at how much he was looking forward to it. Just being with Tess and Boone. Making a home. But there was room for Stefan in his dream. "Maybe you could take over the business. I'd have to show you the ropes, things like getting around inspections at the hyperports and avoiding the Legion." That way, he could still keep his hand in a bit. Share some of the excitement with his brother the way he'd shared it with Shaun.

"Sounds interesting," Stefan said. "I'd need a ship."

"I've got one. She needs some work. And a new cargo bay."

"That sounds expensive."

"Not a problem, little brother. Credits I've got."

Shaun and Lilly blasted off soon after. They took Boone and Ky with them. Boone had his toy starship clutched in his hand as he boarded the ship. Also on their ship was Tess's loom. Lilly had played a big part in convincing Shaun that it should go. She was fascinated by it.

Ruben decided to forgo the cryo for their trip. He fixed up the co-seat as best he could and made sure they had enough food and drink to get them through the journey to Oasis.

Tess turned out the draft horses and sent them downstream. She opened all the gates so the chickens could forage for food.

"What about Joah?" she asked as she took one fi-nal look around.

"He's in the winery," Ruben said. "I'm going to burn it."

"I think he'd want to go that way," Tess said. "Up in smoke with his wine."

"Are you sorry he's dead?"

"No," Tess said thoughtfully. "I'm just sorry he was so . . . wrong about things. I think his intentions had been good when he first came to this place. They just got messed up along the way. Maybe when his wife died. I really don't know."

"You don't have to worry about it anymore," Ruben said. He wrapped his arms around her. "You don't have to worry about anything."

"They came here to escape technology," Tess said. "They thought it was evil. It turned out the evil was already here."

"The Qazar isn't evil. It's what man did with it that's evil."

"I guess it all comes down to the choices we make."

"I choose you," Ruben said.

Tess leaned against him and realized that for the first time since she'd come to this place, her worries were gone. And then she laughed.

"What is it?"

Tess pointed upstream. "The heifer," Tess said. "She's come home."

They took off over the flames of the winery, circling the farm so Tess could have one last look, not that she really cared.

Ruben programmed Eli for autopilot and pulled Tess into his lap as he propped his boots on the com.

"Incoming message," Eli said. "From Port in a Storm."

"That's Shaun," Ruben said. "Receive," he told Eli.

"Boone needs to talk to his mema," Shaun's voice said.

"Is he all right?" Tess asked.

"He's fine. We put Ky in cryo but decided to let Boone experience spaceflight for a while. He's a quick study. He'll probably know how to fly before we get home."

"Is that supposed to make me feel better?" Tess asked.

"Talk to your mother," Shaun said to Boone.

"Mema? Are you there?"

"Yes," Tess said.

"I forgot to tell you something."

"Go ahead."

"Remember the night that Ben crashed?"

"Yes."

"We saw the shooting stars and I made a wish?"

"Yes."

"It came true."

Tess looked at Ruben and smiled. "So did mine."

"Safe Stars," Shaun said over the com. "Out."

"Out," Ruben said. "Safe Stars." He looked at Tess, her eyes glowing happily, as bright as the stars shining through the plexi behind her head.

"My wish came true, too," he said as he kissed her.

*S*targazer
Colby Hodge

DO NOT REVIVE WITHOUT AUTHORIZATION

Those are the words stamped on the cryo tube holding the prisoner. Gazing in fascination at the bulging muscles of his arms, Lilly wonders if the heavy cables binding his wrists and ankles will be enough to hold him when he awakes from his enforced sleep. Yet she ties her fate to his when their ship is attacked. But how is he able to penetrate her mind, filling it with teasing suggestions and hotly sensual images, when that talent has always belonged exclusively to the gener-ations of gray-eyed women in her line? Is the devil with the silver gaze the key to saving her beloved garden planet or is he just a common criminal?

Whirlwind

CINDY HOLBY

As the last remaining bachelor among all his friends, Zane Brody can always be counted on for irresistible charm. So when he sets out for New York to retrieve a valuable thoroughbred mare to Laramie, he has no doubt he can handle any female he encounters, whether equine or human. What he doesn't reckon on is an independent-minded schoolteacher named Mary Dunleavy. A goat butts him off the train and eats his hat, while the woman bats her eyelashes and appropriates his heart. As Mary takes off across the plains, Zane finds his head spinning, and his love life in a...

Whirlwind

PATTI O'SHEA

Eternal Nights

Capt. Kendall Thomas has been plagued by dreams of blood, dreams so horrifying they leave her trembling in the night. Kendall has good reason to be afraid. She's discovered thieves are stealing artifacts from the alien city on Jarved Nine, and the smugglers will do anything to protect their lucrative sideline—even commit murder.

The last man Kendall wants to endanger is her best friend Wyatt Montgomery, but the stubborn Special Ops captain followed her when she went to gather evidence, and the smugglers trapped them both in the city's ancient pyramid. But they can no longer deny the powerful force drawing them together, the passionate dreams that leave them aching with need, the touch of skin on skin that makes them long for…

Eternal Nights

- -